baby doe

a novel

H. William Taeusch

Baby Doe

Cover and interior design by Lori Conser

Published by Wheatmark®
2030 East Speedway Boulevard, Suite 106
Tucson, Arizona 85719 USA
www.wheatmark.com

ISBN: 978-1-62787-813-5 (paperback)
ISBN: 978-1-62787-814-2 (ebooks)
LCCN: 2020909085

Bulk ordering discounts are available through Wheatmark, Inc. For more information, email orders@wheatmark.com or call 1-888-934-0888.

Baby Doe is a work of historical fiction. Names, characters, hospitals, events, and incidents are either the product of the author's imagination or used in a fictitious manner. The novel imagines what it may have been like for parents or caregivers for cases that engendered the use of the term "Baby Doe" in the media. The actual events that inspired this novel occurred in the early 1980s in the United States and are summarized in the appendices. Any resemblances to actual persons, other than public figures, events, or places that are part of public record are purely coincidental.

For Mel

PROLOGUE

Boston, December 1983

My son and I killed time in my office in Boston Lying-In Hospital before a Friday-night game downtown. The ragged Cleveland Cavaliers were taking on our indomitable Celtics. Billy dug through the mess of junk I kept under the examining table to keep him occupied when we were stuck in the office for a while. Billy was nineteen, IQ about sixty-five. His features didn't much resemble mine. He looked more like people with Down syndrome

I put my feet up on my desk, leaned back, and reread the letter with last week's date. The medical school in Cleveland wanted to consider me for chair of pediatrics.

"Dear Dr. McKennen," it began. "Dr. McKennen" was crossed out, and "Mac" handwritten above it. "We are delighted," the letter continued, "that you will be able to visit us and meet with the search committee, the dean, and other members of the department." It would mean a three-day trip: meetings, giving an afternoon seminar, having dinners with various bigwigs and students.

I didn't have any ready-made friends in Cleveland, though I knew Sophia Shulder there. Her lab was down the hall from mine before she left Boston a year ago. I liked the way her mind worked. She took in things and processed them behind luminous brown eyes. The tip of her nose was flat, as if pressed against a window while she analyzed life's problems on the other side. Long dark hair, pale complexion; black and white, like the way she saw things. Never any lipstick that I could see; she didn't need it.

My phone rang, the direct line. Professor Ellen Larkin, not only my department chair and boss but also mentor and friend. I would have walked over a bed of academic hot coals for her.

"Mac, haven't heard from you in a while." I dropped the letter as if it were on fire. "I need you," she said, "to help entertain Harold Hazeleton tomorrow night. At the Harvard Club. My treat. He's giving grand rounds on Thursday, so turn out your people and be sure to ask if he's got a shred of hard data on his neonatal scoring system, the one the nurses are gaga about. Okay?"

"Dinner would be fine," I said, wondering whether I could ever work for any other human being.

I hung up, eased back in my chair again, and pushed my fingers gingerly toward the letter, certain Ellen would call again the instant I picked it up.

She enjoyed being a department chair. The same intuitive, analytic acumen she applied to her research got her through administrative quandaries. The department's interpersonal issues were harder for her. She'd told me that taking care of preemies was easy compared with prima donnas.

Was I a prima donna for wanting to move on?

Most of my job as a division head was great, particularly the variety of it and not having to deal with departmental budgets. But chairing a whole department would give me a chance to test some of my ideas about medical education. And to find out whether we really rise to our level of incompetence. Was it fair to move Billy and use Cleveland to check out my potential—or lack thereof?

I surveyed my spartan office. A well-worn wooden desk recycled from some retired professor's office. Photos of my residency days. The usual diplomas. A picture of my son and me sailing off the cape. A ratty oriental rug from a yard sale. A dirty window overlooked the physicians' parking lot and the Boston Latin School next door. Some perks would be nice. A hefty salary increase. A nicer place to hang my lab coat and stethoscope.

"Hey, kiddo, what do you think of Cleveland?"

"Who's he?" Billy asked.

"Not a he, at least not anymore. It's a city in the Midwest."

"How come?" Billy said, riveted on the structure he was putting together with pieces of wood. When preoccupied, he always had the same answer to every question. "How come?" he repeated.

I wondered how he would fare if I took the job. With my wife long gone, I already felt guilty about finally placing him in a residential home for kids like him. If I took the new position, I'd have even less time for him. "How come it's in the Midwest?" I asked. "Or why would anyone would want to live there?"

My son looked at me, pondering.

"Next," he said. "Next" meant the second of two options. Like, would you like to go to bed now or watch some more TV? Next!

I knew the lily pad philosophy of some of my academic friends: leap to the next one before the one you're on sinks beneath you. It had a certain wisdom.

"Hey, guy, it's easier to get good seats at the basketball games in Cleveland."

"How come?" he said, pausing over the choice of a red block or blue one.

I crumpled some papers from my inbox and lofted the wad toward him. He waved his hands for the catch. It bounced off his head.

"Oops," I said.

"Oops," he said, smiling. He'd never be the one to support me on an NBA salary, that was for sure. Billy added a third tier to his growing tower of uncertain purpose.

I picked up a grant application that had a due date looming, but my thoughts drifted back to Sophia. Her husband had snagged a job as an instructor in English literature in Cleveland, and she already had a promotion in the biochemistry department there. Smart couple. *Bright* was their only word for *good*.

My son half listened to my mutterings, intent on his building.

"Hey, guy, let's put all that stuff back in the box and go get a Big Mac. Whaddaya say?"

My secretary was closing up his desk as we came out of the office. Elderly and orderly, Allen liked to depart after I did so he could see what I dropped in my outbox, leaving no surprises for the morning.

"Everything's all set here, Dr. McKennen. What have you two fellows been doing in there all this time?"

"Well, the kid's been into castle building, and I've been explaining it all to him—life, the universe. What it all means. He prefers castles. I should have been working on the damn grant like I was going to."

"You know he's doing better than anybody expected, and

he loves listening to you talk, even if he doesn't always understand."

"Kind of like my medical students," I said.

Allen helped me into the battered raincoat that I wore summer and winter. Lining out, lining in. I bundled my son into his loden coat and reached up to pull a wool cap over his head. He was a half foot shorter than me.

I searched my pockets for my gloves and his mittens.

"Go on, you two," Allen said. "If you hurry you can avoid the pregame traffic and watch the warm-ups. A dollar says the Celtics are overrated." Allen, the big risk-taker. My son and I looked at him in shock. Allen was smiling. That partially redeemed him.

At the elevator, Billy turned and regarded me seriously. "Game, Dad," he said. On some weekends, when I wasn't on call, I checked him out of the home. It was more than a month since the last time. Father of the year, I wasn't.

This early in the year, the Celtics already looked like a sure thing for the playoffs, and the game proceeded without much enthusiasm. Finally, late in the last quarter, with Cleveland ahead by one point, the pace quickened. With lazy elegance, Bird passed the ball between his opponent's legs. On a flat-out run, Bird caught the return pass and drove toward the basket defended by a Cavalier half a foot taller than him. At the last second, Bird flipped the ball behind his back to Parrish, who slam-dunked it for the win just as the final buzzer sounded. We whooped and hollered in the faces of a few disgruntled Cleveland fans. Once again our guys had pulled it off in the last moment. Billy and I pounded each other on the back. "Cheated death!" I shouted.

PART I

Birth or Death? There was a Birth, certainly …
—T. S. Eliot

1

Cleveland, February 1984
Three Weeks

When Sophia Shulder reached the well-plowed lot behind the chemistry building at only a little past seven in the morning, she had her choice of parking spots. As she backed her Karmann Ghia into a covered space that would offer some protection from more February snow, someone yelled, "Stop!" She jammed on the brakes and opened the door. A shaggy grad student came up to her.

"You almost ran over a damn dog. Look where you're going!"

The student turned on his heel and walked away. Behind the car, a dog, midsized, lay on the frosty asphalt. A beautiful mutt with a lot of cocker spaniel in her, sick and shivering.

"Ohhhh, poor thing. What's going on?" Relieved that she hadn't hit the dog, Sophia got down on her knees and continued talking in that high, gentle voice people reserve for animals or small children. She patted the dog's head. When the animal licked her hand, Sophia didn't pull away, her attention caught by a nasty mass with blood and pus on the dog's abdomen. The dog struggled to get up, but its hind legs didn't move.

Sophia poured out the remnants of her coffee and filled the cup with water from a half filled bottle she found under her car seat. The dog lapped with effort, then lay back with a grunt, panting and looking at Sophia.

"Come on, pup. Stop using those big brown eyes on me. I've got a grant to finish." This evoked a few flaps of the tail.

Sophia could leave the dog for somebody else to take care of, but why would anyone else be less rushed than she was? The fur around the dog's neck was matted as if someone had removed a collar. Maybe someone unable to care for her. Did a child cry over a lost pet somewhere? Sophia remembered the funeral of her dog, Boots, too slow to avoid a car by the time she was fourteen. Sophia's mother, slightly sloshed, composed a poem and coerced Sophia and her brothers to each read a few lines at Boots's backyard grave.

"Why me?" Sophia said as she picked the dog up in a blanket she'd pulled out of the car trunk. The dog weighed no more than a bag of groceries. She eased the dog onto the back seat of her car. Blood soaked through the blanket.

She'd take care of this immediate problem, and there'd still be time enough to fax a draft of her grant renewal to her friend Mac in Boston, to get his comments on it before the weekend. The dog sniffed her old-car smell and then fell half asleep, panting less. The dog tugged at something inside her. After Sophia's father died, Boots was the only family member whose love remained. Sophia had walked Boots, played frisbee with her, eaten ice cream with her, slept with her, dressed her up, did her homework with her, and protected her from Sophia's brothers' pranks.

This dog could be a problem with their white rug and furniture. Though she and Martin were away all day, they could fence the backyard and make do.

As she drove, she half turned and murmured to the dog, "It'll be all right, puppy. We'll get you to a vet and get that nasty infection cleaned up. You are the sweetest thing. Don't you worry. Hey, keep your spirits up … Heard any wonderful dog stories?"

Sophia stopped at a pay phone and after several tries found a nearby vet whose office opened at eight. Then she called Martin, still at home, and asked him to meet her.

Sophia helped lift the dog onto the stainless-steel table and murmured reassurance while the vet did his examination.

"Sophia?"

"Back here, Martin."

Hauled out of bed early by Sophia's call, a disheveled Martin entered the clinic and took in the vet, Sophia, and the dog.

"Found the pooch in the parking lot," Sophia said, relieved to see him. He was at times her better, emotional half, six feet tall with devilish blue eyes, curly black hair, and an air of enough confidence to still charm her.

"God," said Martin. "What's the matter with her? That thing on her belly is disgusting."

"It's not good," the vet said. "A solid tumor of some sort, ignored too long. It's breaking down, infected. Probably metastasized."

Sophia held the dog's head in both her hands.

"C'mon, Sophia, be careful. You heard what he said. You could get an infection."

The vet patted the dog. Martin stood in the corner of the examining room.

"What can we do?" asked Sophia.

"Sophia, it's not our problem," Martin said.

"The choices," said the vet, speaking to Sophia, "are to load her up with antibiotics, then do surgery and hope the tumor hasn't spread, or put her down. Even with surgery, the chances aren't good. She's running a fever. We'd have to x-ray her. The costs would be high."

"So what can we do?" Sophia asked.

"Putting her down would be the kindest thing," the vet said.

Sophia felt a flash of anger. Antibiotics, a few x-rays, some excisional surgery. What's so hard?

"Or I could do a fine needle aspiration of one of the lymph nodes to look for malignant cells that have spread," the vet offered.

"Do it. Please," Sophia said, before Martin could say a word.

He put his hands in the back pockets of his jeans and shrugged.

While Sophia held the dog's back pressed against her breasts, the vet did a rapid push-pull with a needle and syringe. The dog craned her neck and tried to lick Sophia after the vet withdrew the needle. He retreated to his lab, holding the syringe with a millimeter of milky fluid aloft.

Martin shook his head. "I dunno, Sophia. You sure get into some damn strange situations."

"That's the way it goes," she said, not wanting to talk about it till there was some resolution.

They waited in silence.

The vet returned. "Malignant, and it's spread."

"So with drugs and radiation, what are her chances?" Sophia asked.

"Not good. Not good at all."

"I need a number," Sophia said.

"Maybe ten percent survival, and the dog is old. We'd have to keep her here for weeks, that's several thousand dollars, but I don't think she'd make it. And it would be painful. If we gave her enough medication to control the pain, she'd stop eating."

Sophia turned to Martin and leaned on him.

"It's okay, Soph," he said, putting his arms around her. "You can't fix everything."

She wanted to slam doors, break something. Why couldn't the vet fix her? Except for the wound, the dog looked well enough. She buried her face in Martin's chest. She had already imagined a dog door from the backyard into the garage. Walks in the evening and on weekends. Driving to the lakefront for romps on the beach.

The vet said, "I'll leave you alone for a few minutes."

"Sophia, you've done all you can. I didn't even know you liked dogs that much." Martin continued to hold her, but Sophia broke free and paced up and down in the small examining room.

"Putting her down," she called aloud to the vet in the back room. "How is that done?"

"An injection. I could do it here, now," he said, sticking his head out of the curtained lab.

"Could we leave her here for a few days and see if antibiotics helped, or try the surgery or something?" Sophia asked. The dog raised her head.

"Sure you could. But I wouldn't feel right about it. It would just prolong her dying for a few days or weeks. And more pain. I can recommend another vet who'd pull out all the stops for you."

"I think we should do what the vet says," said Martin.

Sophia held Martin's hand.

"I'll just draw it up, and it will be over in a few minutes." The vet waited a moment. With no response forthcoming, he disappeared and came back a minute later with a syringe. He wrapped a tourniquet on the dog's right foreleg. A vein stood out like an ancient tree root. The vet wiped it with an alcohol pad. Holding the leg immobile, he released the tourniquet and looked up at Sophia with a wordless question.

Sophia bent over the table, and again held the dog's head in her hands. Looking away from the syringe, she leaned down and kissed the dog on her dry nose. "Martin? Say something kind."

Martin stared at the ceiling lights for inspiration.

"When once [this] heav'nly-guided soul shall climb,

Then all this Earthly grossness quit,

Attir'd with Stars, he shall forever sit,

Triumphing over Death, and Chance, and thee O Time."

Sophia leaned up and kissed Martin's cheek. She nodded to the vet, who injected the lethal liquid. The dog sighed a long exhalation, shuddered, and slumped on the table, lifeless.

"Man, that looks like great stuff," Martin said, wiping his cheek with his hand.

Sophia shot him a glare, patted the dog. "Thanks," she said to the vet.

"No problem." The vet waved off their attempts to pay him. "Thanks for bringing her in. Most folks wouldn't have gone to the trouble."

2

Four Weeks

Sophia's boss, Professor Adam Stanton, chair of the department of biochemistry at Western Reserve University in Cleveland, had asked her to host a party. Stanton led the search committee for the new head of the pediatric department. His wife needed to tend to her sick sister in Los Angeles, so Stanton asked Sophia if she could handle the evening for the leading candidate, Dr. McKennen. Stanton knew this McKennen was a colleague from her Harvard days; maybe she could help recruit him.

The evening, done well, could help Sophia's own career too. Hosting a recruitment party could be one of the few advantages Sophia had over her peers in the biochemistry department. As if designing a complicated new lab experiment, she had managed her way through the intricacies of party planning. The dean of the med school paid for it, and Sophia dragooned Martin into helping.

"Martin, are the ice and glasses ready?" Sophia asked, as she needlessly bustled from room to room. The caterers ran the operation smoothly and with touches of elegance that Sophia appreciated.

"Yup. All done, checked, and rechecked." Martin saluted Sophia. He'd already sampled the punch.

Sophia went back to their bedroom to finish dressing. Her black hair, rolled back in a soft twist, showed off scalloped gold earrings. She did a quick survey of her closet. An uncharacteristic pink blazer—an impulse buy in Filene's Basement years ago and never worn—had potential. Elegant with a cream silk blouse and a dark pleated skirt. A little racy, but not over the top. Light eye makeup, a bit of blush. A woman with no hint of insecurity returned her look in the bathroom mirror. She tucked an errant strand of hair behind her ear.

Downstairs she walked through the living room and inspected the display: cheese plates, fruits, canapés. All the deck lights were on, and the yard and park beyond sparkled with the afternoon's light coating of snow.

By eight o'clock the guests arrived in bunches, having negotiated the wet, sticky snow on the drive from Cleveland without incident. The somewhat rusty Plymouths and Chevys that reflected the genteel poverty of Sophia's biochemistry colleagues soon lined the road, admixed with the Dodges and Buicks of the pediatric department's senior faculty. Martin, glass in hand, directed the arrivals to kick off their boots in the vestibule and head up the stairs to the living room, where Sophia greeted them. Sophia's male colleagues gave her sidewise looks of admiration, which didn't linger long enough to put their wives or dates on alert. Sophia was the only female faculty member in the biochemistry department. If the renewal of her NIH grant was funded, she'd be well positioned for promotion. In 1984, being a woman could even be an asset, at least for the more emancipated promotions committees.

"Mac!" Sophia said. He came up the stairs, handsome as

ever, in a gray turtleneck and blue blazer. He was flanked by a nervous-looking pretty grad student in a black cocktail dress. "Mac, I'm so glad to see you. Sorry about the snow."

"I always knew you were a responsible person." McKennen gave her a warm smile. "But even you can't take responsibility for a little snow. Besides, Abby here, my designated driver, is assigned to protect me."

McKennen held Sophia's outstretched hand for an extra beat before it progressed into a half hug. She'd always had a good feeling about him, and his seminar that afternoon had confirmed it. She hoped he'd take the job. There might be some collaborative research ahead. Despite rumors of a chaotic home life, Mac never seemed to have a problem working with women. On the other hand, the notorious Charles River fever—the feeling that nowhere else could ever compare—prevalent among her former colleagues in Boston might prove an obstacle to his recruitment.

In a flurry, Sophia introduced Mac to a gaggle of graduate students who'd been shuttling their attention between the punch bowl, Professor Stanton, and Sophia's young, attractive postdoctoral student, Byria Marchand. Byria hailed from Toulouse, and her eyes matched her teasing French accent. Sophia heard her end a conversation about the Red Sox's prospects and segue into a compliment on McKennen's seminar.

The party was off to a good start until Martin strode by, ignoring the guests. Lab rats, he called them. Once they left the Esperanto of the Red Sox, they spoke a different language. When the conversation turned scientific, he felt excommunicated. "Fucking Philistines," Sophia heard him mutter to no one in particular. She headed after him, ready to soothe. His ordeal would be over soon, but then she saw him add half a bottle of brandy to the wine punch. The caterer raised an eyebrow. Martin dipped himself a serving in one of the little punch glasses and took a gulp.

"… Barré-Sinoussi at the Pasteur Institute has found a virus that causes the immune deficiency," Stanton said. "So within a year or two, we'll see a vaccine that will obliterate this disease."

Bypassing the group of scientists, Martin stumbled on someone's foot, and launched half a cup of blood-red punch into an arc that landed on their new off-white shag rug.

Sophia saw the crowd in the living room draw back, quiet, then restart forced conversations. Martin lurched into the kitchen in search of a towel.

"Don't worry, Martin. I'll take care of it," she said to his back, while her mind said, Shit, shit, shit. She leapt to sop up the wine already soaking into the rug. What she hated more than an accident itself was the sloppy thinking that caused it and the chaotic response that followed it. The stain would never come out.

Someone beside her rubbed the stain with a wet rag. McKennen, down on his hands and knees. "Never mind, Sophia. I've got lots of practice; I'm always spilling things in my lab."

Spurred by his example, some of the grad students began swabbing with napkins until the caterer took charge. McKennen helped Sophia to her feet. "There. Now your living room is properly baptized."

The next day Sophia had no choice—her car was in the body shop getting a new back seat installed. Martin was slow getting started, and Sophia was going to lose at least a couple hours of work. There was little snow left but no signs of spring. The car had been filled with silence for fifteen minutes. Martin asked Sophia about her lab experiments.

"Going okay," she said.

"You starting a new project?"

"Maybe." Sophia flipped the pages of *Science* while he drove.

"What are you reading?"

"A magazine."

"I know. Anything interesting?"

Sophia tucked the journal into her briefcase. If she read anymore, she'd get carsick. Then she looked out her window at the same scene they passed every day on the way to work.

He asked, "Anything wrong?"

"No, not particularly."

"You're still mad at me for spilling the punch."

"I'm just mad at myself for having unrealistic expectations."

"About what?"

"Specifically? Drinking."

Martin admitted to himself that he did have a bit of a hangover. "So maybe I got a little loose last night. It was a bunch of your friends after all."

"Look, Martin. The point is that last night I—we—were working. These were people whose opinions mattered. Some of them think a woman is just a wasted investment. She'll get knocked up and raise babies instead of raising grant money for the department. It was not a party for us to have fun."

"I thought parties were to have fun. Maybe getting promoted in a science department is different from the humanities. I thought scientists just had to discover something. Less style and more substance?"

"Right." Sophia set her eyes straight ahead. "I should get drunk when I'm with your friends. Help your career along."

"My friends wouldn't mind—and they can talk about more than sports and molecules."

"Writing. They talk about writing. And themselves. Endlessly," said Sophia. "And it's not just last night. You drink too much."

Martin didn't think he drank too much. Sometimes he thought he didn't drink enough. Certainly not as much as some of his buddies in the English department. "So what do you want from me, Sophia? Sobriety on demand?"

"Yeah, that would be a good start."

Martin gripped the steering wheel. Nothing more to be said. He stopped and got out in front of Milton Hall to walk to his office so Sophia could drive his car to the underground garage where she had free departmental parking.

3

Six Weeks

Sophia stared as a drop of her urine darkened a spot on a pregnancy test. She shouldn't have been so surprised. She didn't merely know what everyone else knew—that making love leads to conception. She grasped the process in every aspect of its microscopic detail. Her PhD was in molecular genetics. She knew damn well that birth control was imperfect—even more imperfect when you forgot to take the damn pill.

She threw the blue-splotched strip of paper in the toilet and flushed it away. She repeated the test with the same result. Her hands shook. She couldn't avoid a glimpse of the frenzied woman in the bathroom mirror with scrambled bed hair. Her face was drawn and tense, her posture stooped. Her bathrobe was old and pilled, her reflection the very opposite of who and what she held herself to be.

When Sophia charged into the bedroom, Martin raised their quilt so she could slip back in beside him.

"No, no, no, no. No!" she said.

"What?" he said.

"It's the third morning in a row. Every time the same

thing." She stood over him and waved the scrap of cardboard in his face.

"What's that?" he asked.

Clueless. What it was, was *his* fault. Sophia stamped her foot. "A pregnancy test."

Martin sat up in bed. "I thought you needed a rabbit for that."

Her face crumpled, and she toppled onto the bed, face-down. "It was our trip to Florida."

"But that was—"

"December."

She waited for more from her husband, but all she got from him was a weak, "Geez."

Sophia, who had to remember everything, forgot the pills on their vacation with his parents. Martin pulled her close.

"Hey, hey, my fairest one, it'll be all right," he whispered. His hand slipped through her bathrobe onto her flat abdomen. He always thought things would be all right.

Later that day they headed to a deserted trail around the town's small lake. The February wind blew through the weave of Sophia's winter coat, a hand-me-down from her mother. Sophia hurried to keep warm, limping slightly on the stony trail. Though there were only a few patches of snow, no spring was yet in evidence—no hint of new green on either side of their path. The horizon glowed orange and yellow, silhouetting the hills on the far side of the lake.

They'd rambled along this same circuit of the lake last summer, debating whether to buy their small redwood house in Chagrin Falls, twenty miles outside of Cleveland. Although the house came with a dated yellow kitchen, more windows than Sophia liked, and mortgage payments almost double what they could afford, they'd barely made it halfway round the lake when they decided to take it. Now they'd nearly circled the entire lake, with no decision. They neared the parking lot where Martin's Alfa Romeo stood alone.

"Oh God, Martin. How can I have a baby, run a lab, teach, and compete with the male sharks who'd love to see me take time off and get out of their way?"

"In my department, it seems like more of the sharks are female," Martin said. "But look. *Abortion*, there I've said it. Granted, it seems, what? Unsavory. But this is modern times. *Roe v. Wade*. It's an option. We've just got to make a decision."

Sophia faltered on the path and let him have his "we." Far better than "you." But when he reached to steady her, she shook him off.

"On the other hand, if we don't have this baby," Martin continued, "we will never have one of our own. In a few years, with all due respect, you'll be, ah, too mature to have babies."

Sophia's thesis had described the microstructure of the zona pellucidum of newly fertilized ova. She knew more about fertilization than most obstetricians in the world. She gave Martin a look that backed him up a step.

"I'm sorry, Sophia. I know it's your field, but hey, I was the willing instigator of our little conundrum. If we wait till your tenure is secure, we'll have to adopt." He paused. "And if we wait for *me* to get tenure, we'll be dead."

Sophia had never thought of adopting someone else's child, but Martin's apology made her feel better. "I'm only thirty-four," Sophia said. "Not as old as you. It's just my reproductive machinery that's 'maturing,' as you put it. My lab is starting to go well. If I cut back, I'll lose my shot at promotion ..." Sophia's sentences began to drift off. "But if we don't have a kid soon … I don't know. I didn't like having an older father."

Now and again they'd played with fantasies. Martin wanted their child to be the poet laureate, professor of English literature at Harvard, or an actor, Robert Redford as the Sundance Kid. For Sophia, it would be enough for their child to win a Nobel Prize, be the first woman on Mars, or head a major university. But they always shared the same tacit conclusion: children would come later, when all was ready.

"In some ways, I feel as if you got me, Martin."

"Of course I *got* you. We're married."

"I mean by getting me pregnant. It's like you've had me on the outside, but now you have me on the inside too." Sophia knew her thinking was definitely not linear.

Martin looked at her, his wholly rational wife. "I don't *get* it," he said.

Sophia took a deep breath and smelled the wood smoke rising from fireplaces in lakeside homes. She shivered and led Martin down the trail closer to the shore, toward a stand of pines that protected them from the breeze. She took Martin's mittened hand. "Remember that feeling of monsters hiding under the bed? I knew they weren't really there, but it was as if they could get me anyway."

"Excuse me, my beloved?" Martin made his monster face. "Are you comparing me with glabrous dragons playing croquet with dust balls under our bed?"

Sophia punched him on the shoulder and smiled for the first time that day. "I do not allow dust balls under our bed. I mean, in a family sense. Like when I was little, my mother worried that my father's affection for me might get out of hand. Monsters from the id, that sort of thing."

Martin rubbed the spot where Sophia had hit him. *"Ja, ja, Frau Freud, und vas ist dis* new theory, *du machst?"*

Sophia didn't know whether to be amused or irritated. She'd always adored the attention she stole from her father. He had limited tolerance for children, for family. But she vividly remembered the day when she was eight and walked into the kitchen with him, proudly carrying a bag of groceries. Her mother's face became livid, scrunched up. She yanked Sophia's arm. "You think you're his perfect little wife, don't you!" The bag ripped. Oranges and apples bounced across the kitchen floor. A bottle of milk crashed on the floor.

"Frau Freud? What's going on in there?" Martin gently tapped the side of her head.

"Sorry. Just that families can be scary," Sophia said. "At least my family." She'd told Martin just the bare outlines of her childhood: Her mother drank; Sophia wasn't close to her brothers; and she felt responsible for her father's death when she was eleven. "And plenty of blame to go around," she added. "I don't want that for us." She hugged Martin, then stepped back, eyeing a hole in his crewnecked sweater and the frayed cuffs of his corduroy jacket. "Not good," she said, fingering the sleeve. "I'll get these fixed next week."

They started a second circuit, following the path along the beach, the waves pressing against a scrim of thin ice. Last summer, she and Martin had swum inside the buoyed ropes, dodging splashing kids with their shouted games of Marco Polo. Later she lay on the beach while Martin competed in weekend Sunfish races. The Sunday ballgame coming from their radio was a bit muffled; she'd wrapped it in a towel to keep out the sand. Soaking in the sun, she was barely aware of the broadcaster's voice rising and falling inning by inning as the hapless Indians tumbled in the midseason standings.

Now she saw the Sunfish on the beach, upside down without their masts, stacked and chained to a wooden rack for the winter.

"Sophia? Hey, buddy? You blame me for the pregnancy?"

Sophia looked at her husband, his black hair tousled from the chill wind off the lake. She jumped up and down for a minute; her feet were becoming numb. She gave him a sideways hug. "So will you still love me when I'm lumpy and misshapen?"

"Skinny or plump. Not the point," Martin said. "Mostly I just want to support the hell out of you. I can be happy either way."

If Sophia ever doubted it, she knew at that moment that the decision was hers. If things turned out badly, it would be her fault. "The thing is," she said, "the timing is wrong. And I'd feel better about it if we'd *chosen* when we generated this pregnancy."

Martin threw a stone, aiming at a tree in front of them, a one-handed basketball shot that missed. "I remember my dad trying to get me to catch a football. I didn't like football. What do you think a kid of ours would be like, what with my brains and my beauty?"

Sophia ignored the joke and walked on, looking out at the elephantine hills across the lake. Then she swung around, facing him. "We raise him together, fifty-fifty. And we let him decide whether to be Jewish or not. No bullshit on this, Martin."

"All riiight! Done, my feminist chickadee. We can even let him choose if he wants to keep his foreskin, provided it's a he, of course." Martin hurried ahead. "It's a good thing we've decided because I might have frozen solid with another circuit of the lake. We can take another walk this summer to

decide names. I kind of like Ezekiel, after my great-grandfa-
ther. Whaddaya think? Let's go home and warm up with a
brandy."

The idea of taking care of three of them—Martin, herself,
and the baby—was oppressive. But maybe better than having
an embryo the size of a pomegranate seed scraped out of her
womb?

Martin cakewalked down the trail singing "We Are the Cham-
pions," his voice cracking on Freddie Mercury's high parts.
Was he happy just because they'd made a decision? Or because they were going to have a baby? Only a couple of weeks
ago, at their party for McKennen, she remembered exactly
how much wine she'd needed to loosen up. From now on,
Martin would have to be doing the drinking for both of them,
not that he'd mind.

4

Ten Weeks

In mid-March, Sophia arrived for work at the medical school. With a feeling of relief, she walked up the stairs to her lab on the seventh floor of the new biochemistry building. She dropped her briefcase on her desk and saw that Byria and the lab tech had left the lab in good order. Two work counters impervious to acids and solvents lined the length of the lab. There were freezers, sinks, electrophoresis equipment, smaller centrifuges, and Sophia's most recent acquisition: a reverse phase liquid chromatograph, plus an ultracentrifuge inherited from an aging professor whose grant had not been renewed. Sophia was always anxious that its rotor might disintegrate when the thing was powered up to over one hundred thousand rotations per minute.

Sophia's office was adjacent to the lab. Through a window containing chicken wire to prevent shattering in case of explosion, she could look into the lab and keep an eye on her technician and Byria Marchand, her postdoc. Today both Byria and the tech hovered over their chromatograph, its operating manual open on the lab bench. The wall beyond was segmented by huge glass panes offering a distant view of downtown Cleveland and the Terminal Tower, beyond the poorer Hough neighborhoods that supplied many of the medical center's patients. Sophia sat down at her desk. The door was closed, the phone nestled under her chin, and she dialed.

"Amy?"

Amy was her best friend, the only one from college days, who now, inconveniently and inconsiderately, lived in Manhattan while enjoying a life with no room or desire for marriage or children.

"Sophia? What's wrong?"

Amy was never a morning person, and despite being a senior manager at a major PR firm, she had not changed her habits. They hadn't talked in over a month.

"Why should anything be wrong? I know it's early, but I just thought I'd call. How's everything with you?" Sophia asked.

"It's okay. New York is getting to me. The whole winter is gray and everlasting. It's time for another Caribbean holiday, like that one we took so long ago when we were forever young. So, Soph? Why'd you call, really?"

"I'm pregnant."

Amy paused. "How far?"

"Maybe a couple of months."

"And now you tell me." Amy was pissed.

"Yeah," Sophia said. "You want to make something of it?"

There was a long pause on the phone. Finally, Amy said, "Knowing you, Soph, I thought you'd have it down to the hour." After another pause, Amy relented. "Sweetheart, you depressed?"

"I'm not sure I'm doing the right thing. About having the baby."

"Yikes."

"Amy, just tell me right now that you love me more than anybody, that I'm the smartest person you know, that this won't hurt my career, and I'll be a great mom."

"Sophia, take a breath. Once rung, this bell can't be unrung."

What was she saying? *Not* to have the baby? "C'mon, Amy. This is what you signed on for, being my best friend."

"Okay," Amy said. "I just need a minute here to get used to the idea that *my* best friend, my smartest friend, who knows everything, is reneging on winning the Nobel Prize like she promised me."

Sophia slammed the phone down and put her hand over her face so Byria and the lab tech couldn't see her crying.

For the next hour, Sophia stared at her lab book, pretending to make sense of some recent data. Finally, in an attempt to help someone else if she couldn't help herself, she tapped on the window and beckoned Byria into her office.

Byria retrieved her lab book and sat down beside Sophia. "I have been over and over it," Byria said. "The data make no sense at all."

Byria was more given to career building than creativity. But shown what experiments to run, she was tireless. Sophia rubbed her blurry eyes and studied the figures. Took a deep breath and concentrated. After twenty minutes, while Byria fidgeted, Sophia sat back. "Look." She circled blocks of numbers and letters from several columns. Byria peered over her shoulder. "What?"

"Look."

Byria studied the page. "Hmmm. *Mon dieu*, Sophia, you're right! It's a protein, not a mess of contaminants. Unique sequence, maybe. We've been looking at different segments, but there's an overlap. You found it."

"Nope, you found it. I just drew a circle around some different sequences. You saw the fit."

"Sophia! Dr. Shulder, you're a genius. We'll have a publication. I'm famous! When can we present the findings?" She kissed Sophia on both cheeks and nearly skipped back into the lab.

Sophia remained at her desk, smiling. She wiped her face with a Kleenex. *Well*, she thought, *if I can do it for her, maybe I'd better do it for myself too.*

But after her second hour of matching DNA sequences on the IBM desktop, Sophia needed a break. Her eyes felt green, her skin felt green, her hair felt green. Standing and stretching, she waved to Byria through the window and mimed drinking from a cup. Byria tossed her lab coat onto a chair and poked her head into Sophia's office. "Coffee, *mais oui*. You buying?"

In the hospital cafeteria, they hunched under fluorescent lights at one of the long tables where a smattering of researchers, physicians, trainees, staff, patients, and their families could be found at every hour of the day and night.

"Why so very gloomy?" Byria asked, biting into a gummy slice of pizza. She had given up French cuisine for anything she deemed American. "You have everything—a lab, maybe tenure someday. The world's best and soon-to-be famous postdoc working with you. You're *fantastique*! I wish I could have more of what you've got."

Byria. Her meticulously plucked arched eyebrows somehow jarred with the row of tiny earrings that perforated her left ear. Sophia played with her coffee spoon, debating whether to tell Byria the news that she had to tell her chairman later that day. Hardly a confidante, Byria had just finished her PhD and, working alongside Sophia in the lab, was avidly picking up new techniques. Her career closely tracked Sophia's, though she was at least four or five years behind. Byria seemed perniciously, malignantly happy, and she worked like a dog.

Sophia shook her head. "Thanks, Byria. But I feel I'm just doing mindless DNA searches on the computer today. I'm stuck."

"Hey, grad students get stuck. *Certainement*. But assistant professors like you just need to ponder now and then," Byria said.

"Nope. Stuck." Sophia took a tiny piece of donut and a sip of coffee. "I think I can sort of infer the sequence for the protein that I'm after. And I know I could prove it if I had the whole protein like you do, and just dump it in an amino acid analyzer."

"So you could get a cDNA that would hybridize?" Byria asked.

"Right. And I know I have the protein partially pure. But I'm still getting a lot more bands on the gels than you did, and I can't sort them out."

"*Zut*. No way around it. Just the strong force approach."

Sophia thought for a moment. "Brute" force was what Byria meant. Isolate tiny amounts of protein over and over until there was enough to analyze for amino acids and get the sequence of the end terminus. Inelegant. There had to be a better way, but the technology was just not there yet.

"And I'm pregnant," Sophia said.

Startled, Byria seemed ready to express any requisite emotion. Happiness for the kid-to-be, sadness for this complication in Sophia's career. As in the lab, she'd willingly follow any cue. "And that's not good?" she tried.

"It isn't good, and it isn't bad. If it were one or the other, it would be easy. It's kind of a surprise—Martin and I wanted to have a kid, but later. Now is definitely the wrong time for me, careerwise. But I'm almost thirty-five, and I don't have much 'later' for this."

Byria smiled—somewhat too brightly. It occurred to Sophia that by the time she got back from pregnancy leave, Byria would probably have Sophia's research grants and data books memorized.

Byria looked at her watch. "I had an abortion last year," she said helpfully.

Sophia gagged into her napkin as she caught a whiff of the morning's fried bacon wafting from the kitchen.

"Geez, Byria, an abortion isn't birth control."

"*D'accord*. But sometimes accidents happen. That's what it's for."

"It was kind of an ..." Sophia almost said *accident*, but stopped herself. "... kind of a surprise."

"So why not have the *bebe*?" Byria asked. "You're married; you have a good income."

Sophia saw Byria looking at her diamond engagement ring, almost half a carat, subsidized by Martin's parents. It had always embarrassed her. She covered it with her other hand. "The honest answer? What I'm after? Science is my first love. You know how hard it is for a woman to make it in academia. If you don't, you need to find a better mentor than me who can tell you. A baby, a kid, takes a chunk out of your time, out of your life, while the men just motor past you in their careers." Sophia found herself tearing up her napkin. "And I'm scared of raising a kid. I don't really know how."

Byria looked at Sophia with amazement. "You're a most intelligent and competent person. If you don't know how to raise *un enfant*, then nobody does."

Flattered but wary, Sophia blushed. There was something calculating about Byria.

"Thanks. But my skills with DNA may not be the best ones for raising a kid." She slid her chair back. "C'mon, let's get back to the lab, where I know what I'm doing."

Early that afternoon Sophia sat facing her boss, Adam Stanton. On his office wall were multiple red-sealed diplomas alongside photos of his colleagues on the steps of the research building for which he'd raised the required millions. Adam Stanton was about sixty-five, trim from biweekly squash games. It was said he was a contender for the Nobel Prize.

"Pregnant?" he responded politely.

"Yes sir."

"Well," he said, positioning a small gold Chinese dragon, the only object on his desk, so that it bared its teeth directly at Sophia. "What are your plans?"

It was a question open to multiple interpretations. Abortion? Sophia wondered. Grant writing? Teaching schedule for the next semester? Suicide? Resignation? Would she breed regularly?

"It is somewhat awkward, of course," she answered.

Her boss got up, turning his back to Sophia. He looked out the window into the quadrangle below, now teeming with students on noon break.

His secretary scooted in with a mute apology and placed his sandwich and coffee at the far-right side of his desk.

"In about seven months, you think?" he said, not looking at Sophia.

"Yes sir," she said, withholding the apology that seemed expected.

"After the start of the next academic year then?"

"Yes," Sophia said.

"No trouble with the NIH about your grant resubmission, I don't suppose."

"No," Sophia said, "we think our score is just within the fundable range."

"Be good to check directly."

"Of course, sir."

"And the sixty-four-thousand-dollar question, how much time …"

Sophia sensed his reaching for and rejecting several endings to his sentence. Finally, he faced her again and let it hang.

"A month, I think." She saw him almost sigh with relief. There was no slack in the teaching schedule to allow for sickness or pregnancy. This was the first time it had come up among faculty members.

Stanton returned to his desk and took the teaching schedule out of a drawer. He drew some arrows among the boxes. "The guy who may come here as chief of pediatrics owes me, and he said he wants to do some teaching. I think he's sharp enough even though he's a clinician. He could take over your course for a month or two."

Sophia knew McKennen could do it. He'd already helped on her grant resubmission.

"Thank you, Dr. Stanton."

"No problem. But just to be clear, for now we'll assume that you'll be relieved of your teaching responsibilities for six weeks, and you'll maintain your lab during that time. You'll receive full salary, and we'll expect you back full time after that.

"That's perfectly clear."

"Dr. Shulder." The chairman stood, took her arm, and walked her to the door. "Sophia. And please start calling me Adam. You women are amazing. Able to care for a little tyke while all the time taking care of a husband, running a lab, and teaching. You've done well since you joined us. I am very pleased with your work. You've timed things well enough, and I think you'll be an excellent role model for women who come to our department in the future. I wish you all the best, and thank you for letting me know in a timely fashion."

The door closed. With a stupid grin on her face, Sophia stood in front of Stanton's puzzled secretary.

"How'd it go?" Byria asked when Sophia returned to the lab. Again, Sophia sensed mixed feelings behind Byria's need to know. Would Sophia continue to be her supervisor? Would there be a surprise opening in the department for a shiny new PhD like Byria?

"Surprisingly well," Sophia said, pulling reagents off the shelf for the next morning's experiment. "Though he didn't give me a hug or anything." Department members knew hugs were reserved for the postdocs when they published a paper or received a training grant. "But he didn't refer me to an abortion clinic either. I think he's actually trying to join the twentieth century."

5

Fifteen Weeks

Dieter had only four more courses to finish before he could apply to medical school. To support himself, he worked evenings in the lab of Women's Hospital. After drawing the day's blood tests and completing the lab tests, all he had to do was log in the specimens for special chemistries and prepare them for mailing or pickup the next morning. The lab was generally quiet after normal working hours, and on this early spring evening, Dieter had a new date. He planned to take her to *An Officer and a Gentleman*, get her in the mood. He had to hurry.

The radio moaned a monotonous Beatles song. The linoleum floor hadn't yet been mopped free of dirt, paper scraps, and spilled blood from the day shift. Dieter peered into a binocular scope, finished clicking off a differential white cell count, then called the results down to the patient's floor. For the last task of his shift, he started dealing with the samples that had to be sent out. There were eight. Six blood specimens for a variety of fancy hormonal immunoassays that would go to a commercial lab after Dieter separated the serum from the blood cells. Two specimens of amniotic fluid needed to be put in shipping tubes for chromosome analysis. Routine handling of specimens was really secretarial work, and Dieter didn't love doing it. He looked at the clock again, lit a cigarette. He put the last of the serum samples in the Styrofoam box and slid it into the mail cart.

Dieter had not always wanted to be a doctor. It was his mother's idea. She was raised in Schwabhausen, a small town outside of Munich, and spent her teenage years riding her bike with friends around the Bavarian countryside, flirting with the German soldiers on passing military convoys. Only a nearby town, called Dachau, was ruled off-limits by her parents. As an edgy teenager, Dieter asked his mother if she had known what went on at Dachau when she was a kid. Looking straight at her son with her clear blue Bavarian eyes, she answered, "It was all so secret. We were just told to stay away. Besides, we had plenty of problems of our own to think about during the war. I hope you never, never have to be in war. You are going to be a healer." And then she changed the subject.

It took a while until Dieter decided to fulfill his mother's ambitions for him. Now he regretted not having taken pre-med courses during college. He also regretted not having gone to Vietnam, a soldier like his father. But he'd been too young; all he could do was participate in peace demonstrations.

When Dieter made his rounds in a white coat to draw blood, he liked being mistaken for a doctor by the patients. He should have asked his date to meet him at the hospital so she could see him as a doctor-to-be.

He stopped daydreaming about the past and future and turned his attention to the amniotic fluids, which had to be packaged separately. Dieter took the two twenty-five-milliliter tubes of amniotic fluid and put them in a test tube rack. Finicky, the lab required that the fluids be transferred into special shipping containers. Following protocol, Dieter took the shipping tubes, placed them behind the original tubes, and one by one carefully transferred the fluids, capping them securely. Why the obstetricians who collected the fluid could not send them directly to the chromosome lab was unclear, but it made extra work for the lab technicians. Dieter copied the patient information onto labels for the shipping tubes:

08235488
Sophia Shulder
DOB 9/2/50
Obstetrics
Dr. L. Stackpole

08235487
Arlene Gibson
DOB 7/6/58
Obstetrics
Dr. J. Kitzmiller

Worried whether he had enough gas to pick up his date and find the Panorama, Dieter took the original emptied tubes and tossed them in a bin for biological waste. When he stubbed out his cigarette in a petri dish, the dish slipped off the edge of the lab bench, spilling live ash and cigarette stubs on Dieter's slacks. Damn! His best ones.

He brushed himself off. They'd pass for tonight. He found a broom and swept pieces of the broken petri dish and detritus from the day shift into a pile and dumped the mess in a wastebasket. While several of the lab workers smoked, it was absolutely verboten to do so in the lab.

Dieter stood up and looked at the fluids sitting in the

two unmarked shipping tubes. The labels were gone. He must have knocked them off the counter along with the petri dish. "Oh no!" The exclamation came from deep in his guts. This wasn't like he had dropped a tube of blood and could go back on the ward to draw another, telling the patient the doctor had ordered additional tests. An amniocentesis was done under ultrasound with a six-inch fine needle pushed through the abdomen of a sedated pregnant woman. Private obstetricians would not like to ask their patients to come in for a repeat test. This was not going to help Dieter's chances of getting into medical school.

He bent over and fished the labeled tubes out of the biological waste bin and put them in the rack next to the unlabeled tubes. There were a few drops of amniotic fluid in each of the tubes that he had retrieved. The one for Sophia Shulder looked a little more opalescent than the other. He picked up one of the unlabeled tubes filled with amniotic fluid. Sure enough, the contents looked similar to the Shulder tube. Chromosomes in amniotic samples were rarely defective anyway. He pasted a new label for Sophia Shulder on the tube that matched the labeled one, then stuck a new label for Andrea Gibson on the remaining tube. He put them both in boxes for pickup in the morning.

Disaster averted. Making one last inspection of the lab, the floor, and his slacks, he turned off the lights and locked the lab on his way out.

6

Sixteen Weeks

Twenty minutes after the scheduled time for her second ob/gyn appointment, Sophia was still sitting outside her doctor's office, wishing she were back in her lab. Routine prenatal visits should not take so much time. She'd stopped a key experiment to keep this 10:00 a.m. appointment downtown. She was possessed of good health and income and had been married for seven years. She had little reason not to be having a baby, and picking at a fingernail in irritation, she thought that the processing of pregnant women, as if they were widgets, could be simplified.

A nurse in a cap and white stockings entered the waiting room. "Sophia? Mrs. Shulder?"

Sophia stood. For some reason, the only other occupant of the waiting room, a teenager, grinned at her as if to say, "If you have to take a test, it's better to be last."

In the pale lime-green examining room, Sophia stripped off her clothes, remembering her brothers who delighted in barging into the bathroom when she was sitting on the toilet—one shouting, "Air attack!" and the other switching the bathroom light on and off while imitating a siren. When she was old enough, Sophia repaired the lock on the bathroom door herself. Now she moved a chair near the door, a habitual early warning signal.

Shivering, Sophia sat on the edge of the examining table, swinging her legs. On the wall opposite her hung a calendar with a pretty, smug-looking housewife. In the background, her husband, minimized by perspective, washed the dishes. "Domestic foreplay," Sophia thought. The calendar advertised birth control pills.

Almost thirty-five years old, Sophia suddenly felt young again. Waiting alone for Daddy, for the school principal, the professor, the thesis advisor. Absently, she felt the roundness of her abdomen. It was too late for her and Martin to rethink this whole thing. After a single knock, the doctor banged the door into the chair and entered the room.

"Hey, Sophia, my friend. How's it going?" He grinned. "How's the tennis?"

At her first visit, she'd asked him how long into the pregnancy she could play. She pictured herself lumbering around a tennis court, her elbow straight out to avoid her big belly while she returned a backhand serve. Dr. Lennie Stackpole, her obstetrician, chuckled. "Didn't the nurse show you the right way to get into that gown?"

Lennie had gray hair and an avuncular paunch. His rumpled blue scrubs, mostly covered by a long white coat, were open enough to bare a gold chain resting on curly chest hair. Sophia wanted the baby and her to pass this exam because Lennie would be pleased.

White Stockings came back into the room to be sure that no naked patient of Lennie's would get away with telling a lawyer unsubstantiated fantasies for the sake of a million-dollar malpractice case. Three ex-wives were problem enough for Lennie.

"Lie back, my friend, and let's look at the little guy."

From the past visit, Sophia knew that all fetuses were little guys, and all women were friends. He took an ultrasound probe in his right hand and plopped a mound of cold gel onto her abdomen. White Stockings dimmed the light in the room and rolled up a console, all flashing lights, switches, and screen. Ultrasounds were new in obstetrics, and Lennie loved them. He stuck the probe in the goo and swirled it around. An array of white speckles, a bright swarm of bees, appeared on the dark screen. Something moved, and she felt as if someone had poked her insides with a finger.

"Cute little guy. Heart seems to be doing its thing. Head looks okay. Let's just get some measurements. Hold still."

Sophia didn't know if Lennie was talking to her or the fetus. A pair of crossed lines appeared with a shimmering object in the center of the screen. Lennie flicked some switches, and a cursor moved the lines onto the oval.

"Good. The little guy looks great. Here, I think he's waving at us."

A flickering image, something like a Popsicle stick, skidded across the screen. Perfect, Sophia thought, perfect, and relaxed as much as she could. She took a deep breath. It was as if one of her lab experiments suddenly came together after months of preparation.

But this unknown being, deep in a hidden space inside her, was separate. In a sense, she wasn't doing it, this pregnancy. It was happening to her. But she would have to care for it, look after it, keep it safe. She felt sweat trickle down her armpit to her side.

"Not to worry, Sophia. Everything looks fine. Feel any movement yet?"

An alarm rang in one corner of her mind, and she felt

a little adrenaline rush. Lennie's gentleness reminded her of one of her professor's benign opening for a devastating line of questioning that almost derailed her PhD oral exam.

"I don't know, Lennie. I've never had a baby before. Why? Anything wrong?"

She reached across her belly and pulled at a hangnail. She sucked her finger as it started to bleed.

"Nah," said Lennie. "I'm just starting to use this thing for routine exams on all my patients. It's sure better than a stethoscope, but the more shadows you see, the more there is to wonder about. I like it because I can send you a fatter bill. This first cousin of a TV set shows a fair bit of amniotic fluid. You sure of the dates?"

"I told you the day and the hour, if you have faith in birth control pills."

"We'll keep an eye on things. Now put your feet up in these miserable stirrups, and I'll get a pap smear. Should have done it on your first visit."

She tried to deconstruct Lennie's comments the way Martin would, but she could come up with nothing ominous. With a sigh, she lay back, feeling fat, while Lennie pulled on a pair of gloves. He extricated a duck-billed stainless-steel speculum from a drawer and ran warm water over it in the sink. He gently inserted it into Sophia's vagina. She grunted.

"Now that's a cheerful, plump little cervix. The little guy won't be coming early if things continue like this."

"Early would be nice for me, if not for it," Sophia said.

He removed the speculum and inserted two fingers, mashing down on her lower abdomen with his other hand.

"Hmmmm. Perfect. You've got him just where we want him. I guess you and Martin have good genes."

Sophia played the role that she'd assigned herself with

Lennie—the tough reporter dame of the '40s noir films, trading quips with the other reporters in a busy pressroom, a cigarette dangling from her lips. Somehow she didn't want Lennie to know that she only had to close her eyes for a moment to see her daughter, a three-year-old girl standing in a garden on a summer day, a large bow in her golden hair. She didn't want Lennie to know about her trite fantasies. She wanted to be smarter than that.

"Would you like an educated guess at gender of this little guy?" Lennie asked.

"Yeah, gender would be nice to know, Lennie. Then we could get right down to choosing a correct name. For the family, it's important to Martin."

Lennie replaced the probe on her abdomen, and Sophia watched her baby's image reappear in glittery gray snow on the screen.

"Well," said Lennie, waving the probe in the air, "It's too early to really tell, and unaccustomed as I am to making medical pronouncements that I may one day wish to backpedal on, I think I can say with some certainty that calling 'it' Peter or even Dick would be not be out of place. Of course, I also know the chromosome results because you were more than a tad insistent on having me do the amnio. Now you can alert the grandparents not to buy pink."

"A boy," said Sophia, relaxing. She closed her eyes and saw a dusty five-year-old at the plate, tugging his cap, looking grim and all business. He spits on his hands, picks up his bat, and swings it menacingly at the pitcher. Sophia sits in the bleachers, her knitting forgotten in her lap. Then she opened her eyes and shook her head. She didn't think she watched that much TV.

"How on earth do you raise a boy, Lennie? I mean, I've

never understood men. My brothers were to be avoided at all costs. How can I raise one?" She wanted the pregnancy not to be so serious. She wanted the hard parts to rush by and the good parts to slow down.

"We're not so complicated, Sophia. I look on the Y chromosome as half an X chromosome. Just look on us as incomplete females, lacking in some important particulars. You know, the toilet-seat gene. Raise the kid one day at a time. You'll do great."

Sophia smiled at Lennie's primitive lesson in genetics, developmental pediatrics, psychology, and early childhood education. Genetics was *her* field. Lately her reading had gone beyond early embryogenesis, wading into descriptions of fetal-maternal interactions—the baby as parasite taking whatever nutrients necessary to grow and develop, regardless of its mother's needs. Maybe not the baby, but the DNA, its pernicious, virus-like molecules only waiting to be passed to a new host.

In recent months, she'd begun studying infant behavior and child rearing. But the books she was reading were either too simplistic, like Spock or Brazelton, or too theoretical, like Piaget and Winnecott. The trouble was that once the pregnancy was over, the kid began. What, dear God, would that be like? It was like overload in the lab; her instinctive response was to seek the one clear line in a chaos of data, to build on the significant and push away the rest without thinking about all of it together. Gaining small increments of understanding, not becoming overwhelmed. Work and study, that had been the key to every problem in the past. Somehow that didn't feel like the right approach to raising a baby.

The past week had brought her anxiety dreams, one after

another. The invisible baby was sick. She hadn't studied for an exam. The baby needed her, and she was locked in her lab. She woke up every time with a stiff neck and a jaw sore from grinding her teeth.

But last night she dreamed she held her baby in her arms. There was a brightness to the baby, an essence of what she wanted to create in life.

Later, when she'd told Martin about her dream, he murmured, "'… the brightness shining in darkness which darkness could not comprehend.' Sounds more Christian than Jewish," and hugged her.

Lennie stopped his pushing and kneading, rolled off his gloves, and gave a sympathetic cluck about her impressive hemorrhoids. He picked up her record again.

"Speaking of boys, Sophia, how about if Martin comes in with you next time?" He looked at her over his half glasses.

"Why? No problems, are there?" she asked.

"No, no, no. Just to keep him involved. I'd like you two to go together to prenatal classes as well."

Sophia looked away. How did Lennie know she had ignored his advice to start the Lamaze classes?

Unperturbed, Lennie continued reading from the chart. "Lemme see here. You don't have anemia or syphilis. You have a respectable titer of rubella antibody. No Rh problem. Blood pressure and urine are fine. I mentioned the normal chromosomes. Weight gain is good. Uninteresting family history, as far as medical baddies go. From a purely medical standpoint, Mrs. Shulder, you are dull. I should give you a rebate. No challenge at all."

"Many thanks, Doc," she said, accepting his help sitting up. "That's the way I like it too." She played her role.

41

"Could you give me the name of a good pediatrician, a good day care center, and a cheap nanny?"

Soon she was back on the street, heading for her car in the public parking garage. In early April, winter was leaving Cleveland reluctantly. She should have asked Lennie more questions, but he was an empiricist, not a scientist. If he thought things were okay, then they were okay. She skirted a homeless man on the sidewalk outside the garage entrance. Though seated, he held himself awkwardly and grinned up at her. He wore a blotched dashiki, an open navy pea jacket, and torn jeans. She dropped a five-dollar bill in his cup and waved aside his offer of pencils.

Not so bad. Good checkup. I'm going to be a good enough mother.

⌒

That same morning, Mac McKennen waited in the wood-paneled waiting room on the fifth floor outside the office of Doctor Kennelly, the dean of Cleveland's only medical school. This was Mac's second visit to Cleveland to check out the job of chair of pediatrics. Marjorie, the dean's receptionist of advanced years and impeccable makeup, answered the phone with a hushed English accent.

Mac had arrived the previous afternoon, between thunderstorms. They'd put him up in a nice hotel next to the Terminal Tower, a surprising replica of the Empire State Building but somehow more impressive because of its splendid isolation in downtown Cleveland. Mac took an hour to shop at the May Company, where he picked up a nifty tape player for Billy. Designed for kids, it had big colorful buttons for play, stop, and eject. The latest thing.

Mac's appointment was at 10:00 a.m., prime time on most dean's calendars. On the short list, Mac hoped that they really wanted him despite his handicap of white maleness. Now they would want to know what he might demand in the way of academe's three fundamental keys to organizational strength: space, people, and money. God only had to worry about two of the three when He was creating the world. Don't bother taking the job, God might have advised, without having the resources to make it work. Almost all problems can be solved with enough of the old S, P, and M.

"Mac!"

Dean Kennelly came out of his office, grinning familiarly. No jacket, sleeves rolled up, and two cups of coffee in his hands. Mac hadn't met the dean before.

"Here you go. Heard you like it black. Come in, come in."

Marjorie had prepped the dean well.

He led Mac into a corner office and waved Mac into a leather chair. Through the windows behind his desk, Mac could see the greenery of a park, which he knew was the entrance to the art museum, permanently guarded by a large cast of Rodin's *Thinker*.

"Good sleep? Marge give you the itinerary for today?" The dean handed Mac the coffee. "How are things in Boston? Not so good that you'd want to stay there, I hope?"

Dean Kennelly implied that Mac was already their first choice, that they just had a few details to clear up first. He avoided the topic of Mac's ex-wife and child.

"Excellent," Mac answered. "Duffy sends regards." It was a crafty ploy on Mac's part. Duffy was the dean of Harvard Medical School, and this was a hint that there were counteroffers to keep Mac in Boston. Not that there were yet. But if Cleveland called, Duffy wouldn't say goodbye to Mac easily. He was tired of Cleveland's periodic raiding of his faculty.

"We're really excited about the prospect of your coming," said the dean. "Now tell me what you think you'd need …"

The dean and Mac batted around some specifics. It was clear that Kennelly could ante up more or less what Mac wanted. Mac had already consulted with many people, of course—chairs of other departments—who told him that Kennelly hated adversarial negotiations. Mac's discussions over the phone with two associate deans had already limned the contours of a recruitment package and so, with the tact of a Versailles courtier dealing with the Sun King, Mac requested only what he knew the dean had to offer. But Mac's grant support was tied to Harvard and might not transfer to Cleveland.

No problem. The dean indicated that Mac would simply have to come up with several million dollars of grants within his first two years on the job. "A good goal," Kennelly said.

Trying not to choke on his coffee, Mac forced a grimace into a warm smile.

As Mac left his office, Kennelly patted him on the back. Mac looked at his itinerary, and set forth to meet the associate dean for research. At the end of the day, Mac wanted to squeeze in a meeting with the pediatrician who cared for kids with developmental disabilities. Mac needed to know whether there were any good local facilities for Billy. If Mac became her department head, it would be a delicate conversation; the woman would inevitably see Mac's needs for Billy as potential leverage for her underfunded, overextended division.

The day's meetings went well. No surprises. None of the people Mac talked with wanted to rattle the guy who was slated to be their new boss. He had time to walk down the corridors of the biochemistry wing of the medical center in search of Sophia Shulder. He wanted to thank her again for the welcoming party, but a postdoc with a French accent—he recognized her from the party—told him that Sophia, Dr. Shulder, was home packing for a trip to Chicago for a research meeting at the Federation of American Societies for Experimental Biology. The postdoc watched to see whether Mac was suitably impressed.

Maybe Mac could work with Sophia again, even tangentially. It would be good to have a colleague from Boston to talk with. Reserved and a bit clumsy socially, Sophia was maybe a little lopsided—all cognitive sophistication. Maybe it was the academic stress that siphoned off her energy for emotional development, not an uncommon phenomenon among Mac's medical students. But Sophia was oh-so-smart. That coupled with her being drop-dead attractive with an enthusiasm for hearing anyone's last best ideas, made Martin a lucky man. Sophia reminded Mac of a young Ellen Larkin. Among the positives for a move to Cleveland, Sophia was definitely on Mac's list.

7

Seventeen Weeks

Sophia had just delivered her paper in Chicago. A good one: "ACTH effects on transcription of hydroxylases in fetal adrenal cortical cells." On a high, she left the Thursday morning session early and walked back to the Palmer House, classier but no more expensive than the large business hotel where the conference was taking place.

Saturated with discussions of biochemical pathways, she was too wired to nap. She had time enough to call Byria later to see if anything in the lab was still working, before listening to the plenary session later in the afternoon. En route to her room, she joined a knot of students in the elevator. They were identified by printed nametags and were clearly headed to a meeting of some sort, with markedly more enthusiasm than Sophia's compatriots back at the Hilton. She followed them into a hallway, read the bulletin boards, and realized it was a national convention of medical students. Outside one door, she noticed a session was about to start: "Ethical Dilemmas in Medicine." She walked in and sat down.

A few video monitors were scattered through the large room. The student chairing the session professed no particular knowledge of the subject; he'd initiated the meeting, he announced, because he felt that ethics were not given due consideration in medical school curricula. After brief remarks by a priest and a social worker, they would screen a case study.

The priest was up first, and Sophia relaxed in her chair, happy she didn't have to absorb every detail as she had been doing all week. She popped some sugarless gum into her mouth. The social worker was tall and good-looking. Sophia enjoyed watching him present without paying much attention to what he was saying. After a while the lights dimmed, and a videotape started. After days of listening to densely packed data, it was a relief to listen to the social worker describe a human story. It was about a man in his twenties, a former high school athlete, who had just joined his father's real estate business in the Southwest. The two of them had driven into the countryside to assess some undeveloped land. Not quick to develop the plot, Martin would have remarked.

After examining the property, the father and son, joking and tired, got back in the car. The son turned on the ignition, but the car wouldn't start. The father got out, walked around the front, and lifted the hood. He wiggled some wires, then waved his hand at his son to try it again. Neither of them knew the car was parked over an abandoned gas line that was leaking propane. When the wires sparked, the explosion blew the son out of the car into a massive fire feeding on the leaking gas.

Sophia sat up in her seat.

The father died in the ambulance on the way to the hospital. The son suffered severe burns over 70 percent of his body.

After a year or so in the intensive care unit in Albuquerque, the son refused more surgery and demanded a lawyer to force the hospital to discharge him so he could die at home. A psychiatrist was called in to judge whether the son was competent to refuse surgery. Most of the videotape showed the psychiatrist talking with the son while the camera panned across the son's scarred hands and feet and bandaged body. They showed him being lifted on a tray into a whirlpool bath so that the granulation tissue could be soaked off. Later they showed his agony as the therapist peeled away softened necrotic tissue and applied medication.

Sophia stopped chewing her gum. One of the reasons she'd opted for a PhD instead of medical school was her volunteer stint at Boston City Hospital, where emptying bedpans seemed to be the major aspect of her work. That didn't bother her. It was the anguish and the suffering that she couldn't take.

After the videotape flickered off, the priest on the panel said that two years after the filming, the son, now blind, was thinking about attending law school. Sophia shook her head to free herself of the horror. She thanked the gods for guiding her to a PhD instead of an MD.

8

Nineteen Weeks

Sophia went alone to her mother's home on the Cape before the Easter break. Martin stayed in Cleveland, immersed in his frustrating search for a single philosophical antecedent for both hope and decay in early twentieth-century English poetry. "Be good for you," Sophia had said. "Get to know yourself some more, then you'll see what you want to write about." He needed to find that focus for his book that just might lead to tenure.

Still nauseous every day from morning until early afternoon, Sophia made her way through two airports en route from Cleveland to Hyannis. On the final stretch—a short flight on a small plane from Boston—she fell asleep and dreamed of walking into a biophysics exam, totally unprepared. The plane landed with a jolt and lurched in the crosswind. Sophia jerked against her seat belt. "Can't," she yelped. Her seatmate released himself and leapt into the aisle. "Sorry," she muttered, relaxing her fists, "sorry."

Sophia's mother was at the small airport, waiting, arms wide open for a hug before Sophia could put down her bag. "Sophia, you're big as a house already."

"Gertrude ... Mother." Sophia put her bag down slowly and hugged her mother, who was thinner than ever.

After Sophia's father died, Gertrude drank more and ate less. She was sober for now, driving Sophia through the clogged weekend roads, through the traffic circles where Sophia and her brothers used to play bicycle tag among the tourists' slow-moving cars. Gertrude was a nervous driver, her foot bouncing back and forth between accelerator and brake.

"I'm reinforcing the seawall in front of the house again, dear," she said.

Sophia realized she and her two brothers would face yet another cost for the house their father had left them.

"We just did that five years ago."

"I know. Now you mustn't get excited. We'll have plenty of time to talk business."

Sophia sat on her hands to ease the pressure on her hemorrhoids. Approach-avoidance, Gertrude. When are you ever going to finish anything? Even a conversation.

For years Sophia's family had spent their vacations outside of Quisset, near Wood's Hole. Their summer place was a gray-shingled house that sat too close to an eroding cliff overlooking the sound. Her brothers, James and John, and their wives and kids all still lived in the Boston environs. With or without Sophia, they maintained the tradition of family gatherings that Sophia had never enjoyed after their father died.

Drinks for the family were served before dinner when James, John, their wives and kids assembled in the living room, some launching a game of hearts or Monopoly, two kids struggling at chess. As always, Sophia felt like the alien in the family. Lying on a large horsehair window seat, she read a paperback as the competition at the Monopoly board escalated alarmingly. Jimmy Jr. upturned the board, some of the bills fluttering close to the fire. John Jr., Sophia's older nephew, marched upstairs. "Asshole! You always do that when you're losing." The scene, common enough, stiffened Sophia's resolve to opt out of these reunions.

"Hey, Jimmy Junior, come over here," Sophia called, "and I'll tell you what your primary heuristic is." Still sniffling with outrage at the effects of capitalism on his hotels on Boardwalk, eight-year-old Jimmy came over and accepted a hug from Aunt Sophia.

"What?" he said.

"It says here that you come into the world equipped with your primary heuristic intact for survival and ... uh, procreation, but you need to be looked after for a while so you can learn all sorts of stuff, which lets you adapt to new situations."

Jimmy Jr. looked over at his father for him to respond.

"Bullroar, Sophia," the schoolteacher said. "Find meals, mates, and then the morgue. That's our genetic heritage, and that's where it stops."

"It says here," Sophia continued, "that schools, libraries, teachers, culture—all of that enables us to adapt to the unpredictable. We're wired to find out new stuff. Those are our secondary heuristics."

James warmed to the importance of teachers. "Whassit you're reading?" he asked.

"Something by Plotkin." Sophia turned the book over and showed him the title: *Darwin, Machines and the Nature of Knowledge.* It was a plod, but Sophia agreed with the basic thesis. Jimmy plopped himself down on the floor in front of a mass of Legos.

The next day, lunch was also communal, by tradition. Bernice served them around the dining-room table. That was traditional too. Bernice had been serving the Shulders for two decades, at their home in Brookline and here on the Cape. Bernice gave Sophia a huge BLT. "I can't eat all that. I'm getting fat," Sophia said, giving Bernice a sideways hug. While Bernice always favored Sophia's brothers, she was the one who'd shaken Sophia out of her depression when her father died.

Bernice stared down at Sophia. "You're eating for two now. Going to be a big boy, honey. Choke it down."

John and James turned the conversation to memories of their father.

"Dad wasn't here much in the summers," James said. "Pop came down for long weekends but stayed in the city working. Sometimes he would bring authors for a night or two on the cape. D'you remember Joyce somebody? He said she was his 'best find.'"

Gertrude took a long drink from her wineglass. James looked up, surprised, as Sophia kicked him under the table. Their father's field was modern Jewish literature at Brandeis. Midcareer he'd left his tenured, low-paying professorship to become a slightly better paid editor at a Boston publishing house.

"What did she write?" asked John Jr., over his sulk, with a surge of momentary interest. He wanted to be a poet.

"Novels. Women's stuff. Popular. Made a mint for the publishing house Dad worked for."

"Trash, nothing but trash," Gertrude stated. "Why your father gave up a prestigious professorship to work in the marketplace, I will never understand." Gertrude glared into her wineglass. "I had hopes that one of you would follow his academic tradition. The arts," she added, pointedly looking at Sophia.

Gertrude shuddered. "Joyce!" Sophia read the logic of her mother's drama. Sophia, her father's prodigy, had failed. If she'd been smarter, better at literature, her father wouldn't have sought an attachment outside the family. If Sophia had known what to do on the boat, her father wouldn't have died. It was sick, it was twisted, and it was justified.

The day had started well as eleven-year-old Sophia and her father motored into Buzzard's Bay from the marina near the Cape Cod Canal. A light wind blew from the east. Sophia's father, still spry enough in his early fifties, shut down the engine and raised the mainsail. Sophia sat with her feet over the bow and hanked the jib on the forestay. "Nice work, Sophia," her father said as he pulled up the jib smoothly. For once her brothers had been left at home, and Sophia had her father to herself.

The sloop hissed through the water at an easy four knots. "Aye, and ye better pull a tad to port, matey," her father directed. Sophia pushed the tiller over and screwed up her face in her most piratical fashion. "And we'll be sacking Troy before noon," she said, confusing books foisted on her by her hard-to-please father.

"Arrrgh," he said.

They sailed to an uninhabited island known locally as the Fortress because of escarpments that towered behind the narrow beach that encircled the island. They set anchor, the only boat in a protected cove. Sophia swam while her father read the *New York Times*, keeping a lazy eye on her. When they got hungry, they went ashore, their dinghy pulled above the tideline. They ate their peanut butter and honey sandwiches on the beach while Sophia's father told her that he was going to divorce her mother. He planned to live with Joyce, one of the authors he represented.

The noonday sun around Sophia dimmed. She heard her father's voice as if from a great distance: "Still love you … just work hard at whatever you do … life pretty much like before …" Blah, blah, blah.

For the next hour, Sophia sat on the shore building elaborate sandcastles. She stood looking at her work for a long time. Carefully, she put her foot through the moat and crushed through the outer wall. Then she mashed the topmost turret. Seawater, poured out of a trashed Coke can, dissolved the last remains of her creation.

They sailed out of the cove in the early afternoon, the sloop bobbing in confused waves deflected from the shore. As they rounded the island, the full force of the wind hit them, gusting to over twenty knots. The sailboat heeled and accelerated. With the mainsail let out all the way, her father held tightly to the tiller. The boat, a Pearson named *Conocimiento*, thirty feet long with a deep fin keel, was sufficiently stout for the conditions.

"I should have reefed before we left the cove, I guess," her father muttered.

Sophia didn't look at him.

"I can just make out the lighthouse at Red Brook," he said. "With this wind, we ought to make it less than an hour."

Sophia hunched farther down in the forward corner of the cockpit, as far away from her father as she could get. She wished he were dead. No other boats were in sight, unusual for this part of Buzzard's Bay on a weekend afternoon in early summer.

Though Sophia's father was a good enough sailor, he was

not as lithe as he should have been for what was rapidly becoming a storm at sea.

The wind shifted more to the south and hummed through the wire shrouds. Sophia looked up at the top of the mast, swinging below dark clouds. She felt sick, so she crouched in the center of the cockpit, bracing herself between the seats. Staring ahead, she burped peanut butter as the sloop dropped from the top of a wave into the trough, the bow shouldering green water. The dinghy towed behind them was half filled with water and swinging like a surly dog on a leash. At the last moment, the sailboat's delicate stern somehow rose above the surge. Her father gripped the tiller, intent on keeping the boat steady as it streaked downwind. She sensed he was proud of her, the way she was handling it, the way he insisted she manage everything. But she was not thinking of sailing. She was still thinking of Joyce. Fucking Joyce. The new verb, adjective, noun she'd just learned from the brothers.

Above the wind, Sophia's father roared something about the "anarchy of chaos damp and dark." He winked at her. She turned away.

Coming off the top of a wave, the boat slewed to port. Tired now, her father overcorrected and the bow came to starboard, too far. The boat jibed, the boom swung across the deck and cracked in the middle. The vang tore out of the cabin top and banged wildly, suspended from the broken boom. A sudden rip tore out a seam in the mainsail, spilling more wind. They lurched to starboard, tossing Sophia into the green water. Her father grabbed for her, lost his balance, and pitched headfirst into the cabin. On the roll back to port, Sophia slammed into the side of the boat just below the cockpit winch, lacerating her forehead. Blinded, dazed, choking on seawater, she hung suspended alongside the hull by a strap on her lifejacket that snagged on a cleat. The boat shuddered and rolled, abeam to the wind. The torn mainsail slatted, its insistent hammering mixed with the racket from below where cans, bottles, and tools clattered on the cabin floor as wave after wave swept under the boat. With the roll, Sophia was plunged underwater, then lifted again and banged into the side of the boat. The seawater stung the gash on her forehead. Instinctively, she reached for the lifeline and pulled herself up until she collapsed onto the cockpit sole. Flat on her stomach, she looked through a bloody haze for her father. She whimpered. Her father lay head down, only his feet visible in the cockpit. Sick from the blow on the head, the pitching, and the rolling, she slipped on the companionway steps and fell into the cabin, fracturing her left leg. Her father was bleeding, she couldn't tell from where. Broken glass, vomit, blood, and seawater sloshed around his head. She lifted his head onto her lap. The pain in her leg felt purposefully malignant.

"Daddy, Dad, please …"

His eyes widened as he stared at the cabin top. "You stupid idiot!" he blurted out, and then he died. He was right, of course. She had wished this would happen.

James walked toward her along the beach. She felt a moment of sisterliness, almost maternal in warmth. James was the centripetal one, always trying to unify them. But he was dim when it came to family dynamics. For most of his life, he'd been his older brother's foil, slave, admirer, and punching bag. And a too-willing accomplice when it came to bullying Sophia.

"What ho, noble sister?"

"James."

With no prelude, he launched his roster of complaints. "You're being a drag, Sophia. You don't talk with us, you don't play any games anymore."

Startled, Sophia took a deep breath and kept walking. James fell into step beside her and continued his litany. "You rag on Mom. You're a negative spirit over the family gathering. No one can have any fun when you're around."

Her anger flashed, then subsided as quickly as it began. In a sense, he was right. The one family member to whom she'd related was her father. She remembered his swinging her around, teaching her tennis, walking with her on the beach. It was John, not James, who knew the full story of Joyce.

She kept walking fast, the wet sand cold on her bare feet and sticking uncomfortably between her toes. She watched a wall of fog, immobile, half a mile off the beach. She'd always known she was meant for something special in life, but now the "what" was confused, impenetrable. She wasn't good at family. She wasn't sure if she was good at marriage. And it scared the hell out of her to think how she would be as a mother.

James clopped along in his flipflops half a step behind her.

"Jimmy, what was it like to have a baby, a son? How did you do it?"

"The usual way, I suppose." He grinned at her mockingly.

"I mean, what did it feel like after the baby was born?" Sophia held her brother's arm and pulled him closer as they walked, a conscious effort at family togetherness.

"Kind of cute. Domestic. My wife actually liked it so much she wouldn't let me do much with the baby."

"I worry about how I'll be," Sophia said. "How I'll feel. I'm scared I won't like it."

James yanked his arm away. "Christ, Sophia, that's exactly what I've been saying. With an attitude like that, you're going to be a really stupid mother."

She stopped dead for a moment, then reached down, picked up a piece of water-logged kelp, and swung it round, hitting him hard on the back. Irate gulls flapped off the waterline and shrieked. James stumbled. Tears started from his eyes. He turned and stalked back the way they'd come.

Sophia spent another half hour walking on the beach before returning to the house. Alone in the living room, Gertrude was rereading *Madame Bovary*. She looked at Sophia, who paused in the doorway vainly hoping to avoid all family members. "Your brother just came in. He says you're in a very bad mood."

"He's right, Gertrude. I am."

"Then I think it might be better for you to go, Sophia, and not make everybody else so miserable. I remember I was particularly unpleasant when I was pregnant with Jamie."

"Go? Where?"

"Back to Cleveland. Yes, now would be a good time." She picked up her novel and adjusted the table lamp against the waning afternoon light. "I love you, dear."

Sophia changed her reservation for her return flight to Cleveland. The following morning Gertrude got up to say goodbye and drifted around the kitchen in a silk kimono, pulling coffee and sugar off the shelves and dumping the unmeasured grounds into the filter. Voices of her grandchildren and their parents, occasionally punctuated with an offended cry, drifted indistinctly downstairs. Gertrude made a peanut butter and jelly sandwich for Sophia and put it with an apple in a brown paper bag, as if Sophia were going off to school.

Awaiting her taxi, Sophia stood on the porch beside her mother. Sophia sensed the pent-up feelings Gertrude could not articulate: a mother's love mingled with anger and oppression. Sophia refused to let herself feel the loss of her mother as well as her father. She gave her mother a hug. Sophia smelled cigarette smoke on her mother's kimono, stale wine on her mother's breath. "Mother, Mom, you're going to be a grandmother."

"I'm already a grandmother, dear. Of two wonderful boys, and the nieces, of course."

Sophia took a breath. "I just hope the baby brings us closer." It was one of those things daughters were supposed to say.

"I hope so too, dear."

Sophia wondered whether either of them meant it. Being a mother and not being a mother—was it a condition that was genetically transmissible? Her mother moved down the steps and searched the road for the cab. Shading her eyes, Sophia stared at the whitecaps topping iridescent blue waves. A perfect sailing day, wind steady at fifteen knots. So beautiful, and so scary.

The day after Sophia returned from Cape Cod, a cold rain splattered over the windowsill of Martin's small office on the third floor of a very ordinary red-brick building not far from Sophia's new science building. Once an apartment building, it now housed the English department at the edge of the campus. A breeze rattled the miniblinds, snatching random papers from Martin's inbox and scattering them onto the floor behind his road bike that still waited for a warm day. He placed his seventh-grade debating trophy onto the errant papers and closed the window. Martin abhorred grading term papers. The rote, mindless work made his head ache. Cleveland's damp April air didn't help. He forced himself to contemplate the stack of work ahead of him. His students were a varied lot, and he preferred talking with them rather than reading their attempts at writing. Some were blatantly uninterested in English literature, merely fulfilling a freshman requirement en route to careers in medicine or engineering. Some had clanking minds, no idea how language worked, in the same way that Martin did not understand internal combustion or how an embryo becomes a human being. What he did like were the occasional students whose epiphanies on first hearing Milton, Keats, or Eliot burst open their minds, a dramatic moment that was almost sexual in intensity. When they first met, Sophia had loved to hear him recite Donne.

Martin looked at his watch. Wednesday afternoon, 4:30. According to department regulations, he held office hours twice a week. Not likely any student would show up in the remaining half hour. He turned to the bookshelves behind his desk, planks supported by bricks, and pulled out a draft of his PhD thesis along with a thick manila folder. He blew the dust off the folder, and the notes inside gave a little shudder. Fine research. He liked culling the ideas of others from books deep in the library stacks. He wanted to extend his thesis into a book. Catch his career up with Sophia's. But the hundreds of three-by-five cards, product of years of research, somehow resisted all attempts at organization; they failed to reconfigure themselves as innovative ideas. The most creative thing he'd written in the past month was a to-do list. Face it, he told himself, he might never have enough new to say about T. S. Eliot and his gang for the world to pay particular attention. Sophia hadn't read much Eliot. She thought he was an anti-Semite who wrote only for males.

A tentative knock at the door was followed by a female voice. "Professor Shulder?"

One of the first-year graduate students pushed the door open and hesitated. Martin never knew whether to correct students when they called him professor. He was only an instructor. Angela Mott, one of his favorite students, tentatively stuck her head inside his door. She was literate, tall, blonde, and totally aware of her good looks. Perhaps it was unfair, but she also had talent. She wore a tight workout top under a baggy man's shirt. Martin wondered vaguely who had given it to her. Blue jeans and a red bandana around one thigh. Moccasins, no socks. Martin had read that morning that Christie Brinkley was dating Billy Joel, and Martin wondered whether he'd settled into marriage too early.

"Look, I know it's late, and I don't want to take much time."

"It's okay, really." Martin straightened and waved at the chair alongside his desk. Angela slowly approached the desk, put both hands on it and leaned over, looking behind Martin at his books.

"Wow. I didn't, you know, think that you were into the twentieth century so much."

Martin's eyes glared straight ahead. Why, why, why, when he was so obviously being manipulated, did he respond anyway? As if the gods had not fulfilled their quota of males necessary for the propagation of the species.

"Sit, Angela." He didn't play games with his students. "What can I do for you?" Martin already knew the answer. Like a few other ambitious, career-minded students in his seminar, Angela was hustling a good grade for the midterm exam he'd given them earlier that week. She curled into the straight chair, her legs tucked beneath her. Earlier Angela had told him that she yearned for a graduate degree in English that would lead her to a job as a fiction editor with a prestigious New York publishing company.

"I just wondered if you've had time to look at my blue book. I'm here for spring break, so I thought I could review it this weekend if you've graded it by now."

Twelve students in his seminar, and the exam was only two days ago. She expected him to have all the exams graded already?

His phone rang. He raised his hand for a moment. She pointed to herself and then to the door, asking a question with sign language. Martin indicated a chair and indicated the call would take just a moment.

"Sophia, what's up?" She'd returned the previous night and hadn't yet told him why she was back so soon.

"Late lab work. Sorry, Martin. Chicken potpie is defrosting on the counter. Put it in the oven at three seventy-five for twenty minutes. I'll be home around nine. Love you. What are you up to?"

Martin watched Angela prowl his few square feet of office space, taking in the photograph of Martin and Sophia lying on the beach. She spotted the blue books stacked on his desk with hers on top. She moved behind him and browsed the titles in his bookcase.

"Nothing much, just finishing office hours. A student's with me. See you later, Sophissima … Me too. Bye."

As he put down the phone, he sighed theatrically. "Where were we?" Martin looked at Angela, who had nestled back into the office chair across from him. He folded his hands, then unfolded them when he noticed he was inadvertently hiding his wedding ring. He straightened some papers on the desk, put his hands behind his head, and leaned back, then dropped his arms again in case of perspiration stains. Whenever such a strikingly beautiful woman walked by, his father would recite a Jewish prayer of thanks: *Baruch shekacha lo b'olamo.* Blessed be He who has such in His universe.

"The blue book?" she reminded him.

"Right, the blue book. Not yet, Angela. I'm tied up with a book I'm writing. I'll be grading next week."

She unfolded herself from the chair. "I'll be around all next week too, so if you don't mind? Could you give me a call when you grade it? And maybe we could go over it?" She placed a piece of folded beige notepaper on his desk and shot him a backward wave of her hand. "Bye."

Martin was sweating lightly. He unfolded the notepaper: Angela 218-3542. Purple ink.

"Goddammit, Angela. Stop right there."

She paused, half out the door, a salacious Mona Lisa. "What?"

"You don't have to pull this act. You're a good writer. Just put as much effort into your writing as you have here in my office."

Angela mouthed a small, soundless "Oh" and left hurriedly.

Martin stared at the wall, feeling angry and virtuous. Sophia was so much better at supervising people—of either sex. He got flustered when he had to give face-to-face feedback to students, especially when it was negative. Angela was good, erratic but good. So why did she need to practically strip in his office? He picked her blue book off the pile and read at random. "Something to live for is born out of desperation to know what you will put with your name." Where does she get this stuff? It was exactly how he felt—about his job, his book, the pregnancy, his marriage, his goddamn life. Whatever it was, he was still waiting for *it* to be born, and it was not the baby that Sophia was carrying.

Five o'clock. He could go home to an empty house now. But he sat there gazing at the raindrops. Leaves made trees in the quadrangle less skeletal. A few coeds moved slowly under umbrellas, hips swinging. Here and there, even a miniskirt.

He repositioned the picture of him and Sophia on his desk. He liked looking at her, especially when she was naked, which she didn't like. So he found he could observe her surreptitiously through their glass shower door. Tall and sleek, her head back, facing the jet of the shower, her eyes half shut, her body merging with clouds of steam. She murmured small sounds of languid comfort, the soapy luffa between her breasts, water sluicing from her shoulders. The baby pooching her belly. It was rare that Martin saw his wife so relaxed. Though she wasn't particularly emotional, Sophia enjoyed being in bed so much that Martin, his experience before marriage derived mainly from Western European literature and *Playboy*, felt his erotic needs were largely met, in quality if not in frequency.

He replaced Angela's midterm exam under the pile and repositioned his thesis on the bookshelf. Sophia had told him to redo his outline for his book, discuss it with colleagues, and come up with new insights linked to all the scholarship he'd already invested in his thesis. Really not that much different from writing a grant, she'd said. He stood up, stretched, then drove home to wait for his wife.

9

Six Months

Iris Malone and her classmates draped themselves around the small office of Dr. Sophia Shulder, eyeing the doctor surreptitiously. Now and again, Iris directed a smoky look, one she'd practiced in the mirror, across the room toward Tyrell. Ty and she were now special friends, and she wanted to be certain Ty remembered.

About ten of the biology students from Hough High School had elected to visit a research lab instead of being bussed to the science museum downtown. The day's purpose was to get an inside look at the job of a real scientist. Iris thought it was a fine way to get out of school by one o'clock on a spring day. She liked biology more than most of her other subjects, so after high school maybe she'd become a physician's assistant if she and her mom could scratch up the tuition.

"Call me Sophia," Dr. Shulder said after their biology teacher introduced her. Sophia's starched white lab coat only partially hid her pregnancy. The doctor wore a plain white shirt, dark skirt, loafers, a ring with a small diamond. No other jewelry. Though she looked pretty good, like she could be advertising a feminine hygiene product on TV or something, the lady could use some styling.

"She's not a doctor. She just plays one on TV," Iris whispered to the friend sitting next to her on a credenza neatly stacked with scientific journals. A few of the others stirred and snickered. Their teacher leaned forward in her folding chair and glared at Iris.

"You're right," Sophia pronounced, having overheard Iris's remark. "I am, and I'm not a 'real' doctor." She explained how she was different from a medical doctor. How PhDs study stuff in depth. "In my case, it's the way we are formed as a fetus—the way we inherit things," Sophia said. "Sex, if you like."

This brought on a general resettling of the students, signifying they were too cool to say, "Oh yeah, man, I do like it."

"What would you like to know?" Sophia asked with apparent sincerity.

"How much money do you make?" Jerome wasn't hostile, but his question was rude.

Sophia chuckled. "Now, about twenty-five thousand dollars a year, which is pretty good by most university standards. But I did four years of college, four more years for my PhD, and three years as a postdoc. Then it took me some more time to get a promotion with a shot at tenure."

Postdoc? A shot at tenure? Iris tried to deconstruct the unfamiliar terms.

"Would you earn more if you was one of the 'real' doctors?" Doc asked.

Doc got his nickname on the football team, defensive right tackle on varsity. You needed to call a doctor if his more than two-hundred-pound frame ran over you. It paid to keep Doc as a friend. He wasn't generally mean but could be.

"An MD does generally make more money, the kind of doctor most people think of when you say 'doctor.' Surgeons earn the most. But doctors come in all different flavors."

Sophia described the variety of medical specialties—surgery, radiology, pediatrics—and their training. It sounded to Iris like an awful lot of schooltime.

"What's a radiologist do?"

Sophia smiled. "Radiologists read x-rays, but sometimes they do special tests like barium swallows and enemas."

Embarrassed for Sophia, Iris listened to the guys' whispered fart jokes for a minute.

"So how do you work if you're gonna have a baby?" Iris asked, looking at her feet. Iris had missed her last period. She felt Ty looking at her.

"Well, that takes some thought," Sophia said. "I can work up to the time the baby comes. I'm being careful with the kind of chemicals I handle in the lab. The evidence says I probably shouldn't drink or smoke or have a lot of x-rays. I don't do heavy lifting, and I'm taking it easier with my schedule. The real problems will come up after the baby is born."

"What do you do in here all day?" another student asked.

"Today we're trying to separate chromosomes from some mice eggs and see if we can find regions on the chromosomes that are undergoing transcription."

Several of the students looked around the room. No mice in sight.

"Wait, let me try that again. You're near the end of your year of biology. You know the drill. DNA, chromosomes. The genes are lined up on the chromosomes like Christmas tree lights. Each gene has control elements that turn it on or off.

When we spread the chromosome out on a slide and look at it with an electron microscope, we can see the chromosome 'telling' the cell to make a protein. And why is that important? What do proteins do in your body?"

That was an easy question. "Lots of things," Iris said.

Sophia looked at her. "Right. What sorts of things do you have in mind?"

That wasn't so hard. "Make chemical reactions go faster so we have some energy," Iris said. Her teacher smiled at her.

"Right again," the Sophia said. "Some proteins are catalysts. An analogy is adding some yeast to flour and water to make bread rise faster. But how big are proteins?"

"Tiny," Doc said.

"How tiny? Could you see a protein under a regular microscope?"

"Naw. Too small."

"You guys are good. That's generally true. How small?" Sophia asked.

A friend of Iris's said, "Nanometers."

"Very good. Again, generally true." Sophia kept at it. "And final question. What are proteins made of?"

No answers.

"Iris'll know. She's the smart one in our class." That was Ty. Sweet.

"It's a trick question," Iris said. "You could mean atoms, molecules, or amino acids."

Ty punched her lightly on the shoulder. "Good one."

Sophia seemed pleased. "You folks are brainy. And your teacher deserves credit too." Iris thought maybe Doc S had been easy with her questions. As if reading her mind, Sophia lifted a photograph lying on her desk and held it up." The point of our research is to find proteins that control how an embryo turns into a fetus, and see how certain proteins do their job, particularly how the brain starts to develop. Have you ever listened to a choir singing with an orchestra? All those voices and musical instruments working together to make a wonderful complex sound? The proteins we're after are all those elements that control the development of the embryo that becomes the fetus, then the baby."

"Look at this photo," Sophia continued. "It's a picture of a chromosome from a mouse egg. We've lit up DNA sequences that we think are telling the cell to make specific proteins. This process is called transcription."

Iris's classmates were interested. Iris looked closely at the shadowed photograph.

"How come there's those places with no transcription?" Iris asked.

"Good question. I don't know," Sophia said.

Peering at the photo, the students jostled each other.

"Whaddaya mean, eggs from mice? Ducks have eggs."

"Yeah, and what do you got?"

"Testules ain't eggs."

"Sperm's spit. Who needs it?"

"You do, Penis Breath. It's stuck in your hair."

Sophia raised an eyebrow to the teacher, who said, "Maybe we need a little more show and less tell." Sophia led them into the lab.

"Beyond cool," Iris said, fingering the instruments. Sophia signaled to a young woman in a dirty lab coat who trailed the group, resetting every turned dial.

On the way out, Iris and her classmates shook Sophia's hand. "So how far along are you?" Iris asked.

Sophia smiled at her. "We have a draft of our latest research findings in manuscript, and I just resubmitted my NIH grant."

Iris shook her head. "No, the baby."

"Oh," Sophia laughed. "I'm coming up on six months now."

On the way out, four or five of the students muttered, "Thanks, ma'am." Sophia looked relieved. Relieved but pleased. Iris could tell that she was not used to being around kids.

"You know, if any of you have any questions," Sophia said, "or want to come back and spend some more time looking around the lab, that's okay with me. In fact, I'd like that."

Nice, Iris thought. "Malignantly white," as Arsenio Hall put it on late-night TV, but nice.

Dear Dr. McKennen,

We thank you for your visit and seminar a few months ago. You have a lot of supporters here in Cleveland. Unfortunately, we have been advised by the dean to take a few more months and widen the search somewhat to meet new university rules regarding affirmative action. Just wanted to give you a heads-up to let you know our thinking, and why there have been delays in the search process.

Sincerely,

In her dark paneled office, the formidable Ellen Larkin handed the letter back to Mac and gave him a sly smile.

"Well, hell," he said. "I thought the dean at Cleveland was eager to have me sign immediately."

Ellen already knew Mac was interested in the position; he'd told her after he came back from Cleveland. But given her vast network of contacts—colleagues and former trainees in every ranking medical school in the country—it was probably old news to her by then. Had she talked with the dean in Cleveland? Mac was too cowardly to ask, but it was inconceivable that she hadn't. She probably knew this letter was coming, even knew what it would say before he came by her office, fuming.

"You know, don't you, Mac, that affirmative action is taken pretty seriously these days? Despite the fact that Reagan wants to dismantle it. Or maybe because of that."

She was right, of course. As usual, she made him feel better. She prioritized helping her staff and faculty move up, so there was a throng of students, residents, and junior faculty who idolized her. Meanwhile, there were some senior faculty people who felt that the needs of the department—and theirs in particular—were getting short shrift.

"Yeah, but does the dean mean it, or is he just unhappy with the search committee's short list?" From Mac's own considerably less-developed grapevine, he'd thought it was a done deal.

"Who's to know?" she said, knowing full well that Mac knew she knew. How much had affirmative action helped Ellen get her own position? It was clear to her that women in leadership roles had to be better than the males. Mac knew the handful of really good ones, like Ellen, were treated like royalty so they wouldn't yield to blandishments from other universities.

The job in Cleveland was still being advertised; Mac had seen it in the *New England Journal* with the usual note appended: "The university is an equal opportunity employer ..."

"There are no black or womenfolk with my credentials," Mac blurted out. Ellen raised her eyebrows as she once did in Mac's first year of training when he'd announced he planned to write the definitive monograph on the disease Ellen had studied for decades. "Young pup," was the only part of her withering response he remembered.

"Give it some time, Mac. We like having you here. I'm sure it will work out for the best."

Sophia didn't enjoy bridge or games in general, but it was a good way to pass an evening with the in-laws. Martin's parents were passing through Cleveland on their annual pilgrimage from Philadelphia to their summer home on Mackinac Island. Sophia had been there after the wedding; Martin wanted to show her all the places where he'd once slain dragons and discovered pirate wealth. They'd had a good time—bicycling, hiking, horseback riding, tennis, all things she loved. They learned a little more about sex too. Martin's ease about life translated into frequent calls for lovemaking.

Martin's cuddly parents embraced Sophia as a daughter unreservedly. Both parents were gray-haired, their age illuminated by the lamps beamed onto their playing cards. Though no longer an observant Jew, Martin's father, Nathan, wore a small yarmulke at home. He held a cigarette almost permanently, ash falling in his lap. The elder Shulders seemed so much less judgmental than Sophia's family. And almost no tension. Nathan loved playing games, jokes, talking, drinking. Martin's mother, Edna, from a prosperous Reform family, had married somewhat beneath her station. After getting her BA from Brandeis, she'd given up graduate studies to marry Nathan before he shipped out as a tactical support officer during the Korean conflict. The house in Mackinac had been in Edna's family all the way back to the early 1900s, when rich Chicago industrialists like her grandfather—the inventor of those curved steel curtain hooks—built manorial summer homes on the island. If Sophia's in-laws had a fault, maybe all that money made them too easygoing.

Sophia had spent almost two days preparing their dinner, finally opting for a simple menu of roast beef, mashed potatoes, green beans, and a lemon meringue pie. Nathan and Edna appreciated every mouthful. The patio doors were open. A light breeze blew indoors as their bridge game heated up. Unwary insects hurtled into the electric bug killer outside and sizzled with an acrid smell. Sophia was dummy on a bid of four hearts as Nathan, her partner, sweated out the contract for the first rubber. She riffled the pages of their wedding album, remembering the moment Martin proposed. There were the pictures of their camping trip in the Adirondacks.

Sophia remembered awakening to a fine gauze of cool fog. From the door of their tent, she could see only the ragged lower boughs of pine trees looming over them. The upper branches dissolved in the mist, but she heard them swaying in the wind. Huge, scary sounds but somehow soothing too.

Sophia dozed, only to feel Martin's arm under her red-checked pajamas. Sleeping bags that zipped together were one of the great products of twentieth-century technology. She lay still. Sex was best for her when she wasn't quite awake, when her analytical edges were dulled, and she didn't feel compelled to make it work. She relaxed into flannel and warm solid flesh. Inside their orange tent, their breath came fast, intense. Hot wet kisses, urgent nestling.

They were the only two people on earth as they lay together in the snow-patched immensity of the forest. Martin said drowsily, "Marry me. I love you."

Sophia felt like she did when a biochemistry exam came back with an A plus. A surge of warmth and contentment diffused through her body. An achievement. She wanted to tell someone, to show off the grade on her paper.

"So what kind of ring did you have in mind?" she asked, only half joking.

"Can't. Not yet. Impecunious grad student," he said, pulling the sleeping bag up around his head. She poked him so he wouldn't fall asleep again. This was an important moment.

"No poesy?'

"Too tired," he murmured. "I love you. Marry me."

But soon Martin raised himself on his elbow and gently combed his fingers through Sophia's hair.

"'Desdemona. My fair warrior!'"

"More," she said, fitting her body to his. "More!"

"'It gives me wonder great as my content / To see you here before me. O my soul's joy!'" Martin blew gently into her ear. "'If after every tempest come such calms, may the winds blow, till they have wakened death."

Sophia's eyes closed.

"Yo! Death. Wake up!" Martin shook the sleeping bag off Sophia's now nude body.

"Stop that, stop!" she said, pulling the cover back over them both. She settled into the recovered warmth, wanting more.

"'And let the laboring bark climb hills of seas, Olympus-high, and duck again …'" Martin buried his head between her breasts and quacked loudly.

Sophia giggled. "We weren't that strenuous."

Martin surfaced, waving in the air to mark the iambs. His finger tapped now and again on Sophia's nose. "'I fear my soul hath her content so absolute that not another comfort like to this succeeds in unknown fate.'"

"Oh, my Othello!" Sophia exclaimed, feeling an importunate bulge on her smitten swain.

⁓

"Two no-trump!" Nathan opened the bidding with a Shakespearean wave of his arm.

Oh Lord, Sophia thought, putting aside the album, brought back to the present by her histrionic father-in-law. Nothing appealed to Nathan so much as a grand gesture, a trait that had made and lost him several fortunes during his brokerage years. She wondered whether he really had the points necessary for his opening bid.

"You couldn't make one no-trump, you riverboat gambler?" Edna ribbed him genially. "I'll double that."

Nodding absently at her mother-in-law, Sophia bid four hearts, giving Nathan the Jacoby transfer option.

"Double," Martin said, distractedly.

"Four no-trump," his father countered without a pause, looking pleased with himself. He completely missed Sophia's bidding convention.

"Double," Edna said, smiling as she recounted her cards. "Oh boy, Martin, we're going to cream them." Looking at Sophia, she added, "Sorry, dear, I should tamp down my competitive urges and treat you more like my enormously dear and very pregnant daughter-in-law."

Sophia considered the slam possibilities. Edna was the challenge. Hearts or spades? Sophia held the ace and queen of spades.

"Six spades," she said, a small slam. Martin passed. Nathan looked startled but had the sense to pass. After tapping her hand on the table for a minute, Edna doubled again.

Bingo, thought Sophia. Pass, pass. "Redouble," Sophia said, all in. But she'd have to play the hand.

Martin led a small diamond that played to Sophia's singleton ace. Then it was just a matter of time till his mother lost her final trump, assuring Sophia and Nathan's big win.

Sophia sat back, trying hard not to look smug. Nathan announced, "This will go down in the annals of our family history. Our first grandchild will be telling the tale to his grandchild in the next millennium!"

"We'd better let you quit while you're ahead," Edna said, just a bit grim at their loss. It was 10:30 on a Saturday night.

Elated, Nathan was in no mood for having the evening end. "So do you have a name for that grandchild of ours yet? Personally, I think Ezekiel would do. My grandfather's name."

Martin grinned at his father. It must have been an old family joke.

"How about a name based on his personality?" Edna chimed in.

"Personality? Mom, he hasn't even been unwrapped yet," Martin said.

"I dunno," Sophia said, "How about Dopey? It's the way he's been acting the past week or so. Kind of quiet in there." She smiled. "I think he's going to be laid-back like Martin and not wired like me. Fortunately."

76

"Oh, sweetie." Nathan looked over his half glasses at Sophia. "We like you fine. I told Martin this afternoon we want him to be just like you when he grows up."

Sophia poked Martin in the ribs and thought how she missed her own father.

10

Seven Months

Iris Malone stepped off the Carnegie Street bus near the hospital. She was twenty-six weeks pregnant. In the dim yellowish light that followed a thundershower, she walked the half block from the bus stop to the medical center's emergency room.

The receptionist at the registration desk was Molly, according to the nametag that hung askew on her massive bosom. Iris eyed her. Molly raised her arched eyebrows in return, barely glancing at the glittery words on Iris's T-shirt: "What's Love Got To Do With It?" Iris tried to stand up straight in her faded jeans and look as if she were not having cramps while Molly typed.

NAME: Desiree Matone
ADDRESS: 1428 Scovill
PHONE: None
CONTACT PHONE: None
SS NO: None
TIME: 16.35
INSURANCE: Medicaid (undocumented)

REL.PREF: Baptist
PERSON TO NOTIFY: None
PRIMARY CARE SITE: None
PRIOR VISITS: None
CHIEF COMPLAINT: Bleeding down below

Molly hit a key and an eight-digit hospital number emerged on her screen. She pulled a sheet of paper from the printer, attached it to a metal clipboard, and placed it in a slot labeled "Waiting Room, STAT."

Iris found a restroom. Breathing through her mouth to avoid the stench of urine and vomit, she bent over in the locked stall to change her pad, her eighth that day. When she came out of the restroom, a few men watched her stumble back to a seat. In a corner across the room, Iris recognized a furtive drug deal being transacted. A man, a boy really, not more than twenty, gesticulated soundlessly. Others were spread out, trying to sleep on the chipped plastic seats. The early news on a TV suspended in the waiting room showed Reagan addressing his fellow Americans. Iris didn't feel like one of them.

Forty minutes later they called out the name Desiree. Iris looked around the waiting room to see what Desiree looked like before she realized they were calling her fake name. Bent over, she entered a small room with unpleasantly green walls, a gunmetal desk, and a table with a thin mattress covered with a paper sheet. Iris lay down on the table, thankfully.

An emergency room resident in a short white coat and picture ID, Thomas Nichols, MD, entered the examining room.

"Desiree, is it? What seems to be the trouble? Your mom here with you?"

"No. I've been having some bleeding down below."

Nichols picked up her wrist and took her pulse. He took her hand again, then dropped it hurriedly.

"Okay, we're going to have to do some stuff here. You just hang tight." Iris felt dizzy. A gray-haired nurse appeared. Nichols barked at her. "We need an IV, type and cross, CBC, blood culture, chemistries, a temp, and a BP right away. Let's set up for a pelvic. Christ, Stella, she looks shocky. Let's go, let's go, let's go."

Stella put a thermometer under Iris's tongue and wrapped a cuff around her upper arm. She pumped it up, then listened with a stethoscope as the pressure hissed out of the cuff. Shaking her head, she puffed up the cuff a second time and let out the pressure more quickly before recording some notes on a chart.

"Don't worry, honey," Stella said. "Just stay down. We'll get you feeling better."

Iris mumbled some thanks when Stella removed the thermometer and trotted out of the room, returning in moments with a cart laden with equipment. She hit the intercom button and Iris heard her say, "Stat page the ob/gyn resident on call." Stella reminded Iris of her mother.

Nichols poked his head back in the room, ran his hand through his hair, and waited.

"Stella, stat page the ob/gyn resident, and put her up in stirrups. Desiree, we're going to have to do a pelvic exam and check you out, okay?"

"Uh, Doc," Stella said, "I already paged the resident. The BP is seventy over thirty, so how about we get some volume running?"

"Right, right, let's do it."

They were just finishing drawing the blood and puncturing Iris's forearm for an IV when a young woman walked in wearing a white jacket.

"Hi, I'm OB on call. How come you interrupting my supper?"

Dr. Nichols explained the bleeding problem and listed the vital signs.

"Hi, um, Desiree? I'm Dr. Ment, Claudia to you, local expert on female problems. How many pads today? You pregnant? Where's your mom?"

Iris felt kind of high and detached. Was this a real doctor? Doctors didn't come from her neighborhood.

"I dunno, I've missed some periods, I guess," Iris said.

Claudia kept up a cheery chain of questions as she stretched latex gloves onto her hands and started the pelvic exam. "Women's work," Dr. Nichols muttered, and left the room looking for some flesh to stitch up.

"Son of a gun, honey," Claudia said, her hands pushing on Iris' lower abdomen. "This uterus of yours is about twenty-seven weeks pregnant. We've got to bring you into the hospital. You've lost a lot of blood. This is not good. Now tell me your real name so's we can call your folks. 'Desiree' sounds like a hooker."

Obstetric delivery note: *A 17 y/o black G1 para 0 to 1 entered from the ER with vag bleeding and crampy abd pain. Vital signs in ER: BP 70/30 pulse 93, temp 38. No prenatal care. Gestation estimated at 27 weeks. Uterus tender. Cx exam deferred because of poss previa. Rule out abruptio placenta. Brought to delivery floor where fetal heart rate of 140 dropping to 60 with contractions was noted with bright red vag bleeding. Patient given two units of blood and taken to the DR, where patient was found to be in active labor with cervix dilated to 9 cm and the placenta partially lying free in the introitus.*

A crash CS was carried out under general anesthesia and at 9:10 PM a liveborn male premature infant was delivered. Apgars of 2 and 5 noted. Infant weighed 920 g. Post-partum hemorrhage continued per vagina after suturing the uterus, so despite usual measures, hysterectomy was performed. (See Dr. Stackpole's note).

The newborn was handed to pediatrics. They intubated and ventilated and later transferred to Children's NICU with a dx of prematurity with respiratory distress syndrome.

No foul-smelling lochia and temp was normal p delivery. Cultures and CBC sent. NPO till morning with D5 saline 2 liters over 12 h. Mom consented to prenatal labs and drug testing.

Claudia Ment, MD, OB. 3rd-year

At first Iris wasn't even allowed to get out of bed to take a pee. They shot something into a vein that made her shaky, then something else that made her sleepy and weak. The nurses told her that she had lost a lot of blood. They had to take out her uterus because the bleeding wouldn't stop. They asked her about drugs. Coke could do that to her, they said. But, hell, she couldn't afford that shit. Didn't like it anyway. Ty gave her a little but not much, said he had to save it for the white folks.

Her mother, Mattie, came too. "Honeybabysugar, whyn't you tell me?" And she cried. Iris said she was sorry and repeated it about a dozen times and tried to comfort Mattie. And then she said to herself, "Isn't this some shit, just who's the mother here?" until she thought about that some. "Who's going to want you now?" asked Mattie, not expecting an answer. "Seventeen years old with your own baby, and the little thing come early and might die or might never be right in the head, weak and sickly? What were you thinking?"

Iris watched the soaps on the little TV above her bed in the university hospital's public ward. She remembered doing sex with Ty, who was on the football team, big, and cool with his hands, not to mention other stuff that could heat her up just thinking about it, so maybe he'd come round and it was worth it and all. I can do this, I'm cool, I'm totally together and shit, but she sure wished Mattie would've stopped crying when she visited and would have taken her in her arms and told her Honeybabysugar, it's going to be all right with a fine baby that we can both love and care for and never mind if that shit that did it to you never comes around.

The day after her C-section, they said Iris could see her baby. They put her in a wheelchair, and a nurse's aide pushed her to the neonatal intensive care unit. Waiting to be buzzed in, Iris sounded out the letters. NICU. Nick You?

The majority of infants were housed in waist-high Plexiglas incubators, some of them under bright fluorescent lights. Several babies were attached to green respirators that resembled skinny, half-finished robots. All activity was focused on the occupants of the plexiglas boxes. Iris thought it looked like a scene from a science fiction movie.

A nurse wheeled Iris to one of the incubators. The nurse pointed inside the clear plastic. "Yours," she said, by way of introduction. Iris peered down. The infant, smaller than one of her slippers, looked like a toy baby. Tiny. Eugene, she'd call him. Eugene, after her favorite uncle in Detroit. "Eugene?"

she whispered. "We're going to take some getting used to each other."

Iris sat in a rocking chair next to the incubator, watching the baby and the activity in the unit. They showed her how to put her hands in the incubator's portholes and feel his legs, the only place she was allowed to touch him. With all the equipment surrounding them, it was as if Iris and her baby had been beamed onto some other planet where they were doing experiments on mothers and their babies. But Eugene was a baby all right. Her baby. She had to believe that all the staff buzzing around were doing right by Eugene. Faith, as Mattie would say. You had to have faith that it will come out okay. Iris had never been able to have Mattie's faith, but Iris could hope. She stayed as long as they let her despite the ache from her stitches. When an aide came to wheel her back to her hospital bed, Iris took one last look. Baby Eugene was attached to an awful lot of tubes and wires.

The day after Iris Malone's emergency Caesarian section at Women's Hospital, Sophia drove up a long driveway to Professor Stanton's house. Sophia wedged her aging Karmann Ghia behind a long line of sleek cars. Sophia wasn't certain why she'd been invited to stop by for drinks at the home of her chairman and his wife, Juliet. Maybe for a meet and greet for some visiting professor.

Maple trees sagged overhead from the August heat and humidity. Despite a sleeveless shirt, last summer's purchase at a sports store, she was sweating. Martin's white dress shirts were more comfortable, but she couldn't wear them to work, and she refused to pay the prices at those downtown boutiques for the "Lady-in-Waiting." Her bra was too tight, her stringy hair felt greasy, and her head and back ached.

A seltzer on ice would be nice. Just one. She dragged herself up the flagstone steps to the door of an impressive Shaker Heights manor, not bad for a professor in biochemistry. The wife must have money.

The wife, Juliet, opened the door, and a blast of air conditioning froze Sophia's sweat. Juliet welcomed Sophia with a two-sided kiss before taking her hand and leading her into the living room. Dark wood bookcases on either side of a brick fireplace. Above the mantel hung an English hunting scene, the fox still alive and running. Under her feet lay a thick Berber carpet. A rustling sound came from the dining room as if a wave were beginning to break, then a female chorus of "Surprise!" blew into Sophia's face, pushing her back a step.

"Sophia, Sophia, forgive us. We knew an old-fashioned baby shower would be *de trop* for the eighties, but we decided to do it anyway," said Juliet, guiding Sophia to an easy chair, one she could get out of without assistance. Twelve or so women, some of whom Sophia knew, filed out of the dining room, smiling at her and nudging each other. Byria, her postdoc, was among them, already looking a little high. Wrapped presents were stacked under an expansive coffee table.

"Ladies, let's give this working woman some punch and cool her off before we have a go at her."

Juliet was plump but sophisticated in a long silk Furstenberg dress. She bustled around making introductions, handing Sophia her frosty seltzer, and serving more wine or punch for the others.

It gave Sophia a minute to tell herself, I can get through this, I can do it. It comes with motherhood. She was sorry she hadn't taken the time to drive home first and shower. She concentrated on breathing evenly. She would adapt. She remembered the secondary heuristics that she would model for her son.

"So how is the pregnancy going so far?" Another department chair's wife stood over Sophia, who couldn't sit up straight in the cushy leather chair.

"Well, not so bad, not so bad," Sophia answered automatically. Something more was called for. "I had a lot of vomiting in the first trimester, and I've gained thirty-two and a half pounds." She searched a creaky part of her brain for something positive to say to this mother of three. "But my blood pressure is remaining normal."

"Isn't it weird to be pregnant when you're actually working on the mechanisms of reproduction?" the woman persisted.

Sophia felt the implicit intent. "That's hard to answer. I have lots of expertise in the lab but not much when it comes to being pregnant and actually having a baby."

"Oh, you'll do fine, dear. Mostly things go well. My second was a 'blue baby,' but we took him to Hopkins. He had an operation, and now he's twenty-eight and just fine. Runs a mile every morning. But Juliet was telling us about your lab work. I mean, you understand how all the molecules in the embryo can get screwed up and everything."

Sophia felt that she was being criticized, but for what? Working? Ignoring the ugly possible outcomes? Being different?

"I don't think about it, the things that can go wrong," Sophia lied.

The conversation finally swirled away down the rapids of popular science. How you'd eventually be able to mandate the color of your baby's eyes. Byria, taking center stage, explained how, with some small help from Sophia, that someday it might be possible to engineer embryos of mice with fluorescent spots that glowed under black light.

"But why would anyone want to do that, dear?" Juliet asked.

Relieved to be out of the limelight, Sophia thought about her pregnancy, which was increasingly unpleasant. But that wasn't the issue. Pregnancy was a limited state, a means to an end, like graduate school. Sophia liked challenges but preferred achievements. Even more than that, she liked to discover the meaning of things. Her paper on chromatid exchanges had been turned down earlier in the week by the *Journal of Clinical Investigation*. Peer review was difficult but surmountable. Being pregnant, walking the walk, doing what had to be done to produce a genuine live baby—that was something no peer reviewer could deny. She was scared and excited. Like taking a difficult exam: if you'd done your homework, you knew you'd pass the test. She'd put together a Lotus spreadsheet for the schedule during the countdown. Nursery curtains were juxtaposed with control experiments and the resubmission of her paper. Martin's list included the insurance policy and baby-proofing the house. Last summer Martin had accidently killed Sophia's young prize roses with turpentine that was still under the kitchen sink. Never mind that the baby wouldn't be crawling for months.

The doorbell rang, and an elegant young stranger brushed past the hostess and through the room of surprised women.

"Amy!" Sophia cried, and put her hands up for a hug.

"You bet, Soph." Amy hugged her tightly. "Martin told me about the shower. I'm on my way back from a meeting in

Chicago. You'd better feel some guilt, kiddo. You never let me know about this shindig."

"But I didn't know either," Sophia almost wailed, holding up her arms for another hug. She tried to speak once, twice, but there was a huge lump in her throat and her eyes were wet.

"I've been scared," she whispered.

"No more reason to be. I get it. I'm here."

"Game time, gang." Juliet's pronouncement stopped all conversation. Game? Sophia was new to baby showers. She dried her eyes surreptitiously.

First came the string game. Everyone cut a piece of string, the length they guessed would match the exact girth of Sophia's seriously protruding abdomen. The woman with the blue baby waved a string at least twice Sophia's size. Amy grinned and winked at Sophia from the back of the crowd.

For the next game, Juliet placed a number of baby items on a large tray and passed it around. Then she took it out of the room, and all the women had to write down as many items on the platter as they could remember. Sophia won easily. Since all the presents stacked under the table were for her, she was declared ineligible for the prize, and instead the runner-up was awarded a gift massage. While Juliet served a gooey, multilayered chocolate cake, fruit salad, and coffee, Sophia opened her gifts. The first was a certificate for a shop that bronzed baby shoes.

Amy whispered to Sophia, "Will you give me one of the shoes to hold my vibrator?"

11

Eight Months

Baby Eugene, Iris's baby, lay in the NICU across an enclosed bridge that connected it to the obstetric wing of the medical center. Alicia Mendez, the nurse caring for Eugene, unaware his morphine was wearing off. Alicia didn't know she was hurting him when she disconnected Eugene from the ventilator and suctioned his trachea through the endotracheal tube. The resulting irritation in Eugene's trachea caused sufficient pain to cause a surge of epinephrine from his adrenal glands that transiently raised his blood pressure. Already weakened by asphyxia when Iris's placenta separated, capillary walls couldn't withstand the increased pressure and leaked blood into Eugene's brain tissue. The senior resident, Dr. Eli Kurz, did a quick exam on Iris's baby, and ordered an intravenous push of bicarbonate along with some normal saline to treat Baby Eugene's decreased blood pressure and increasing acidosis. A marble-sized area of the infant's brain died within minutes.

"Damn, this kid is unstable," said Alicia as Baby Eugene's heart rate dropped again. The baby went into shock.

Kurz, Alicia, and the on-call intern, Steve Calvert, responded by the book. They ordered an immediate blood transfusion, continued the antibiotics. Within an hour the acidosis resolved.

"That was scary. Glad you were here. Why'd the blood pressure tank like that?" Steve asked Dr. Kurz.

"Good question, Steve. Micropreemies do this sometimes. We did the right things. We'll get a head ultrasound. Sometimes we never know."

Nobody had done anything wrong. They had done the right things, but they hadn't done the right things right.

It was 3:00 a.m. when Iris was shaken awake with the news. She'd been at the hospital with the baby till 11:00 p.m. The nice nurse, Alicia, had told her how well he was doing.

Mattie, her mother, yelled, "Iris, Iris honey, get up now! C'mon, you gotta get up, *now*, hear? Get in here and take the phone. It's the hospital, Baby Eugene has had a bad spell."

Iris pulled on her bathrobe and took the phone, stretching the cord right across the living room.

A nurse she didn't know was on the line. The situation, she was saying, was not good. Last night Alicia had said that Eugene had "turned the corner," but this wasn't Alicia on the phone. "Baby Eugene had a sudden 'downer,'" the voice told her. It was serious. She'd better come immediately.

Iris and Mattie got into a cab, holding one of the vouchers the social worker had given them in case of emergency. At 3:00 a.m. the streets of Cleveland were deserted. The cab driver deliberately kept his eyes on the road, avoiding whatever tragedy was pulling his two fares to the hospital at that hour.

In the NICU, Alicia took Iris and Mattie into the conference room next to the nursery and sat them at a large table littered with textbooks, knapsacks, hospital charts, Pepsi cans, oranges, brown paper bags, coffee cups, and stethoscopes. Alicia took a chair opposite them and reached across the table to take Iris's hand.

"Since you were called," she began, "the baby's stabilized. We have him on medication and he's getting a transfusion. His heart rate and blood pressure are okay. I have to get back in there; we're still working on him. As soon as things are settled a little more, you can talk with the intern and the resident."

The nurse's words came out too fast for Mattie and Iris. They sat silently, stupefied from shock and fatigue. Twenty minutes later, they were taken to Eugene's incubator. He was attached to more wires and tubes—taped to his chest and abdomen, extending from every orifice. Iris's baby was pale and still, breathing in sync with the ventilator, not the squirmy, cute little thing she'd left just hours earlier.

"He looks awful, Momma."

"I know, honey. Well, look, they're doing everything they can for him."

A young man dressed in whites entered the room and surveyed them tentatively.

"I'm the intern, Dr. Calvert. Steve. You are?"

"I'm the momma, and this is the baby's grandmother."

"Well, what we think has happened is that the baby may have had a little bleed into his head. He destabilized, but we got him back."

"Is Eugene going to live, Doctor?" Iris asked.

"He's very small, and this is a setback. We don't know. We'll just have to wait and see."

If they didn't know, who would? Weren't they supposed to know? Isn't that why they were here? This doctor looked awfully young. Maybe Iris should ask for an older doctor? But they had her baby. Maybe it wasn't a good idea to piss them off.

"Anything else?" the doctor asked.

"No, no. Thank you. You just go on caring for Baby Eugene as best as you can," Mattie answered for the two of them.

Iris turned, hugged Mattie, and rested her head on her mother's shoulder. Mattie stroked her hair. "It'll be all right, sugar. That baby of yours is strong stuff."

The next morning in Boston, Mac called Ellen Larkin as soon as he opened the letter. "I got the offer from Cleveland."

"Oh, Mac. I'm glad, and proud of you too. I knew it would come through."

She was so cordial, and so capable of behind-the-scenes politicking, that for a split second Mac doubted his own success. Had she manipulated the whole deal just so she could find someone new and jazzier for Harvard? Maybe a molecular biologist? There was no regret in her voice. But then, maybe she wanted to hear a bit more regret from Mac.

"Ellen, how much of your fine hand was in all this? What do I owe you? What do you know?"

She and Mac loved gossiping about the personalities in pediatrics, the people they worked with. It was part of Mac's education in how the real academic world worked.

"I didn't do much. All I know is you'd better be nice to Stanton, their head of biochemistry. When the dean was re-considering the woman on the short list, Stanton marched into the dean's office and announced that there would be a faculty revolt if recruitment standards were subverted by some debased view of affirmative action. The dean called me for my opinion, and I supported Stanton."

"Ellen, how am I going to survive without you?" Mac asked.

It was not flattery. When Mac had to deal with a balky administrator, all he had to do was suggest that he'd have to confer with Ellen. That always solved the impasse.

"You'll do just fine."

"I don't know. You're The Boss. You're so much smarter than I am."

"True, true enough, Mac. But this is Harvard. In Cleveland the wants and needs of the Bible-belted ones are so much simpler."

Mac laughed. Though he knew she would always be there for him, he'd bet that she already had one or two women in mind to replace him. Her department would be a model of affirmative action.

"So what's the offer?" she asked.

Mac told her, a bit sorry he hadn't asked her to help him formulate his conditions. But she was frugal to a fault. Mac suspected she would urge him to lower his salary proposal, modest though it seemed.

"Sounds all right to me. Just find me a good hotel in Cleveland," she added, "so I can visit from time to time, and a great place where you can take me to dinner."

Ellen was a savant and a rare, genuine sweetie. Mac wondered yet again whether he could or would make it in the big world out there without her protection.

12

Nine Months

On an October afternoon, Sophia sat in sunlit bleachers overlooking center court. Martin was tied up at an all-day retreat of the English department, and she'd skipped out of the lab to watch the finals of the Crestwood Tennis Tournament. The match was sold out, and she paid a scalper twenty-two dollars for a ticket. Nastase was down two games in the fourth set. Bjorn Borg had won the first set, Nastase, the next two. The players were grinding out the game point by point. It was precision tennis, the way Sophia liked it. But now contractions real contractions this time, were coming every ten to fifteen minutes, or roughly one contraction per game. Eight seats away from the aisle, in the fourth row of the bleachers and the third hour of the match, she felt her membranes burst. A gray-haired gentleman in front of her shouted "Christ!" as warm amniotic fluid splashed over his lower back. Nastase missed his serve and turned to glare in Sophia's direction.

Wetness spread like an apron down her khaki skirt as she lurched to her feet. Mortified, she sidestepped down the row. She reached the policeman guarding the exit at the bottom of the bleachers and gasped, "Baby, now," pointing redundantly to her swollen belly.

On the twenty-minute ride in the ambulance to Women's Hospital, Sophia wished they'd turn on the siren so she could tell Martin about it. The ambulance stopped at the traffic light in front of the hospital. She grunted loudly as a contraction came. The driver cursed, hit the siren button, and shot through the red light, straight up the ramp into the emergency room entry.

By the time Martin charged into her hospital room, the contractions had slowed. He was flushed, excited. After kissing Sophia, and hearing the baby wouldn't be here for a while, he raced down to the lobby and was back in less than five minutes with some yellow and white chrysanthemums. Sophia sent him out to calm down and confer with the nurse.

"We gotta walk," he said, bustling back into the room. "The nurse said it will help the contractions." He helped Sophia to her feet. She held onto the IV pole on wheels, trying not to crush the loop of plastic tubing that dripped dextrose and saline into her arm. They shuffled down the hospital corridor. Sophia was still only four centimeters dilated.

At the end of the hall, she stopped; a contraction sent her slumping onto a molded plastic seat in the empty waiting room of the prenatal care clinic.

Martin put his hand on her abdomen. "I can't remember what Ginger told me to do at this stage." Ginger was their Lamaze coach.

"Forget Ginger," Sophia said through clenched teeth. "Hold my hand."

"I think she said labor lasts about twelve hours the first time."

"Jesus, another six hours? This is a dumb, dumb way to get babies out," said Sophia. "Let's get going."

With her hands on her knees, she pushed herself up. Suddenly, she felt something warm ooze painlessly down her leg onto the floor. She sank back in the seat, feeling faint.

"What the hell is that?" Martin said, staring at a red sponge-sized blob on the yellow linoleum floor. He was as pale as Sophia.

"It for sure isn't the baby, but it doesn't look good. Let's get back to my bed."

She started to head back when another contraction doubled her over, a monster. Sophia panted through her mouth. Focus on breathing. She could hear Ginger's voice.

"God!" she gasped. "Martin."

Martin was at a loss. He couldn't carry his wife—it was nearly an eighth of a mile down the hall to the obstetric ward.

"I'd better get help," he said.

"Don't leave me here!" Sophia cried.

"What'll I do, what can I do?" Martin panicked.

As the contraction eased, Sophia put her feet on the metal base of the IV pole.

"Here, Martin. Help me up. Now hold me and push this thing back, fast."

Martin held Sophia and the IV pole in his arms and with a splayed gait galloped down the hall. Small reddish globs dripped down Sophia's legs, like leaking engine fluid. Leaning together, a bizarre pentapod apparition, they sped toward the obstetric suite and banged through the swinging doors opposite the nursing station.

The head nurse glared for a moment before disentangling Sophia, Martin, and the IV. She eased Sophia back in her bed and attached a fetal heart rate monitor. No heartbeat appeared on the screen, so she applied a chrome fetoscope to Sophia's abdomen and listened intently. Not looking entirely reassured, she reattached the leads for the cardiac monitor.

"That's better," she said. "He's doing okay in there. It's probably not an abruption. Let's just see how dilated you are. Did you come by way of Kansas on that IV pole …? Hey, great … nearly there. Almost time to go to the delivery room. Let's get your obstetrician and anesthesia in here. You're gonna have a baby."

An enormous contraction wrenched, twisted, jolted, and washed all thoughts from Sophia's mind. God, it hurt.

Lennie Stackpole came into the room radiating calm, as if he knew Sophia had what it took to get through this. He looked competent and benevolent in his pressed green scrubs. "Sounds like it's time for a little of the happy drug," he said. The nurse injected it into the IV, and Sophia suddenly felt warmly relaxed.

"Won't be long now. An hour or so. Let's bring Martin back in," Lennie said. The Demerol was doing funny things to the inside of Sophia's head. She retched the remains of a hotdog from the tennis match and looked up to see her husband. Martin reached for her hand, mesmerized by the Doppler heart sounds from the fetus. Lines on paper simultaneously recorded Sophia's intrauterine pressure and her baby's heart rate.

"I'm being squeezed in half," she panted, "and you're doing Physiology 101 experiments. Let's get on with it." Lennie smiled benignly at Sophia and said to Martin, "We'll have him out in less than an hour. Time for an epidural." They walked out of the room. Lennie's hand was on Martin's shoulder. Wait, Sophia wanted to scream, what about me?

A nurse's aide swung into the room and instructed Sophia with a brisk, near-quitting-time tone: "Spread your legs, sweetie." She lathered shaving cream and tepid water over Sophia's genitalia. A few strokes of a razor and the aide was gone, leaving no nicks on Sophia's now drafty vulva.

Another contraction. She was all alone. She panted. She waited. Frightened of the pain that was going to come again. The liars, those Lamaze liars, she thought. Stupidly, she'd believed them. Concentrate on breathing, and it won't hurt, they said. Or maybe it wouldn't hurt so much?

A tall man in green drew back the curtain. "Mrs. Shulder? I'm Dr. Johnson, the anesthesiologist. Sorry for the delay. Emergency trauma surgery had me down in the OR. Let's talk about an epidural."

Sophia screamed, "PLEASE!" and expelled the breath she'd been holding. Johnson backed up a step. A nurse brought in a trayful of vials, syringes, and tubing.

"Turn over on your side," the anesthesiologist directed, leaning over her. Her hand brushed his crotch as she turned toward him. His penis. Oh please, thought Sophia, get it away.

"Other way, Mrs. Shulder. Other side, thanks."

She rolled on her left side, crouched in a fetal position. She felt something cold on her bare back. Alcohol. "You'll just feel a little prick," Johnson said soothingly. She almost smiled, but another contraction was coming.

"Hurry!" A minute later she felt her legs go away. The contraction was already engulfing her, but all she felt was a dull pressure. She let out another breath and whispered, "Thanks. Thanks so much."

Masked faces peered down at her as they rolled Sophia into the delivery room. Johnson had another IV in her left arm and hooked a blood pressure cuff onto her right arm. He was God; he could do anything to her.

Martin, in scrubs and a blue paper hat, was led into the

delivery room and positioned near her head. A bulbous, striated mask made him look like an expressionless extra from the *Planet of the Apes*. He held Sophia's hand, the one without the IV.

"I'm tubes all over," Sophia said. "The well-wired woman." She wanted to be witty enough for Martin to love her, to hold her, to help her.

Martin bent over to put his head near hers. His eyes were tense and worried, but he squeezed her hand.

The anesthesiologist placed a mask over Sophia's face, saying, "This will give a little more oxygen for the baby now." She breathed deeply and felt totally, terribly, out of control.

Gowned, masked, and gloved, Lennie Stackpole walked into the delivery room like a priest mounting the pulpit. He twinkled at Sophia over his mask. Suddenly a jackhammer started banging in a neighboring room. Oh God, oh God, thought Sophia, is that how they get babies out? Lennie looked up and dropped an instrument on the operating table with a clang. "Goddammit! They told me they'd be through by now. Can someone see to it?"

A delivery room nurse scurried away, and a minute later the hammering stopped.

"Sorry, folks," the returning nurse said. "They're building a couple of operating rooms next door for our new cardiac surgeon. Progress."

"Now then," Lennie said. A nurse circled behind him, grabbing the ties of his sterile gown. "Where were we?" He picked up the stainless-steel forceps and clanked them together over his head while doing a little two-step in his sterile booties. "Let the ceremony begin. For I will bring forth the king of all the world."

Startled, Martin looked at Lennie for a moment, then apparently caught the spirit. "Jehovah, Lord of Hosts," cried Martin, "send to me this night out of the womb of Sophia, a son. A son who will pluck the last of the Philistines from the face of the earth."

Sophia guessed that Lennie was usually the sole star in the delivery room, and couldn't see whether he was smiling. Was Martin calling Lennie a Philistine?

She was on a roller coaster, rising slowly to see and think clearly at its heights, rushing down into fear and confusion.

Out of her fears, Sophia heard a familiar voice coming from the corner of the operating room. The woman walked over and looked down. "Sophia? Is that you? My God, what are you doing here? Well, I mean, it's obvious, but what a way to meet again after all these years." She pulled her mask away. It was Jane, Plain Jane, who Sophia and Amy had ridiculed. Jane, their roommate from college. Now she appeared at Sophia's side dressed in beige scrubs. Give her a serape and she'd still look like Janis Joplin.

"Jane?" Sophia clearly remembered that nasal voice and the black, eyebrow-length bangs now hanging beneath an operating-room cap. What the hell was Jane doing here?

"I'm in pediatrics now," Jane said behind her mask. "I'm just moonlighting over here while I finish my fellowship in infectious diseases. I heard you married and left Boston, but I had no idea …"

Sophia let out a little yelp—fear more than pain—as she felt another squeeze, distantly, fuzzed by the epidural. The scrub-suited liturgists straightened, quieted, and faced Sophia's perineum with anticipation.

"Not the time to catch up. Good luck," Jane said, returning to a corner of the room with the pediatric intern, nurse, and medical student.

What goes around comes around, thought Sophia. Now my baby's life is in the hands of someone I used to make fun of. God, she thought, I take it back. Let the baby be fine. Please let Dr. Plain Jane be brilliant.

"Sophia, good, relax, breathe easily," Lennie said, sitting on a stool between Sophia's legs. They were strapped into stirrups on either side of his head.

"Here's another," Sophia heard. She panted. She wanted to scratch her nose under the oxygen mask, but both her arms were strapped down. She didn't know how to push back the terror. The numbers on the fetal monitor rose again. Some start for a mother, she thought. I'm squishing him in there. She started thrashing against the restraints.

Lennie nodded to the anesthesiologist, who injected something into Sophia's IV. It made her feel warm. Her thoughts loosened.

"Scissors, we're going to do an episiotomy," Lennie said.

"Push now, Sophia."

She pushed so hard she thought her ears would burst, then screamed as she expelled her breath. She felt some sort of dull tugging, then a yank, as if they were trying to pull her off the end of the table. Her shoulders scrunched up and hurt, jammed with her strapped arms. She felt a rush and heard splashing water, then she felt empty, vacant, as if a huge boulder had been pulled out of her very foundation.

Those standing around started to move rapidly. Nobody talked. What had happened? She heard suctioning, gurgling sounds.

"Is the baby there? What's going on?"

"The baby's out, Sophia," Lennie said. "He looks good but a little blue. It's a boy all right. There was some terminal meconium. The pediatricians are working on him. We ought to hear something in a minute. Good-sized guy."

Sophia gazed up at the huge operating room lamp blasting light onto her private parts. Where was her baby? Martin was staring at the corner of the room, where there was a huddle of people around their baby. He kept squeezing Sophia's hand, hard.

Through half closed eyes, she looked at the blurred operating room light above her, white, pure, and beautiful.

Sounds, ugly sounds, intruded—repeated suctioning sounds, like someone was angry that the milkshake was all gone. She heard a choked noise, then an offended baby cry. "That's the stuff," she heard Jane say. "Here we go, Sophia."

Jane walked over carrying a mess of bloody green cloths. A baby's head protruded. A round face, looking like nobody, bluish.

"The face is a little swollen and blue," Jane said to Sophia, pulling the swaddling away from the baby. "A face presentation?"

Lennie gave her a thumbs-up. Jane held the baby up for Sophia to see. The baby's chest was moving, and his nostrils flared like those of a tiny racehorse. Sophia felt detached, out of her body. All at once the baby opened his eyes, looked at Sophia. She felt a warm surge, almost like a second birth. She cried, then laughed. She felt dizzy and in motion. She tugged her hands against the restraints. "Oh, let me hold him."

The anesthesiologist unstrapped her wrists, and Sophia took the baby into her arms.

"Help me, Martin. I don't want to drop him."

Sophia leaned to the baby, damp forehead to damp forehead. "I'm sorry, I'm so sorry. I didn't want to hurt you. Not easy getting started, huh, little guy?"

Distantly Sophia heard Jane's twangy voice. "I don't care what they teach you in anesthesiology, and I don't give a goddamn what your attending says. That bulb syringe is no good for meconium. It couldn't suck rhinorrhea from a rectum."

Someone else whispered, "He looked like he was marinated in meconium. But shouldn't we have him in oxygen?"

"Bonding, bonding, my boy." Jane's voice. "It's the fashion. We'll get him back from the mother in a minute."

The baby in Sophia's arms filled with life. He looked irritated, moving his head from side to side. Sophia poked his chest tentatively with her finger. The baby made batting motions with his hands.

"NBA, all the way," said Martin.

"We'll take the baby now and get him checked over and cleaned up," a nurse said, not unkindly.

No, Sophia thought, no, as they lifted the baby from her. Closing her eyes, she felt as if a drawbridge had just been lowered and a melee of revelers tumbled out of the castle. A great cacophony of cheers, songs, shouts. Rhythmic tambourines and blowing of flutes. Giggling clowns and amazing jugglers. Plumes of confetti in cool sweet air. Vendors of candies, sweetmeats from smoking ovens. Dogs barking. Riots of brilliant reds and yellows and greens as young children ran through the crowd, shrieking with laughter, trailing ribbons of silk.

Then Sophia heard someone say that Jane wanted another check of the breathing. A nurse objected; she had to put in the eye drops, do the footprint, put on the ID bracelet. The intern said no, he had to check him first. The nurse said wait your turn. The intern said who's the doctor here? Then Jane murmured something that quieted them all down.

Sophia lay back again. It was complicated, but it was over. She couldn't remember when she had ever given herself over so completely to others. And it had turned out all right. Within waves of disequilibrium, she felt complete and wonderful. Isn't that how mothers are supposed to feel? Distantly, she felt a picking at her crotch as Lennie sewed up the episiotomy.

God, how great, she thought, tentatively. The baby. Martin patted her arm.

Alicia, the NICU nurse, was in her early thirties, the mother of a young teenager. She did not have affairs with the interns or residents who rotated through the NICU. In fact, she did not have affairs at all. With the residents, she acted like a good physician: they were there to be watched, handled, taught, and sent on their way. Attraction was not part of it.

Alicia worked a full week and was always the first name to be called when someone needed extra help on a shift. Living with her mother saved on rent and babysitting costs so her overtime pay could go straight into her daughter's college fund. The great love of her life had been a fighter pilot, the last one shot down over North Vietnam. He never knew he was going to be the father of a child.

But Alicia's attraction to intern Steve Calvert was obvious. He reminded her of her husband, who had also been a philosophy major. Her husband's frequent letters had questioned what he was doing, but he was there by choice, an uneasy mind trained to fly a navy Phantom, strafing targets hidden beneath a green canopy of jungle. He never wrote of the risks he faced.

Steve even looked like her husband. She saw it instantly the first time he walked into the on-call room. Stocky, with thin sandy hair, hanging over impenetrable dark eyes. Unlike Alicia's husband, though, Dr. Calvert radiated insecurity. He seemed surprised to discover the happenings in the NICU, amazed to find himself in a war zone.

Alicia had been called from home at 3:00 a.m. to place a central venous line in one of the preemies. No problem.

She poked her head into the on-call room. "Steve, the line is in, and x-ray is coming. I think maybe it'll need to be pulled back a little. It may be in the right atrium."

Steve rubbed the sleep out of his eyes and sat up. "What?"

Alicia repeated what she'd told him.

"How do you do it?" Steve asked. "I mean, day in and day out? I don't know if I'll make it through the rotation."

Alicia was tired and collapsed in a chair beside Steve's bunkbed. She knew when interns needed to talk. "You'll get used to it. For most interns it takes about two weeks to get used to the NICU routine." Suddenly she realized that she was sitting alone with him in his on-call room. She jumped up and offered to buy him a cup of coffee after he finished adjusting the central line and checking the x-ray.

They talked for half an hour in the dreary cafeteria. Steve had gone into medicine out of survivor guilt. His younger brother had died of leukemia after two years of treatment with anti-cancer poisons. For almost a month, Steve had read adventure stories to Arnie, his bald, emaciated brother as he lay dying in a pediatric ward. The staff there had been of the mind that morphine had to be rationed out to avoid addiction. Sure, Steve wanted to help kids, but in the outpatient department most of them had trivial complaints, and the ones with serious illnesses in the ICU's were frightening. The only really effective options were antibiotics, vent support, or surgery, with pain medication sometimes thrown in for good measure.

Days later they had coffee again at the end of Alicia's shift, and then again, until it became a late-evening ritual. They talked about the death of babies, good deaths and bad. A good death was an inevitable one; the parents were prepared, and everything was done that could have been done. And there was no pain. Preferably with the parents holding the baby at the end. Alicia attended the funerals of the good deaths. She didn't go to the others, like the full-term infant who died suddenly in the normal nursery. It happened about every two years. A baby normal in all respects, then found blue, lifeless, or perhaps with gasping breath, nonresuscitatable. Shrieks from the mother would echo down the hall of the postpartum floor. The on-duty nurse or intern would be in shock for weeks along with the parents. When Alicia knocked on Steve's door late one evening, Steve was shaken by just such a case. Unlike Alicia's husband, Steve could not handle the war in which he found himself. Alicia took him in her arms.

Every morning after her discharge from the hospital, Iris had taken the bus to be with Baby Eugene. Last night, her cousin had partied until three in the morning and bounded into Iris's room when she got home. Iris couldn't remember the last party she'd been to.

A nurse startled her from behind. "Iris, we're going to have to get in there on Baby Eugene. The ultrasound guy is here to check his head again."

Iris backed away from the incubator, wondering what she'd be doing if she weren't here every day. Probably sleeping in. She thought about her typing class. It was dumb, but she actually liked it. Sitting behind that IBM Selectric made her feel that she was an expert at something. She was the best in the class. Not so smart with Eugene. She'd really screwed him up.

Mattie had told Iris, "It's your own fault that child came early. You didn't take it easy. Didn't get the checkups. And damn, honey, now how you expect me to raise that little bitty thing while you're at school?"

The ultrasound tech, a white guy, rolled his machine up next to Baby Eugene and put a big glob of gooey stuff on Eugene's soft spot. The ultrasound screen lit up with an image that reminded Iris of Darth Vader's mask—two huge dark eyes and a grill for a mouth. There was a big white area, like a bright bruise. The staff had told her that that was where the bleeding in the brain was.

"I'll make sure the docs get the report back today," the technician said, wiping the goop off the baby's head.

"Please, God," Iris whispered, "make it be okay."

"Iris, right? I just want to go over what the doctors have told you. I'm the social worker on call today. Is that all right?"

Iris woke up. She'd been dozing with her head in her arms on a little table beside Eugene's incubator. The woman looked like a model in a magazine. A pale blue sweater, maybe cashmere, tossed over her shoulders. A long-sleeved blouse that you could see her lacy bra through. Her soft maroon skirt was slit in front and pinned with an oversized silver safety pin. A pearl necklace, a brooch, bracelets on each wrist, rings practically on every finger. Sweet Jesus, Iris thought, what have I done wrong now?

"Here's the thing, Iris. By the way, my name is Jennifer." Of course it was. The social worker looked at her watch. "The doctors think the baby had some bleeding, some bleeding into his head. Well actually, a lot of bleeding. This is bad. Are you with me?"

Iris thought so. They'd already told her what it was.

"So what does that mean for Baby Eugene, exactly?" Iris asked.

"Well, let me see." The social worker pulled up a chair, knee to knee with Iris, consulted a clipboard, ran her finger down a list. "It says the baby might die. Or he might live. There's a note here about the possibility of brain damage."

Iris waited to hear something she didn't already know. Some news. The woman seemed to want some response. What was her point? This woman, this Jennifer, brought out the street in Iris. "You mean he might grow up and be a social worker?" Iris knew it wasn't funny, but her head hurt and she was so tired.

Jennifer, her shiny lips a single tight line, looked again at her watch and said, "I'll tell you what, young lady. I'll just put a note in the chart that you don't seem to grasp the importance of all this."

Jennifer stiffly walked away, trailing a scent of lilac. Alone again, Iris put her head back down on the rollaway table.

13

Day One

Martin pushed Sophia in a wheelchair up to the viewing window that allowed them to see into the well-baby nursery. Their baby boy lay bundled in white blankets decorated with a parade of small blue elephants. A pink stocking hat that said "I'm a Women's Hospital Baby" was pulled down on his head and his ears stuck out.

"Why does he have a pink hat?" Martin asked.

Sophia stared at the babies. Her baby, a little man, was sleeping with a serious expression, obviously an intelligent child. He stood out from the seventeen much more ordinary babies in the nursery. Some were crying lustily as they approached the 10:00 p.m. feeding time.

Her baby's eyes flickered as if he were watching a movie on the inside of his eyelids. His face was bluish and swollen. He grimaced occasionally. Bad movie.

Martin tapped on the window, trying to get their baby to open his eyes, but all he got was a hostile look from a nurse. Martin put his arm around Sophia. She had the feeling it was for himself, not for her. They'd spent the past weeks working against their deadline, the birth of the baby. All sorts of home-

and work-related projects had needed completion. Awkward lovemaking hadn't been part of their routine.

Sophia shrugged off Martin's hand and tried to think past the searing pain from her episiotomy every time she took a step, the nausea, the dull ache of an overworked uterus. So much of her life necessitated planning. It was her strategy to control the future. With a baby, the immediate would rule.

They had prepared well. Toward the end, she and Martin had come down here every two weeks for childbirth classes with nine other women and their partners. Under the guidance of Ginger, a brusque obstetric nurse, they toured the obstetric suite and the postpartum floor. The nurse made them all feel like army recruits.

Yet the baby, her baby, was an achievement, never mind if billions of women had carried out a similar feat. After her wedding, another one-time life event preceded by months and months of preparation and anxiety, she remembered the feeling of "Now what?" She would have preferred a week alone to recover rather than a honeymoon. Now, too, she felt like a novice ice skater facing the empty sheen of a frozen pond all alone.

A nurse came around the corner and asked which of the babies was theirs.

"The cute one with the pink hat," Martin said.

The nurse did a standard review. Breastfeeding? Sure, give it a try, not sure for how long because of Sophia's work. Pediatrician? Lennie Stackpole had recommended a guy who would probably see the baby in the morning. Martin stood on one foot, then the other, while the interrogation progressed. Help at home? No parents in town, but a private nurse in the afternoons for a week after the baby came home so Sophia could get some sleep. Circumcision? Sophia turned to Martin.

"Sure," he said. Sophia couldn't believe he would be so nonchalant about tissue being cut from the penis of their baby, but she'd promised Martin he could decide.

"Good work, Sophia," the nurse said, ignoring Martin. "Sounds like you folks will be ready for graduation home in a couple of days. We've got reference books if you need help choosing a name. A lot of Skylers and Bransons these days."

Sophia shook her head. Was that it? Where were the directions? The definitive manual? Not just for names. One day at a time. Feeding and watering. What could be so difficult? But how come she kept thinking of the baby as some kind of test?

"Can I take the baby to my room now?" Sophia asked.

"How long do we have before we have to give him a name?" Martin asked.

That night Sophia lay with the baby cradled in her arms. "So, babe, are we going to be friends? Should we try this feeding trick again?" The baby dozed, with occasional jerks in his sleep that discomfited Sophia. The first attempt at breastfeeding hadn't gone well. The nurse said just keep trying.

Sophia watched her baby's breathing, the rise and fall of his chest under his white hospital baby smock. His delicate hair. She flipped the pages of the pediatrics textbook in front of her and read the chapter on physical exams of the newborn. Delicate lanugo on his forehead. Fuzz, check. Punctate milia on his nose—those white spots. A calm, Buddha-like appearance in his sleep. His round face didn't resemble anyone in her family, or Martin's as far she knew. It was still swollen from birth. Miraculous. Beautiful. Those terms weren't in the textbook.

Sophia wasn't tired or too uncomfortable. Her mind was

clear. Unusual. The ordinary millions of thoughts and worries, the to-do lists for home and work, were absent. She was conscious only of herself and her baby. How could she feel so intensely about something that had been just a lump in her abdomen? Several nights before the delivery, lying in bed with a scientific journal balanced on her abdomen, she'd felt another nudge inside, importunate. "So you want stories about tigers and princesses, not reverse transcriptase?" She had absently reached for Martin's hand and placed it on her moving abdomen, but he drew his hand away and turned the page of his novel. Over the months she'd grown familiar with the being inside her, even comfortable with it by the end.

But this sleeping baby. Outside her, now, with so many moving parts. So much more complicated than a bulge in her belly. She wanted to hold and keep the goodness of this moment, but worries snaked their way back into her consciousness. The responsibility for a new life. What if she couldn't breastfeed, didn't have enough milk?

She put down the text and called Martin, who'd left her to get some sleep.

"Heya, mother of the year. How's it going?"

"Not bad, not bad. He's a little slow on eating. Seems he can't eat and breath at the same time."

"You tell him for me," Martin said, "how much enjoyment a little fellow can have at the breast, now and later."

"Yeah, yeah. You know what I think Martin? Next time? You get pregnant buddy, and you go through labor."

Sophia stroked her baby's cheek, her nipple leaking colostrum. The baby turned toward the nipple and took a few sips, then dozed off. It seemed to Sophia like the sucking tired him out.

"C'mon, guy," she said, both to the baby and to Martin

on the phone. "No rest for the weary. Work to do. Gotta eat to live. Not like last week when you could just kick back and get it done for you."

"You tell him, Sophia. What's the poor kid going to do with two teachers as parents?"

"Look, listen, and learn, I guess. I think I'm learning more from him at the minute. Not the other way around."

Martin was still stuck on the name issue. Names. He suggested and just as quickly rejected a few more, then rang off promising to be there first thing in the morning. Sophia didn't understand his problem. Joe, Sam, Bob—any or all would do. She stroked her baby's cheek again with her breast, and he sucked without latching on. Then slept some more. He was so soft and warm lying in her arms. She tried to recall the last time she felt this contented. Lying on the grass at Mackinac before her wedding, watching the fuzzy shapes of perfect white clouds.

She gave the baby a little poke on the stomach. "C'mon, guy," Sophia said. "You're harder to start than my Karmann Ghia on a cold morning."

She felt her breasts gingerly. Instinct was needed here, not intellect.

He's a cute little critter. No cheek has ever been softer. She lifted the upper edge of his diaper to sneak a peek at his penis. It was adorable.

The night nurse swung into the room and caught Sophia mid-act.

"Got all his parts, does he? How's the feeding going? Hm?" Uninvited, the nurse palpitated Sophia's breasts through the gown.

"He's still pretty sleepy, I see," the nurse declared. "And not an avid feeder yet, I guess. Your milk will be in soon. Now it's colostrum. Good for the tyke. Do you want me to take him back to the nursery so you can rest?"

"No, no," said Sophia. "Let me keep him. We're getting to know each other. I guess his choice of mothers doesn't worry him too much because all he does is doze in my arms. Peaceable."

"That's good, Sophia. Some of these babies come out and cry like banshees, like they were wired up wrong or something. I don't know how their mothers can handle it. Looks like you have one of the easy ones."

Probably better that way, Sophia thought. Mellow, like Martin. She wished he were here so he could see how astoundingly cute their baby was.

Mothers from posh Shaker Heights and mothers from inner-city Cleveland all gave birth at Womens Hospital, which was connected to the childrens wing of the medical center. Dr. Donald Kracton, one of Cleveland's leading pediatricians, checked his referrals from obstetricians in Womens Hospital in the late afternoon.

When he saw the Shulder baby, there were six student nurses awaiting him in the 6A nursery. He was rushed; there were five admissions to handle, and he had promised his wife that he'd be home early tonight. But he'd also promised to do some instruction for aspiring nurses. Three of them, buxom young things, were gazing at him admiringly, and he couldn't resist a bit of exhibitionism.

The nursing instructor leaned against the wall and gave a knowing look to the head nurse as Kracton began his performance. He undressed the first infant, a large squalling Jamaican baby, and started the classic newborn physical exam taught to all pediatric interns. As one of the younger nurses leaned over the bassinet intently, he said, "Let's first check the infant's hearing. Now I want you to tell the baby to open her mouth."

The student nurse looked behind her, hoping he was addressing someone else. "Go on," said Kracton. She looked disbelievingly at her instructor, who was now deep in a discussion with the head nurse about the relative merits of dim sum at two local Chinese restaurants.

"Open your mouth, baby." Her peers' snickering turned into a murmur of surprise as the baby opened her mouth.

Milking the moment, Kracton, said, "The skeptics think it's a coincidence. Do it again."

"Open your mouth, baby," the student nurse repeated.

On cue the baby instantly opened her mouth. Clearly Kracton had magical powers of communication with babies. Nonetheless, the students saw nothing but boredom on the faces of the head nurse and their instructor as they observed the baby's miraculous responses. Only one of the students noticed that Kracton was holding the baby's hands during this mysterious act. In fact, it was a slight squeeze of the baby's palms that elicited her palmar-mental reflex—a reflex that had almost no significance whatsoever but never failed to excite student nurses.

Having captivated his audience and awakened the infant, Kracton checked the infant for color, muscle tone, respirations, activity, and posture. He stuck his well-washed little finger into the baby's mouth, looking for a cleft palate. He felt the scalp for fullness, the neck for goiter, and the clavicles for breaks and then turned his attention to the arms, legs, and abdomen, palpating the liver, spleen, masses, and kidneys.

Next was a brief neurological exam—the best test of a

physician's skill with the newborn exam. This was where doctors could be divided between those who "know babies" and those who don't. After checking primitive reflexes like sucking, grasping, and stepping, he picked up the baby, holding her in the armpits with his two fingers supporting the back of her head. She was now peering at Kracton's face. He turned in a circle and saw that the baby's eyes moved in the direction of his spin and snapped back to look with surprise at the doctor, a normal finding in newborns.

Close to the finale, Kracton checked the Moro reflex, clasping the supine infant inches above the mattress of the bassinet, then suddenly dropping her backward about two inches or so. Like almost every newborn, this one flung out her arms, widened her eyes, and threw her arms forward as if grasping a tree trunk or parent. Then she yelled for dear life.

As Kracton indulged in his theatrical flourishes, he noted with satisfaction that the nursing students were still fully with him.

"He's not such a bad old fart," the head nurse was saying to the nursing instructor. "He's done this so many times that sometimes his mind seems to be wandering. But at least he doesn't order lab tests all the time like the younger pediatricians.

For many hard months, the nursing instructor had served on the hospital's pediatric advisory committee with Kracton. He was old guard. He wore a little bow tie at the neck of his button-down Brooks Brothers shirt. Wire-rim glasses above a little brush of a mustache. She'd argued with him repeatedly about the extent of nursing prerogatives. He was hostile to nurses, she concluded, because he wasn't getting it at home.

"I don't know, Sally. His kind is what's holding nursing back. He's a medical reactionary. A total Neanderthal."

Kracton finished his second admission exam. Before writing his note in the child's chart, his pager beeped. A call from his receptionist. His partner had sent one of Kracton's asthmatics to the emergency room.

He decided he could still squeeze in a third exam. Mrs. Shulder's room was close to the nursery. There was nothing remarkable on the Shulder baby's chart except that the first-time mother was a little older than usual. Normal amnio. There'd been a few late decelerations of the fetal heart rate during labor, mild. No blood group incompatibility. Good enough Apgar scores after they had sucked out some meconium.

Kracton hurried down the corridor, his glasses sliding down his nose and his yellow gown slipping off his shoulders as the bow in back came loose. He strode into room 608, where Sophia Shulder lay with her baby on her abdomen. It was dim in the patient's room.

"Congratulations, Mrs. Shulder. I'm Kracton, the pediatrician. Let me just have a look at this fellow."

The baby was crying now. Of course—they cry when you're in a hurry so you can't hear their heartbeat, feel their abdomen, or appreciate their muscle tone. Nothing much on the exam, really. The baby was good sized. Swollen blue face. He had a small umbilical hernia, and that was about it. Kracton would go over the infant again more thoroughly on the discharge exam.

"The baby's good, Mrs. Shulder. Name? None yet? Breast-feeding? Not sure either? Well, the nurses will help you on that one. I'll look in on you tomorrow. Questions? No? Good. See you then."

Gad, Kracton thought again, first-time mom and ambivalent about breastfeeding according to the nurse's note. Social history on chart said mother was married with a PhD. This will take me at least half an hour tomorrow. She'll have a library of questions. He hurried out of the room and across the bridge to Children's Hospital to see his asthmatic.

PART II

In this brief transit where the dreams cross
The dreamcrossed twilight between birth and dying
(Bless me father) though I do not wish to wish these things.
—T. S. Eliot

14

Day Two

When Dr. Kracton entered the nursery the next morning, the head nurse was on him immediately. "Donald, do me a favor and check the Shulder baby first. The intern started an IV and ordered a chest x-ray about an hour ago. Baby's been breathing fast."

Dr. Kracton didn't like being called by his first name. He looked down into the bassinet with the Shulder baby. The baby's face still looked blue and swollen, which was okay for a newborn who came out face-first after a longish labor. A touch of jaundice was apparent. Kracton unwrapped the infant and noticed the respirations: seventy-two per minute. He picked up the baby and pressed his stethoscope to his back. The baby drooped over his hand; poor muscle tone was more obvious than he remembered from his initial exam. Listening to the chest he heard a soft heart murmur, like an overloaded washing machine in a distant room. The baby's palms had bilateral simian creases—single transverse lines, the head line and the heart line combined into one abnormal crease running the full width of each palm. The baby had gaps between the first and second toes on both feet, and his eyes were slightly slanted. There was a skinfold between his eyes and nose, and the small umbilical hernia he'd noted the day before.

"You think so too, I gather," said the head nurse, who had been watching him.

"Down syndrome. I missed it yesterday. I was too distracted by your damn student nurses. You should tell them to dress more appropriately. The baby has pneumonia or heart failure or both. Get me a feeding tube," he said, shortly.

It wasn't possible, of course, but the thought crossed his mind that the nurse was making a rude gesture with the feeding tube before she handed it to him. He inserted the tube through the baby's nose, attempting to pass the tip into his stomach. It wouldn't pass.

"He's probably got a TE fistula, and I'll bet there's an AV canal in the heart, the commonest." The baby's esophagus didn't connect with his stomach: it ended halfway down his chest. The tracheoesophageal fistula, a serious birth defect not uncommon in infants with Down syndrome. It could be repaired by only by experienced pediatric surgeons. The heart defect was another problem, even more serious.

Kracton stood in the middle of the nursery, the yellow examining gown hanging to his knees. He looked at his watch. He was already late for an office full of patients. He inspected the chart again. Dr. Stackpole's log of Sophia Shulder's prenatal visits. Data on her labor, the delivery, and the delivery room status of the newborn—they were all uninformative. Just one entry stood out: "First trimester amniocentesis, normal." What the hell had happened? The amnio results were supposed to be bulletproof. One hundred percent accurate for defining the number of the baby's chromosomes. Down syndrome kids had three number 21 chromosomes. It was a yes or no diagnosis. Not maybe. Not "just possible." If the kid had an extra 21 chromosome, he'd have Down syndrome. No two ways about it. Somehow, someone had screwed up the results, bigtime.

Kracton picked up the phone and dialed the tie line that connected him to the NICU in the medical center. After several holds he heard the pediatric resident on the line.

"Look, Kurz, I'm in the well-baby nursery at Women's Hospital with a jaundiced day-old term infant who has Down's syndrome and probably a TE fistula. Probably a cardiac anomaly. Supposedly a normal amnio in the first trimester.

"What? No, I'm not mistaken!" Goddamn residents treated referring docs like idiots.

"You have room for the transfer?

Good. Keep it on your service. Let your attending deal with the parents and the damn surgeons. I'll tell the mom that you'll be talking with her later today. Yes, of course there's a father—always is. I haven't seen him. Send someone over and pick him up. This kid is getting sick."

Kracton put down the phone, not gently.

Feeling as if finals were over, Sophia lay on her back, toes peeping out from under the sheet. Her bed was buzzed to the "max up" position. Between her feet she eyed the pediatrician at the foot of her bed, the guy Lennie had recommended. He said Kracton was not a liberal, not an academic, and sometimes not much fun, but he'd seen and cared for a hell of a lot of infants. A serious pediatrician. Standing there in his bow tie, Kracton reminded Sophia of the grim Archibald Cox just after Nixon fired him. She was glad to see him again, ready and willing to learn from his expertise.

"Mrs. Shulder, we have a problem with the baby. I could

wait for your husband to get here, but things are going to be moving quickly this morning, so I need to tell you what we're thinking."

The newspaper fell from Sophia's lap as she straightened herself up in the bed. She fixed her eyes intently on the doctor. Unwittingly he stepped backward. The heart? The kidneys? Sophia took a deep breath and held it. The Lamaze approach: with trouble coming, think about breathing. She let it out.

"What is the problem?" Sophia asked.

Kracton closed the skimpy curtain that separated Sophia's space from her roommate's. Kracton moved the vase of yellow mums on Sophia's bedside table so that he could see her fully.

"The problems may be multiple."

She waited.

"We will need the results of a number of tests," he said.

She waited, eyes widening.

He said, "We need to transfer the baby to the neonatal intensive care unit over at Children's."

"Oh please, God, what is the matter?"

"I'm afraid it looks like a chromosome problem, Mrs. Shulder," he said.

"What sort of chromosome problem?" she said evenly.

"I'm suspecting trisomy 21. Ordinarily, I wouldn't be so specific without having lab tests in hand, but …"

"No way, Doctor. I had an amnio. The results were normal. We did it just to rule out Down's."

Kracton blinked and said the test results were really between her and her obstetrician. He listed the symptoms. No real doubt … possible anomalies … checking for other defects …

The pediatrician was still talking, but his voice faded from Sophia's consciousness. She felt as if she were falling down a shaft with sandpaper walls. She had trouble breathing. She covered her ears with her hands. "... Down syndrome ..." Kracton continued. Sophia smashed her pillow with her fist, again and again.

"Nurse, could you get in here quick!" Kracton shouted from the door in the general direction of the nursing station.

Later, Sophia lay watching the motes drift in the diagonal rays of sunlight that were warming her legs. Despite the blurred sounds from the nursing station and the TV game show above the bed, she was enveloped in quiet. Her mind and body felt bruised and numb. She wanted to tell someone how wrong this was. It couldn't really be happening to her. She would be a good mother, she really would, just make the baby normal, not even special, just normal. There had been no warnings. All through the pregnancy, things had progressed well. She'd banned the possible genetic and environmental mishaps from her mind. She could handle a baby with defects. It would be hers. They could work through the problems, she and Martin. She looked up at the screen, where the game show participants were leaping and hugging each other after a big win. She turned away. She heard a moan and was surprised to discover it came from inside her. What had she had won in her life? Mostly she had ground it out. School, training, life. She thought of her college, her PhD training, postdoc years. No end of problems met and overcome. She did things right. She had even worked less toward the end, easing up for the sake of the baby to come. She'd had the amniocentesis. The results were normal. She had done what was required. She should get the reward. Not fair. Not fair! Sophia rolled over and bit the pillow to muffle her sobs.

Martin celebrated the birth of his son over a lunch at a bistro a few blocks from the medical center, where some of his colleagues and the grad students bought him a couple of beers. One of his students, Angela, had eyes on him throughout lunch. "You're such a stud," she announced, "fathering a son. Lucky you didn't have a girl. Yet." The others had laughed and Martin with them.

After lunch Martin headed back to the hospital on his bike. He coasted through a gentle curve, admiring the Shaker Heights homes set back from the street. Probably big backyards for the kids. He and Sophia would have one of those someday, somehow. He slowed on the long descent toward the medical center.

Fallen leaves obscured a sewer grate. Its wide bars and wider gaps paralleled the curb, suddenly trapping Martin's front tire. He sailed over the handlebars, skidded in a heap along the sidewalk, and rolled onto the grass, stunned. For a minute nothing hurt, then he realized his arm was numb. He touched it and felt an electric jolt. Broken!

A car stopped. The driver an older woman, a shocked expression on her face, offered Martin a ride to the hospital. He got up slowly, holding his arm in his jacket, and left his trapped bike as a warning to future bikers.

From the emergency room, he called Sophia. He wore an inflatable temporary splint. It would take at least three more hours till they finished the x-rays and put on a cast.

Later, when Martin entered Sophia's room, he screwed his face into what he hoped was an appropriate look of repentance. The baby wasn't there. Sophia looked wrecked. Her eyes were red, her hair disheveled. Clearly upset.

"The fault of the armor," Martin said. "It failed to protect me in a tiff with the dragon." Martin held out his cast showing it off, a sling around his neck, a large abrasion on his left cheek. "Only a broken arm. All fixed. Nothing to be upset about. Sorry, darling." He leaned in to kiss her.

She turned her head away. "Our baby has Down syndrome."

A shapeless bubble of emotion welled up, as urgent as it was unexpected. Wetness behind his eyeballs, as if someone had banged him on the head. "What the fuck?"

"No joke, Martin." Sophia's voice was a pitiful thread, different. She lay on her back looking at the ceiling. Martin had seldom seen this. Sophia vulnerable.

"It's true," she said. "They don't have the tests yet, but the pediatrician is sure of it."

Martin reached for Sophia and held her awkwardly, the cast not yet dry. He felt her soundless sobs. Of course Martin had heard of Down syndrome. Down in the pits. Down where the IQ is in double digits. Down, down, down.

Sophia slowly breathed in and out. "They transferred the baby across to Children's Hospital around noon. They think he has other problems. His esophagus isn't formed right, so stomach secretions are getting into his lungs. They want to operate. A malformed heart."

Martin had a hard time getting air into his own lungs.

"The baby isn't here?"

His arm ached through the codeine. He wanted to escape from the room. He wanted to run. When he was a precocious grad student sixteen years ago, the *Boston Globe* published a review Martin had written of Updike's novel, *Rabbit Run.*

"Down syndrome? But you had tests. You said he couldn't have Down's syndrome. It was one thing we could be sure of before he was born."

"Yes, Down syndrome," she said icily.

Martin didn't get it. Sophia was pissed off, and at him? It wasn't his fault. "So what now?" he said, plopping into the chair alongside the bed.

"Do a search for the latest journal articles in the med library. Copy those for me, and we'll go from there."

Sophia seemed to be back, laying out a plan of action. That should have been good, but something felt wrong.

"Yeah, but what do we do? What are we going to do about the baby?" This was surely within Sophia's ken, her domain of responsibility.

"I don't know." Sophia, who knew everything, didn't know.

"Shit, shit, shit. How could this happen to us?" Martin slapped his forehead.

Sophia raised her hand, then let it drop and turned her back toward him. "I really don't know, Martin," she said, talking to the curtain on the other side of the bed. "You're right. The test I had months ago was supposed to tell us whether the fetus had this or not."

"Let's sue the fuckers." He was crying. Sophia turned back to him and took his hand. Hers still had an IV taped to the back of her wrist.

"It won't do a damn thing for the baby."

Martin's feelings lay jumbled and immobile. Nothing gave way. Sophia. The baby. Fatherhood. He felt some action was needed. He had to fix it. He had no idea how. They stayed silent for a long while, holding hands, the small TV animated with characters making and solving problems as evening darkened the window.

That evening Martin came back into Sophia's hospital room

and bent over to kiss her. He kept his lips closed so she wouldn't smell the alcohol.

"The baby looks just the same to me," Martin said. "They have a lot of monitoring stuff on him. One of the people said they were just going to do more x-rays, and we probably won't know much more until tomorrow. He said they can get a preliminary chromosome count in a day or so but maybe not, because of something or other. I can't believe that that doctor would give you that diagnosis without lab confirmation. The baby looks so goddamn normal except for his face, still a little blue and swollen."

Martin paced as far as he could in the few square feet between Sophia's table, the chair, and the door. Oppressed by the presence of Sophia's inert roommate behind the curtain, he kept his voice down to an unnatural whisper.

"Honey, I don't think there's much question," Sophia said. Everything the pediatrician had told her matched the little she knew about clinical genetics. "The nurse said they thought he was kind of limp yesterday, but because of his puffy face, the other signs weren't apparent."

Sophia's low-grade fever precluded a trip over the bridge to the neonatal ICU to see their baby. They'd been drizzling sedatives into her, and Lennie had started some antibiotics.

"When I tried to feed him, he choked and sputtered," Sophia said. "I thought I was doing something wrong. I should have called for help then."

They were quiet. Martin rocked in the American colonial chair next to Sophia while her sedatives did their work. He wished he could do something. He wished he had a drink.

Sophia's eyes opened suddenly. "We have to choose a name for the baby."

Her eyes closed again. Her hands were gripping the edge

of the top sheet. Martin held them. He couldn't bear looking at his wife's sadness. His glance fell on a Picasso reproduction above Sophia's head, a skinny bluish mother gazing at the infant in her arms. Martin hauled himself to his feet and gave Sophia, her eyes half closed, a kiss on the cheek.

God, Ezekiel. He remembered kidding Sophia about the name. Martin tried to make himself comfortable for the night, arranging a cocoon in the bedside rocker. The phone rang and Martin picked up. It was the senior doctor, Notestein, in the NICU.

"So sorry to call so late, but just wanted to let you know that the surgery on the esophagus is critical, and the surgeons will be by to explain it all in the morning."

That night, Sophia awoke with a start. She waited for that sense of relief she sometimes had on waking, realizing that the impossibly complex exam she was unprepared for was only a dream. Instead, the events of the day seared her brain. Her episiotomy hurt, but she welcomed it. She didn't want the pain to go away. If there were a finite pool of healing in the world, she wanted it all for her baby. She wanted to absorb the baby's multiple maladies into her own body. She never wanted to feel well again.

Sophia twisted and tried to go back to sleep. In vain. She didn't think she deserved happiness like people in California do. She lived and worked in Cleveland, and she just damn well deserved a normal baby, not too much to ask for after working hard and overcoming her ambivalence about being pregnant in the first place.

Finally, she fell asleep. In the haze of a hot bath, contemplating the island-like belly rising in front of her, she swished, soaped, and rinsed. When she finished and stood up, her belly suddenly fell into the tub in a gush of blood and debris. Bending over to see where the baby had been, she saw nothing between her empty pelvis and her chest except a gristly white spinal column. No more water in the bathtub. She'd accidently kicked out the plug and the baby had disappeared down the drain.

That's when she woke up sweating, and needing to pee. She crawled out of bed, stepped by a sleeping Martin, and shuffled toward the bathroom. After flushing she watched the swirl of water in the toilet. Nausea washed over her.

15

Day Three

At six thirty in the morning, the curtain around her bed was pulled back by a stout red-faced man of about fifty. "Mrs. Shulder?"

Sophia opened her eyes. She hadn't been sleeping. The man wore a starched and spotless long white coat over surgical scrubs.

"Ah, you're the Shulders. I'm Fenderson, Hardy Fenderson, the surgical attending."

Like in the movies. All this wasn't really happening. Sophia wanted to go home.

Martin, awake now, looked up at the surgeon, who said, "I've reviewed your baby's case. I understand you've had some discussion with the neonatology team about the problems and what may need to be done?"

"Not so much," Sophia said. Martin stumbled to his feet. Sophia watched the surgeon. Drowsy, she felt like she was in third grade, in for a scolding from the teacher.

"Sorry for the early hour. The way we surgeons operate." He chuckled at his little joke. "I understand you're a scientist, Mrs. Shulder."

"Yes'"

"And," Fenderson said, turning to Martin, "you, sir?"

"What am I?" Martin said. "Good question. The father, I guess."

Fenderson, not amused, sat in the chair Martin had vacated. "Why I'm here. The surgery represents an interesting problem." He launched into the facts. "As you know, the esophagus is not fully formed. A bit goes up from the stomach and a segment comes down from the mouth, but they are not joined. So the baby cannot get food down to the stomach. In addition, there is a connection from the lower esophageal segment to the trachea."

Dr. Fenderson sketched a cartoon baby with the esophagus anomalously connected to the lungs. "This little connection here is the fistula dumping stomach acid from the lower esophagus segment into the lungs, causing a pneumonia."

On the page where the surgeon sketched the innards of their baby, Sophia saw her name stamped in the upper right corner:

Baby Boy Shulder
08243248
DOB 09/09/84
Neonatology: Notestein
Referring: Kracton
Surgery: Fenderson

"Ordinarily," Fenderson continued, "we just go in through the retropleural space." The surgeon looked up at Martin's blank face. "That's through the back, then take down the fistula and connect the esophagus." He tapped with his pen on the paper. "Problem solved. But in your baby, the upper and lower segments probably aren't long enough to connect. Therefore, we have to do things in stages. In the first operation, we'll just take down the fistula to prevent the stomach juice from spilling into the lungs. That will let us cure up the pneumonia caused by the stomach acid. Then we'll bring a little tube from the upper esophagus segment outside the neck, so this upper segment can drain, then we'll put in a feeding gastrostomy, basically a hole in the abdomen so we can feed him through there." The surgeon poked his pen in the middle of his caricature of a baby. He took a consent form out of his pocket and offered his silver pen to Martin, who placed it on the table near Sophia.

"Complications." Sophia's throat constricted. She coughed. "What are the complications? Isn't it harder to do surgery on a Down syndrome baby?"

"Don't think so. Not much risk for this first operation, Requires some skill though. Occasionally, some bleeding or infection after we go in to ligate the fistula. Rarely, the fistula is hard to find. And we are operating around the aorta and some great vessels." Fenderson wet his lips. "But the real problem comes after. We'll have to stretch this upper segment and the lower segment so eventually we can join them up. If that doesn't work, then we can swing up a graft from the intestines. I've had pretty good success with that. But a primary repair would be best." He paused. "This is the op permit. I think we can do him first thing tomorrow. We want to get this done now because the pneumonitis can get pretty bad, and the anesthesiologists get antsy about that. And the heart thing's not trivial."

Martin picked up the pen and reached for the consent form. Sophia put her hand over his and said, "Why?"

Fenderson looked surprised. He resettled his weight in the chair. "Well, they'll talk to you about all that stuff. You know. Risks. Hard to do anesthesia on a kid with pneumonia, sometimes."

"What about the heart thing?" said Martin. Sophia held Martin's hand, grateful.

"Oh, right. Glad you bring that up. Anesthesia thinks, even with the heart, if we hurry things along, your baby'll probably get through our surgery okay. I expect the heart surgeons will be around soon. Then as soon as we take care of the TE fistula business, they'll get on with all they want to do."

"Can't you just do one surgery? Fix everything at once?" Martin asked. He dropped the pen back onto the table.

"Oh my lord, no. Wish we could." The surgeon smiled again. "But the heart surgery will have to wait. Probably George—he's new here, does the hearts—will want to do it when the baby is bigger. Rather a big deal. Open heart surgery, you know."

Fenderson pushed back from the table with the look of a job well done.

"So. Questions? If I could get your signature, I'll have the nurse call the OR and get him on the schedule." He moved the pen closer to a spot midway between Martin and Sophia.

"Have you seen our baby?" Sophia said.

"No, no. Just the films. My chief resident, who will assist me, has been over him thoroughly. I'll see the baby first thing in the morning on the table."

Sophia tightened her hold on Martin's hand. "We're going to think about this some more," she said.

"Before we sign the consent," Martin said, nodding.

The surgeon started. "Well, yes, of course. Take all the

time you need. But the weekend's coming, and the lung business may get dicier, so I really don't want to wait until Monday. There's always the chance we could be bumped from the OR schedule. OR's been jammed up with emergencies lately."

He looked at his watch pointedly, took his pen from the table. "Sorry, got to run. Just drop the permit off at the NICU. Nice to meet you." He paused. "If you really are having trouble making up your minds, remember that the surgery becomes more difficult with time. This is Tuesday. I won't, I can't, do the surgery after this coming Friday, at the very latest."

Then he was gone, long white coat flapping like the cape of a superhero.

"What now?" said Martin, running his good hand through his hair.

"Just get the stuff I asked the librarian to pull for me."

Later that morning Sophia plowed through the literature Martin had brought. On her lap was a heavy obstetric text. She recognized the terminology. They called it Down syndrome now, not Down's. Either sounded better than the older name, mongolism. That was the term Gertrude would know. Who would tell Gertrude that her latest grandson was a mongoloid? With an amnio that diagnosed Down's syndrome, Sophia could have, would have, had an abortion. No purpose having an amnio in the first place if you're not contemplating an abortion if the amnio is abnormal. She flipped through the text, stopping now and then to read a few lines.

She absorbed the information without thinking, without crying. She needed a clinical genetics text. This one had only a few pages on Down syndrome. Its description of the genetics was superficial. The paired chromosomes are supposed to separate before the embryo is created. Somehow all of the chromosomes for her baby had separated normally except for one lousy pair. An accident. Either she or Martin could have been responsible, though she was the more likely culprit. It could happen again. As if a sperm would ever get within a mile of her again.

Down syndrome wasn't hereditary in the Mendelian sense; there was no single gene for it. But maybe she and Martin both had a touch of some as yet undiscovered Down-like gene, call it what you will—detachment, obliviousness. She hated that aspect of herself, and she hated it when she saw it in Martin. Sometimes her mother personified it, and Sophia was determined not to be like her. Paying attention was key. Constant awareness. She never knew or understood enough. That's what kept driving her.

She tried Bayesian analysis, considering what would be best for her baby, for her, for Martin, for all three of them. Her thoughts raced amid the vague and chaotic choices. Her mind could find no logical way out. Maybe just stop thinking about it as a problem to solve. She touched her face. The lightning had struck. Not her, not Martin. It was the baby, her son, whose body was okay on the outside but whose heart, gut, and brain would never be normal. The gut and the heart could be patched, maybe. The mind, not.

Exhausted, Sophia dozed and dreamed of a psychiatrist sitting beside her baby's incubator, speaking to the baby, intoning questions. "Do you understand what a life with Down's syndrome will mean? Do you know that your mother was ambivalent about getting pregnant? Do you understand that your parents may not want you to have the operations that will save your life? That they would have given you up even if your heart and bowels were okay because your mind will never work well? How do you feel about a mother like that?" The psychiatrist turned the baby's face toward Sophia. The infant's face was huge and darkly blank. Sophia gasped and desperately shook her head from side to side trying to chase away the image. She closed her eyes tight and willed herself to nap.

At lunchtime, Sophia pushed her untouched food tray aside. "Martin. We can't avoid it any longer." He dropped the Cleveland *Plain Dealer* at his side. "Parents, you mean."

"Yeah."

Martin looked at his watch and said he'd try his dad after another trip over to the NICU.

Sophia reached for her bedside phone to call her mom, but before she could make the call, her curtain was pulled back again.

"I'm here, Soph." It was Amy. Martin had called her last night in New York. This morning Amy was in the doorway of Women's Hospital, room 608.

Sophia held out her arms. Amy's hug made her feel better instantly. But a cursory look at her friend brought on a tweak of resentment. With a sleek new hairdo and a shape not so different from Sophia's a year ago, Amy looked like she'd just stepped out of the pages of *Cosmo.*

"I don't want support," Sophia said abruptly. She shook Amy's hand like a rattle. "I don't want help with my feelings. I need to decide what to do. I need to decide about these surgeries."

"Okay. If that's how I can help."

"So?" Sophia combed through her unwashed hair with her fingers and patted a spot on the bed for Amy.

"Listen," Amy said. "In college, they told us about this case. A subway is coming down the track and can't stop. If it continues, it will kill five people. If you throw a switch that forces the subway to change tracks, only one person will be killed. Obviously most students opt to throw the switch and save four lives."

"I don't get it," Sophia said petulantly, though she felt her panic receding with Amy perched next to her. Like in their college dorm room, snug despite a northeaster howling outside.

"Stay with me, Soph," Amy told her. "Then they change things around to make the scenario tougher. Suppose that instead of throwing a switch, you had to push one very fat man onto the tracks to save the lives of the four people careening along in the subway. Same arithmetic, same loss of one to save four. But let's face it, most folks are queasy about pushing someone to his death."

Sophia looked out the window. She could see Children's Hospital, one of the many interconnected buildings of the medical center. The medical school building where Sophia had her lab was connected by a covered walkway to Children's Hospital. Sophia imagined second-year medical students crossing the bridge to get their first look at her baby, a Down syndrome baby, in the NICU.

"The point is," Amy said as she reached out to take Sophia's hands, "they're three people in this problem. You have to look at it emotionally, not just rationally."

"I know, Amy. I got it. But I can't pull them apart—the rational from the emotional stuff. It stays entangled and awful and ugly no matter what I think. Are you saying I should make a decision based on how I feel? What I feel is ... that I want to not have this problem. I want my baby to ... he doesn't have to be perfect, just okay. Not to be sick and needing I don't know how many surgeries, and …"

Amy sat on the side of the bed, took a comb from her purse, and smoothed Sophia's hair. "And what?"

"And, oh God, for him not to be … limited." Sophia hid her face in her hands. "Stupid," she whispered.

Amy put her arm around Sophia. "I know," she said. "I know."

Lennie pulled the curtain back. Amy eyed him as Sophia made introductions. Lennie stood at the foot of her bed as if distancing himself from a bad patient with an untoward outcome.

"Lennie, what should we do?" Sophia asked.

Lennie was dressed in street clothes. "We'll leave you on IV antibiotics for another couple of days. Slight fever. The resident thought you had a touch of dehydration and maybe a smidge of endometritis."

"What should we do with the baby, I mean? The operations? Screw the fever."

"It's a pediatric thing now, Sophia. They're the experts. Trust them, and it will be all right."

Sophia couldn't believe it. Lennie, her ideal of a doctor, was abandoning her. "A little late for trust after the amnio results, Lennie. They want us to sign for the first of the operations. "

Lennie shifted up and down, one foot to the other, his face white. "You could just let nature take its course. Harder to do that these days. I guess you have to go with the docs in the NICU. The amnio? That's on us. The admin guys are all over the lab. I'm so, so sorry. Look. Stay in the hospital as long as you like. I'll get Blue Cross to leave you be while you get things worked out."

Lennie scurried out the door, leaving Amy and Sophia alone for the conversation neither could finish.

Martin came back from the NICU and coaxed Sophia out of bed. Amy had gone to check into a hotel near the hospital so she could stay overnight. Martin helped Sophia into a sexy robe he'd bought for her in the gift shop. They started down the same long hall they had walked when she was in labor.

"We have to get him operated on, Soph. They're pissed at us already for not having signed the op permit."

"Listen, Martin. Fenderson said he didn't think they could connect up the esophagus. He'll need more operations on his esophagus. They think he has a heart problem that will take a preliminary heart operation first, open heart surgery when he's bigger. He has Down's syndrome. I mean, he isn't an Erector set. We can't rebuild him."

"C'mon," Martin said. "Everybody has operations these days. They said just take it day by day. What's the alternative? Just let him die? What if you were the baby, Soph?"

Not a bad question, she thought. But there was no doubt what she'd want. "I'd want to die, Martin."

They locked eyes. "Me?" Martin said, then he looked away. "I'm not so sure. There's new stuff, discoveries every day."

How Martin could be so smart about some things and so naive about anything scientific or even medical. "Martin, I don't think you were listening to what they told you. One or two operations just to keep him alive, then more on the esophagus, and then they start the big operation on his heart. This is a baby, for God's sake!"

"You just think this way," Martin said, "because he has

141

Down's syndrome. I was talking to a social worker over in the NICU, who said some of these kids are almost normal. What if he didn't have Down's?"

"What-if yourself, Martin. What does your mother always say? *A breyre hob ich.* No alternative. It's there. It's part of the picture."

Sophia hated this. Locked onto an IV pole with antibiotics running through her system, she couldn't see her baby. Martin was her interpreter, and she didn't trust him to get this kind of information right

"Let's hold off on the op permit a day or so," Sophia said. "I'll be out of here by then, and we can talk together with the doctors in the NICU."

Martin rolled his eyes in frustration and hit his cast against the wall with a soft *thwock.*

"Who did you talk to about the baby over at Children's?"

Martin thought back. A blur of professionals, part of a hierarchy he didn't understand. The social worker was nice. The guy who drew blood from their baby said he had an aunt in Germany who had a baby with Down's syndrome and the kid had done all right. Nobody really stood out. "Did your buddy, the guy from Boston you had the party for? Did he ever get the job? Maybe he's someone we could talk to."

"Dad, Dad, it's Martin." Martin finally got through on the pay phone in the obstetrics waiting room. The phone cord was short, and he had to balance himself on the chrome arm of the nearest chair.

"Can you hear me? Can you hear me?" Martin's father shouted. His hearing was failing.

142

"Dad, I hear you fine. Sorry to call collect, but I'm at the hospital."

"S'okay, son. Not so good?"

"Yeah, it's bad, and it keeps getting worse. They think there's a bad heart problem on top of the swallowing tube thing. Both need surgery, but the esophagus has to be done in the next few days because it's screwing up his lungs. I don't know what we're going to do. That's partly why I called."

"You need the best doctors. What about flying him to the Mayo Clinic? Your mother and I can help on any expenses."

"No, thanks, thanks a lot, Dad, but flying out of here isn't the solution."

"No?"

"No, the question is whether we have any surgery at all or just let him die." There was a pause on the line. "Dad?" Martin said.

"I'm here, son. Not sure I heard all that, but I'm here. Perhaps, maybe that would be for the best."

Martin assumed his father meant letting the baby die. "Yeah, I know maybe it would be best, but, God, letting him die? I mean what would you and Mom have done?"

"Die? Die? I thought you said 'fly.' Why would anybody let a baby die?"

"Goddammit, Pop. We aren't letting the baby die. We're just not sure about signing on for all the operations."

"What's the difference? And watch your tone, son."

"Sorry, Dad. I'm just really strung out about this. Everybody says, 'Well, if this or that were different, then you could do this or that.' But things are exactly how they are."

"Have you called your rabbi?"

Martin paused. They didn't have a rabbi, didn't go to synagogue, but he had talked briefly with the hospital rabbi. "I did. I did talk with a rabbi. He said if the baby dies, it's God's way. If the baby lives, we can't understand why bad things happen. He recommended a book on good things that happen to bad people. Bad things that happen to good people. Whatever. The rabbi didn't exactly get it. We have to make some kind of decision here."

"Maybe the rabbi did get it. You know what I did for your *bubbah* before she died. Everything. That's what I did. I'd go with what the doctors say, Martin."

"I appreciate it, I really do, Dad, but I don't know … You know what I really think? No matter what we do, it's a shitstorm for life."

"Son?"

"I said, shi—never mind, Dad."

"We trust you, Martin. We know you and Sophia will work it out."

"Okay, okay, thanks. Tell Mom thanks for the *rugelach*."

Martin had done Sophia the favor of breaking the news to Sophia's mother. Nonetheless, Gertrude picked up on the first ring when Sophia called. "Sophia, is that you, dear? How is the baby? Have the tests come back yet? Are the doctors sure? Are you sure they're the tops in the field? Couldn't they operate? You didn't? Martin too? Oh dear. What can we do? Do you want me to come? Martin's mother may come? Oh dear. How rotten. No, I haven't told your brothers. You know how upset they would be … I understand …" There was more, but Gertrude finally wound down. "My friend told me she read about a cure for it. In the *Reader's Digest*, I think. No? I'll send it to you. Okay. Okay. You too. Bye, dear, goodbye."

Stiff with tension, Sophia lay motionless in bed, her obligatory call completed. It was, of course, all about Gertrude, who regularly referred to difficulties as "a muddle." Or "God's will." Up till now, Aunt Ada's schizophrenia was the only real family disgrace. Sophia's father died before he could follow through on the divorce. Sophia herself might have qualified too. According to Gertrude, Sophia had been a high-strung infant, screaming nights with bleeding eczema until she was three.

Gertrude's reaction had been so predictable. Sophia and Martin were young, poor dears. They could try again later. Sophia wasn't really ready for babies yet. She'd married too soon. Martin wasn't even a professor. Gertrude probably had a gin and tonic the minute she hung up the phone. It worked for her. For Martin, too, pretty much. Maybe Sophia shouldn't be so critical.

Later in the afternoon, when Sophia's fever hadn't resolved, they started different antibiotics and moved her to a private room. A nurse named Alicia from the NICU drew back Sophia's bedside curtain and introduced herself.

"Tell me all about the baby," Sophia asked. "I only held him a few times before they took him away. The last time I tried to feed him, he looked like he hated it. They won't let me in the NICU until my fever's down."

"He's kind of cute." Alicia showed Sophia a Polaroid of the baby. "He's bigger than the preemies we mostly get in the NICU. But he's pretty sick, so he doesn't move around much. We may have to put him on a ventilator because of the pneumonia. When can you come over and see him?"

"My damn fever. They won't let me visit. When I held him the first day," Sophia said, "I thought he was fine. I guess he was choking a bit. I should have said something."

She lay back in bed, picking at her nails, and appeared to hear little else that Alicia had to say.

Alicia's heart was pounding when she left the room. She couldn't name her intense feelings, but with just a nudge, she could turn into a fearsome evangelical for all sorts of opinions. Conflicting ones. The thought scared her.

While Alicia walked back to the NICU, Dieter received a call from his supervisor. Dieter had anticipated the call. He drew bloods in the NICU. He knew the story on Baby Shulder—a normal amnio, then born with Down's syndrome. They were asking questions. Dieter handled amnio specimens in the lab. Of course he remembered the time when he dropped some specimens and couldn't tell which label went on which tube. Of course it was him.

He hurried down to the second floor, his supervisor's ten-by-ten office, and sat, unable to scoot his chair in far enough to close the door.

"So, Dieter, this is all sort of routine, but the regional lab wants us to check." His supervisor was an older man, kind enough. It was hot in his closet of an office. He knew about Dieter's aspirations and had already promised a good letter of recommendation to medical school.

"What actually happened?" Dieter asked.

"Like I said when I called, one amnio reported as normal and the mom has a kid with trisomy 21. Another amnio drawn on the same day reported as trisomy 21, and that mom has a normal kid. Obviously some sort of mix-up. I guess even after hearing she was carrying a Down's, the one mom didn't get an abortion. Now with a normal kid, she must feel like she's been kissed on the butt by God Almighty."

"Who screwed up?" Dieter said. He'd guessed what this interview would be about and had prepared himself. "Did the doc who drew the amnios mix them up?"

"Nope. We thought of that. Different offices. Different docs."

"God," Dieter said, resisting the urge to wipe his forehead. "I'd hate to be the tech at Regional who signed them out."

"You bet. But funny thing. Each of the assays was signed out by a different tech at Regional, and the assays were done there on different days."

Dieter felt the back of his neck prickle. A drop of sweat rolled down his back. He sat a little straighter.

"So, obviously," his supervisor said, "Regional wants to lay it on us. We do take the amnios and put them in their shipping vials, which I think is a dumbass thing to do anyway." The supervisor sat back and lit a cigarette, against the rules, but, hey, he was a supervisor. He didn't offer one to Dieter.

"Just one more step that could go wrong," Dieter said.

"Right. When you guys package the amnios, we don't have you log in your names because we don't do the assays. But I got to ask you, just like I've asked everybody. You remember anything about this, Dieter?"

Dieter pretended to give it some thought. "That's months and months ago."

"More like six, to be exact. You were one of the techs on duty when these amnios went through. Usually handled by the day techs, and they don't remember any amnios on that particular day. There were two techs on duty."

"Nope," Dieter said. "Don't remember a thing. Sorry I can't help."

"Okay. Thanks anyway. Regional is probably just trying to cover their ass. Said they're looking into it some more. How's the premed studies going?"

"Good, good," Dieter said with a smile, but he nearly knocked over a chair as he left the office.

Meanwhile, in the NICU, Iris was bored. Day in and day out, she sat in the rocking chair beside Baby Eugene's incubator, an "Isolette," they called it. Iris thought that sounded like a bad way to start a life. She wouldn't let Baby Eugene feel that way, isolated. She came to be with him every day, skipping her afternoon classes. He was on a bunch of medicines and still had an IV in him, but his skin had healed, except for a small mark on his left ankle from the IV.

Iris met once a week with the doctors and nurses, who told her the extra oxygen he was getting was way low now, and he was kind of using it just to coast along with his preemie breathing. His head was the problem. Too big. Just like his damn father's. They said that when Baby Eugene got to be bigger, they would put in a shunt to keep the pressure from getting too high and mushing the good part of his brain. A tube from inside his brain that would run up outside his skull then down under his skin where it would stick inside his belly, and that's where all the water on his brain would go. Iris hoped they wouldn't leave the tube too short so he'd walk bent over or something. The good news was that he was gaining weight, almost an ounce most every day. They fed him, and let Iris feed him too, with a tube down his nose into his stomach. They had talked her out of breastfeeding because she would have had to pump her breasts for months and bring the milk to the nursery. Iris didn't find the thought very appealing.

She read the magazines scattered around the waiting room and did a little homework. She liked Spanish and was getting pretty good at it. She could sometimes talk to one of the nurses in Spanish. Some of them were really nice. Some of the other mothers too. She got to know the ones who had preemies because they all came every day, like her.

The routine of the nursery often made Iris sleepy. When the shift changed at 3:00 p.m., all the nurses paired off to compare notes with one another. The doctors made their rounds in bunches and made her leave while they stood around Baby Eugene's incubator and figured out what they were going to do to him next. Afterward, once or twice a week, Dr. Calvert or Dr. Kurz would stop for a few minutes to tell her what was going on. Technicians came and stuck Eugene's heel for blood. Ultrasound and x-ray folks took pictures.

Occasionally, there were bursts of activity, the doctors and nurses all upset and shouting. That was not good; sometimes it meant a baby died. The nurses would wheel in screens, and she could hear them from behind the screens, talking low to a mother sobbing with a dead baby on her lap. Later Iris would see a little white bundle all covered up like a mummy in scary movies, just lying alone in a bassinet before they took it away.

The baby brought in yesterday created a strange stir in the nursery. It wasn't a preemie, Iris could see that. It was a big baby. She could see the baby breathing fast, and they took x-rays of its chest. The doctors hustled in and spent a long time over the newborn. Dr. Kurz seemed angry, and some of the nurses were clearly upset.

A man with his arm in a cast came in and stood a long

time next to the incubator, just looking inside. He talked with the nurse. His back was to Iris, and she saw his shoulders start to shake. She'd never seen a white man cry before.

⁓

Darryl from Dallas, the surgical resident, who looked like a young Clint Eastwood, entered the NICU with a smile on his face. Seldom in doubt, and from what Alicia heard, he was fearless in the operating room.

"Hi, sweetie," he said to Alicia, who'd just finished putting a new IV in the last findable vein in the Shulder baby's arm. "You got bags under your sparklin' eyes this morning, hon. Better tell your boyfriend he's got the night off tonight."

He put his arm around Alicia's shoulder. Steve was with a group of interns at the other side of the NICU. She saw him look at her and straighten up.

"I'd be happy to give you a thorough restorative exam in the on-call room, but I've seen the x-rays for Baby Shulder, and you've got me a sure enough TE fistula to repair."

"Since when do surgical residents do TE fistulas? I thought a big case for you was excision of a mole."

"Uppity nurse. It'll be my sixth, and I can beat the chief's skin-to-skin time already. What do the cardiologists say about the heart defect?"

"They haven't done an ultrasound yet. They think it's AV canal, but Dr. Kurz thinks it's a hypoplastic left heart anomaly."

"They think he can he make it off the table? I've got a perfect OR record this year. Maybe those effete pediatricians you hang out with aren't screwing up as many preop orders these days."

Alicia explained some of the issues that were holding back the plans for surgery.

"Damn," Darryl said. "I need this case. Tell the parents I'm so good that in twenty years I'll be able to excise the extra chromosome from each and every cell with my bionic scalpel. My advice is to cut. He's human, isn't he? You keep givin' me these peek-and-shriek cases of colitis with dead bowel all over the place, and I'll never get rich or more famous." He grinned.

Alicia couldn't help smiling back. He was truly unredeemable.

But when Darryl put his stethoscope to the baby's chest, his face changed.

He looked up at Alicia. "Geez, you guys. This kid needs a lifeguard at the gene pool. What are you doing here? It may already be too late for surgery."

He scowled and listened again to the baby's chest. After a minute, he groaned and slung the stethoscope around his neck.

"His lungs sound like shit. That pneumonitis isn't trivial. He's going to need to be ventilated. Soon. Now you triple-stat page me when you're over your little moral dilemma."

Alicia was about to say it wasn't her decision, but Darryl cut her short. "All this fuss over informed consent for surgery. Why don't you guys get informed consent when the preemies show up? Tell the moms it's three months of needle sticks, tubes in the trachea, chronic lung disease, brain bleeds. Now those are risks worth talking about."

Alicia said, "We do. We do that," but she knew they didn't. Not really. So she went on the offensive. "You surgeons always on the high road. D'you ever think what it's like for the kid or the family?"

But Darryl was already stalking out of the NICU.

Turning back to the baby, Alicia sighed. She was getting much more tired after every shift. The baby was in a holding pattern. The surgeons wanted to operate, but not until the pediatric cardiologists okayed the surgery. The cardiologists wanted to catheterize the baby's heart, but not until the neonatologists felt the baby was stable enough and the TE fistula was repaired. The residents were deferring to the attendings. The neonatologist was negotiating with the parents, who didn't know what they wanted. They couldn't understand how the baby could have Down's syndrome when the amnio had been normal. The hospital administrators were trying to avoid a lawsuit—and some very bad publicity.

When Alicia signed in that morning, the head nurse assembled her staff together to talk about their feelings. "So what do you think, gang?"

Everybody looked at Alicia, who had spent the most time with the Shulder baby.

"Well, I think we ought to do something. He's dying."

The others' opinions were split. Many of the younger nurses wanted to do everything possible; most of the older ones thought they should let the child go. The head nurse had called the meeting just to let them vent, Alicia thought, not to decide anything. It occurred to her that, if some god checked up on them at that very moment, something awful would happen.

Alicia rolled Baby Eugene onto his back. He still weighed barely more than a pound. Most people think of babies, especially tiny preemies, as fragile. They are in some ways. But as she looked at Baby Eugene, she wondered how many adults would be able to tolerate an endotracheal tube, an arterial line, two IVs, tape all over, skin breaking down when they changed the tape, venipunctures, heel sticks, reintubations by barely competent residents, phototherapy, and a constant attack of noise and light. It was no way to live. She drained the plastic bag covering Baby Eugene's tiny penis and charted his urine output, adequate so far for this shift. She repositioned his head. No preemie under her care would graduate from the NICU with a flat head.

Generally Alicia liked caring for the sickest kids, like Eugene, observing their blood gases and blood pressure, four lines running, and constant vent changes. But taking care of the Shulder infant was giving her no pleasure. Since she was taking some classes this fall and working mostly nights, she missed many of the discussions on the morning rounds. Back and forth, the conversations spilled over into the evening.

"Of course, the parents have the right not to sign the op permit."

"That's euthanasia!"

"Well, I'm not going to be part of it. I want full IVs and antibiotics for the kid's pneumonia. Now. Stat."

"We'll get the hospital administration to sue for custody of the kid."

"Ethics? You want to kill a baby, and you're questioning my ethics?"

Then the conversations started all over, in another distressing loop.

Alicia went back to charting vital signs on the clipboard above Baby Eugene's incubator. She jumped; someone was close behind her, peering over her shoulder into the incubator. She turned. It was only the hospital chaplain, drifting again through the nursery.

"How're you, Father?"

"Fine, my dear. You?"

He behaved as if nothing could bother him. As if there were no questions without good answers.

"Let me ask you a question about a kid in here, Father. What does the church say about letting babies with birth defects die?"

The chaplain looked startled. "Alicia, is it?" he said, reading her nametag. "You have a patient who's troubling you?"

"That's an understatement, Father. What is the opinion of the church?"

"I guess that depends on which church you are talking about, and a more specific question. Sit down a minute. Maybe I can help."

This was not what she'd had in mind, but Alicia perched herself on a stool in hope of getting a concrete answer. The chaplain dropped into a rocking chair, and she gave him an outline of the Shulder case.

"No wonder you're troubled." The chaplain pushed back gray hair on either side of his head. "It's really two problems. One of theodicy, the other of medical ethics."

Alicia had no idea what he was talking about.

"Theodicy. The great problem of all religions is how to explain how a benevolent God can allow all the small and terrible ills suffered by humankind. We call it *mysterium inequitatis*. The common answer is that we humans are just too stupid to understand the ways of God. That's the *mysterium* part. The ethical question is relatively easily answered, emphasis on the 'relatively.'"

"How is it easy?"

"Relatively easy, my child. Church doctrine developed long before NICUs. The church, my church and all religions, are dead-set against active euthanasia. But allowing anyone, old or young, to die a natural death without painful, heroic therapies is acceptable. Unfortunately, between these two poles of black-and-white clarity, modern medicine has created a huge gray zone of uncertainty. That is to say, these days with opiates, nothing needs be to be painful, and almost nothing is 'heroic' anymore." He rocked forward and used the momentum to get up.

Alicia was frustrated. He was being too cerebral. She leaned on an empty Isolette. "That's not enough, Father. You're saying there are not clear answers for this sort of situation."

"You're right. Be patient, child," he said as he smiled at her, "'with all that is unsolved in your heart. I have an unbreakable commitment in the chapel, but come see me afterward if you'd like." Smiling, he continued ambling down the row of incubators, greeting nurses.

You don't get it, she thought. Damn it! How can you not suffer over this? This is not 'easy'! What does God want us to do? How do we find out? Who will tell us if you don't?

Alicia examined her heart. She wondered how she would feel if the baby were hers. Just working in the NICU would put her at risk from unknown viruses, silently affecting the physical development of her embryo, before she ever even knew she was pregnant. In her head, she heard a voice. "The doctors are just letting it waste away ..." Then another: "The parents don't want it ..."

Alicia resented her colleagues' intense interest in how she felt about the baby. On other cases, she often got angry when the residents ignored her opinions on management issues, but on this one she was meekly following their orders. Actually, "orders" wasn't quite the word here. They were coming to her indirectly. "Dr. A wants you to slow down the IV rate to two ml per hour," Dr. B would say. And Dr. A said, "Dr. B wants you to give morphine if the baby is irritable." The nurses too were expressing their opinions through mediators. Even Alicia. On her sign-out rounds, she did not say the baby was lethargic, but that Judy, on the seven-to-three shift, had found the baby was lethargic. It wasn't wrong, Alicia thought. She was just following somebody else's plan. If there was a plan.

That night when Sophia finally dozed off in her hospital bed, she dreamed that Martin took their baby to a basketball game. The baby was dressed up in a little suit and tie. His face was bright yellow. The game was nearly over, the score tied. Fans were on their feet, stomping and whistling. Then somehow the baby was in the game, became the basketball. Up and down the court. The pace intensified. The baby, his round little yellow face laughing, was snapped from player to player. With seconds left on the clock, a panicked member of the home team pitched their baby at the basket from half court. He arced in slow motion toward the basket as fans and players froze.

Score! Pandemonium … as the images dimmed in her consciousness, Sophia lost sight of her baby in the chaos on the court. Sophia pushed herself upright, rubbed her wet eyes, and wondered how she'd survive the coming day.

16

Day Four

Sophia's fever was gone, the IV was out, and she hoped Lennie would let her be discharged home. Early in the morning, Martin wheeled Sophia across the bridge for her first time in the NICU. At the entry, Martin helped Sophia up to see the whole panoply, the moving circus: nurses, aides, the unit secretary, respiratory therapists, phlebotomists, consultants, nursing and medical students, the interns, the junior resident, the senior resident, and if one was lucky, a glimpse of the gods: the attending physician, but more powerful yet, the head nurse, the billing guru, and even a roaming administrator. And sure, also the parents and the patients, their babies. All were interspersed among the bassinets, the Isolettes, the monitors, the sinks, the ventilators, the carts of emergency equipment, the record racks, the chairs, the phones and faxes, the drug storage containers, the supply carts.

With Martin guiding her, Sophia walked toward her baby. She perceived a disorderly sense of order, the sounds—mellow rock music, the chatter of the staff, and the strange syncopation of many bedside monitors. She smelled a complex bouquet of cleansers.

Sophia turned her attention to "the baby," as they now called him. The tubes of a ventilator snaked through a porthole. They hissed in a steady rhythm that, after a few minutes, she found both reassuring and disconcerting.

Coming off her night shift, Alicia came over to say hello, and as nurses do, she explained the various lines.

Sophia reached for Martin's hand on the back of her wheelchair and said, "I want to hold him, but I'll settle for touching him."

"No problem," Alicia said. She opened a porthole and helped Sophia stand. She rolled up the sleeves on Sophia's gown and swabbed Sophia's hands with alcohol wipes. Sophia touched her baby's thigh. The baby startled, and Sophia yanked her hand back.

"It's a normal reaction," Alicia said.

Sophia put her hand back and stroked gently. She smiled at Martin. "He's still cute. He's not a monster at all."

Martin slipped to the other side of the Isolette and snapped pictures of Sophia and the baby while Alicia stood back, out of the frame.

Sophia moved her hand to the baby's head. "So soft," she murmured. "Hiya, little guy. We hardly got to know each other."

After ten minutes Martin asked, "Do you want to go back?"

"I'm good," Sophia said.

She seemed mesmerized, so Martin dropped down in the wheelchair, and Alicia drifted off to other duties.

After half an hour Sophia said, "Okay, let's go back to my room and pack up. I'll come back this afternoon." Martin helped her into the chair. As he wheeled Sophia back to her room, she said over her shoulder, "Maybe Gabriel?"

Martin shrugged. "Nice. But by tradition, Jewish boys aren't named till the eighth day, when they're circumcised. My father would probably like it that way."

Back in the hospital room, Martin threw her things in an overnight bag, and then they poked at the hospital tray with an early lunch and waited for Lennie to okay Sophia's discharge.

"We could name him after me, but Jews don't do that either," Martin said

"Good," Sophia said. "How would we tell the two of you apart?"

Steve Calvert was exhausted. It wasn't supposed to be like this, tiptoeing down a knife's edge between order and chaos. He hated this NICU rotation. Too much data, too many demands, too many devices beeping at once—not only his pager but IV pumps, ventilators, and heart rate monitors.

When he was in medical school, most of Steve's clerkships were in internal medicine. He walked around, talked with his patients, did physicals, and read up on the cases in the library. Then he reviewed the cases with the consultants. It was thoughtful and orderly. Anyone who looked very sick was transferred into the ICU, out of sight.

He remembered his one pediatric rotation, the one that convinced him to apply for a pediatric internship. He spent most of his time on the sick infant ward. The two-year-olds were his favorites, the way they'd sometimes hold up their arms to be held when he came by their cribs. Steve would pick them up and carry them into the procedure room for a lumbar puncture or a blood test. Those who stayed more than a week, the chronic kids, admitted with relapses, weren't so glad to see him in the mornings. He'd never forget one kid. He carried two-year-old Bradley Russel on his hip during rounds. The kid was obese from steroids, yellow with jaundice. He looked like a solemn little Buddha and was dying slowly with inoperable liver failure. There was nothing anyone could do about it. Steve left the rotation before Bradley died.

As a new intern on his first rotation in pediatric cardiology, he had been responsible for working up the young patients who came into the clinic before they had elective heart surgery. Nice kids, not very sick, with interesting heart murmurs and EKGs. Straightforward, totally corrective surgical repair.

But his third rotation, the NICU, was a zoo. Newborns on ventilators, monitors dinging, nurses calling him urgently. "He's turning blue again, Steve. I think he's seizing." Electrolytes, fluid balance, hyperalimentation, and intralipid orders that sometimes had to be written three or four times a day for each patient, blood gases more out of whack than he'd ever seen before.

It was the damnedest thing—some of these infants came in severely acidotic, but just when he was ready to jump on them with bicarb, the repeat tests came up normal, and the kid was out of the NICU. Sometimes, just the opposite happened. The Malone baby, a preemie, was acidotic a day or so after birth. Kurz, his senior resident, pushed bicarb, and the next thing they knew, a head bleed blew out the kid's brain. Sometimes the babies looked fine, but Kurz said to put them on antibiotics and get a spinal tap done, stat. Steve didn't get it.

Parents wanted updates, the delivery room stat paged. The last time his pager bleeped, he was on the john and jumped up so quickly that his pager slid into the toilet.

The Shulder baby. The parents hadn't signed the op permit. What kind of crap was that? Don't all parents get angry and go into denial about a kid with anomalies? A perfectly normal response. They should be helped through it, like Kubler-Ross said. The private pediatrician who'd sent the baby over had reinforced the parents' hesitancy. "Maybe it's for the best that he has an inoperable heart anomaly too," he'd told them. But the surgeons disagreed. "TE fistula? Nearly a zipper operation." The surgeons said that they hadn't lost one of them in the past two years. They could do the job on a three-pound preemie. The heart, they said, could be dealt with by the new whizbang cardiac surgeon.

The chief surgical resident came to the NICU and looked at the Shulder baby several times during the day. He lectured Steve. "Down syndrome ... what's the big deal? There are worse things in life than having a kid with Down's. Leukemia, for one. That's the risk of having babies, for Chrissake—they don't come out perfect every time, and we can't throw them back like an undersized trout. The fistula is dribbling battery acid into his lungs. You *will not* let this baby die when I'm number one for the surgery!" He'd slammed out of the NICU as if it were all Steve's fault.

Some of the staff were sympathetic. One of the lab techs showed up now and again. "Sure, Dieter," Steve said. "Take a look. Right here. Maybe you can fix the baby. Nobody else is doing diddly."

Steve motioned toward Baby Shulder's incubator. Dieter was premed. He frequently hung out with the interns, who were happy to show him some of the cases with interesting findings. So many people seemed to be taking an interest in the Shulder baby, and Dieter was just one more in the parade.

Dieter and Steve looked down at the baby, who seemed to be paralyzed. Only the ventilator was moving his chest rhythmically.

"A classic Down's, Dietz."

"I've never seen one before."

"Well look fast, buddy, because if the higher-ups don't get their asses in gear, this one is not going to be around much longer."

"Why not?"

"He's dying."

After lunch, Sophia felt stronger and walked across to the NICU on her own. Martin left to tend to office hours for his students. Behind the window that looked into the NICU, Sophia finished washing her hands. Neither Steve nor Dieter paid any attention to Sophia, dressed in a yellow gown, like those who patrolled the hospital recording demographic data on their clipboards for billing purposes. Now she walked in their direction.

"How come?" Dieter asked.

"A lot of reasons. But, basically, the mother of the year won't sign the op permit so we can save her baby's life."

Sophia heard them. She stiffened.

"No shit."

"No shit. And we're supposed to be the high-priced babysitters presiding over his slide into never-never land."

Sophia grabbed their arms and jerked them back from her baby's side. "You ANIMALS! Get away from my baby! Don't touch him! Don't even look at him! Get away. NOW!"

Dieter and Steve disappeared into another part of the nursery. The chatter in the NICU ceased, and most of the staff stared at Sophia. Nostrils flaring, she stood beside her baby's incubator and glared at no one in particular.

After the blowup, Sophia sat by the baby's Isolette through

the early afternoon. After an hour, she was calmer, and Alicia came by.

"They're young. Don't let their talk bother you. You got bigger stuff to worry about. A lot of us are upset about your baby's problems."

Soon enough the NICU no longer felt like an alien planet to Sophia. The incubators, portable x-ray, and EKG became as familiar as the instruments in her own lab. She looked down at her son and mouthed, "Hey, little guy," using Lennie's name for babies. She reached through the portholes again and again, touching his arms, his face, his chubby legs.

Sophia reviewed more articles she'd brought in her knapsack. She rocked alongside her baby's incubator.

A social worker came by, doing her job: Would Sophia like to tell her what she was feeling about all this? Pleading a headache, Sophia shooed her off as quickly as she could, though there wasn't much else she could do in the NICU. With his gut anomaly, the baby needed a diaper change infrequently. Very little was going through his system. Every so often the cardiac monitor would sound its alarm, but usually it was just a loose lead, rapidly adjusted by the nurse. Soon Sophia was able to adjust it herself before the nurses responded.

Shortly after three, Notestein, the neonatologist, stopped to say he had some more information about the baby. "The heart is anomalous. But it's not what we thought at first. It's a less typical lesion called hypoplastic left heart syndrome. Also requires open heart surgery for a complete fix. Maybe a little trickier, but our new cardiac surgeon is one of the best at it." Sophia grilled him for half an hour. Something called the Norwood procedure to bring more blood to the body because the left ventricle and aorta were underformed. High mortality. Might have to do some preliminary surgery until the baby grows enough for the Norwood procedure. Several operations. The new technique had only been around for a couple of years. When Sophia finally heard Notestein saying over and over, "Sorry, I really don't know the answer to that one," she let him go.

An hour later Martin came in, ready to sit with the baby until suppertime so Sophia could check on her lab. She didn't have the heart or the energy to tell him that the bad news about their baby was even worse.

Enough was enough. Dieter wouldn't let them nail him for this one minor mistake. He picked up the phone in the blood gas lab and waited for an outside line. Then he dialed the number of the *Plain Dealer*. If everybody focused on the surgery issue, they'd forget about the amnio. The surgery was really the important part of the case. Life and death. The newspaper would love it. He asked for any free reporter. To his surprise, he reached one immediately. Lydia Knowles.

"I have some stuff that may interest you for a story."

Dieter would not tell the reporter his name, even when she promised to keep the discussion confidential and not use any direct quote attributed to an anonymous hospital source.

"So, what's the story?' she finally said.

"The story is that they have this mongol baby in the NICU, and they're just letting it die."

"What's the kid's name?"

"Shulder, baby boy, born four days ago."

"Why are you telling me this?" she asked. Lydia was not really a reporter but an intern, a paid one. She held her breath.

She had little experience with anonymous tipsters who were skittish about talking with reporters.

Distract the hospital from worries about how the lab test had been messed up, Dieter thought. That was a good plan. His hopes for medical school would be in the toilet if anybody found out his mistake. He saw how tense the doctors and nurses were about the Shulder baby. He'd bet they feared any kind of inquiries. But with so many lab tests done in the hospital, everyone knew it was a statistical certainty that a certain percentage of them would be wrong. Mistakes are the price of doing business in a hospital. Holding the phone, he suddenly had no idea why he was calling a reporter. It was a dumb thing to do.

Dieter hung up abruptly and turned to the row of kidney pans with iced, one-milliliter syringes that awaited blood gas analysis. He would work harder to be a good tech. He'd be a good doctor like his mother wanted.

An hour later, Lydia entered the hospital basement through the delivery entrance and picked up a rumpled, somewhat smelly doctor's coat from a laundry cart. In the women's restroom, she put her hair up and put on her horn-rimmed reading glasses. They made her look like a librarian.

She attracted no attention in the elevator up to the NICU. She walked briskly though the doors marked "Neonatal Intensive Care Unit, Mothers and Fathers Only." The secretary greeted her politely and asked which infant she wished to see. "The Shulder baby," Lydia said. She was in luck, the NICU was busy.

"Here's the chart. I finished entering the lab data if you

want it. The father's over there with the baby if you need to talk with him." The secretary turned away and started pasting lab reports in the next chart on her desk.

This was too easy. Lydia flipped through the chart like she imagined any med student would. Some very interesting stuff. Her eye caught the word "euthanasia."

Carrying the chart she walked over to the man indicated by the secretary. He sat beside a baby so attached to wires and tubes that the kid must really be sick.

"Excuse me. Could I talk with you for a minute?"

Martin looked up. "Sure. What do you need?"

"I've been studying your baby's chart and just had a question or two. Says here," Lydia said, opening the chart, "parents not signing surgical consent. And then further down, I can't make it out, but it looks like somebody wrote the word, 'euthanasia.'"

"That's crazy!" Martin said. "We're just in discussions with the docs about the surgery. It's a tough set of decisions. Let me see that chart!"

But before Martin could grab the chart, someone tapped Lydia on the shoulder. "Alicia, RN" her name tag said. "I'm sorry, but who are you?"

"I'm a third-year student doing a renal elective and was sent up by the attending to review the Shulder chart."

"Yeah, but the kid doesn´t have renal failure, at least not yet."

Lydia opened the last pages of physicians' notes in the Shulder chart. "You're right. Must be a mistake." The father returned to the novel he'd been reading.

"By the way," said the nurse, "I didn't think students took renal electives since the head of the division had his bypass surgery?"

Lydia mumbled that her elective had been scheduled for a long time and she must have gotten the wrong patient name.

Alicia held out her hand for the chart. "You're new. Mistakes happen. Just don't forget your nametag next time you're in the NICU."

Lydia hurried out of the nursery.

A few months earlier, a crime reporter had entered the hospital to interview a gang member who'd been shot in the abdomen. The crime reporter, who'd infiltrated the building via the same route as Lydia's, was now being prosecuted by the hospital. Lydia shucked the white coat in a restroom and almost ran through the basement to the exit.

She wished she'd gone into TV reporting, but knew she didn't have the looks. But just think about it: Striding confidently into the NICU with a video man at her back ... interviewing the doctors and even the father on camera about that note on the chart that she'd managed to glimpse. "Refusing surgery ... administration considering custody proceedings ... euthanasia."

While Lydia hurried from the hospital, Henry Perlmutter, the administrative director of Children's Hospital, put his foot down. "We've got to get clarity on this. This hospital cannot be known as the place where they kill babies."

He glared at his two assistant directors, Byrne and O'Connell, Irish Tweedledee and Tweedledum. They both wanted his job. Styrofoam cups littered his office, which was hot and malodorous with the stench of cigarette smoke and stale coffee.

"The problem is Notestein," said Byrne, who handled problems of the medical staff. He was the one who couldn't handle neonatology's cost overrun.

"Christ," said Perlmutter, "we hired a new pediatric chairman. I thought he was starting in August. He's supposed to be the hotshot in the area of neonatology."

"Sorry, boss. McKennen hasn't officially started yet. Notestein is acting head till the new guy arrives, and we have to deal with him. He's also taking care of the Shulder baby."

Henry Perlmutter was in his mid thirties, young to be the chief administrator of a large metropolitan hospital, though his thinning brown hair, placid appearance, and three-piece suits made him look older when he peered at his staff. He managed to please the hospital's board members, who liked him because he followed directions well. The chief of staff, a surgeon, constantly reminded Perlmutter that surgical revenues provided the hospital's main income. Perlmutter acceded quickly to his superiors' requests, sat on committees with good cheer, and kept what little imagination he had under control. His career was advancing smoothly.

"Okay team, what's our approach going to be? How is the baby doing?" asked Perlmutter.

"Not well. He's yellow, has a lung infection getting worse, probably on a ventilator by now, Notestein says he could go on another three or four days," reported O'Connell. Both Byrne and O'Connell studied the table in front of them while Perlmutter pondered.

Finally Perlmutter cleared his throat. "The way I see it, we have only two options. Either we let things ride, or we get a court order to operate on the baby."

"Christ, Henry, if we get a judge onto it, we won't be able to keep the lid on," O'Connell said.

O'Connell was in charge of most legal affairs outside of malpractice cases and also PR. He stuck to the main point. "Besides, what if the judge doesn't force the operation? The heat'll get to him, he'll ask others, and there will be leaks. Our aspiring city prosecutor will gleefully jump into the act."

"Let's pray that things in the Middle East don't calm down," Byrne said, in his Boston Irish brogue. "That's our only hope to keep it off the front pages."

"You're wrong, dead wrong," O'Connell insisted. "Once the reporters get hold of this, even World War III won't make it onto page one of the *Plain Dealer*."

Perlmutter raised his hand. He liked a little competitiveness between his assistants, but not acrimony. "Where's McKennen stand? This is a medical issue, isn't it? He should be taking the lead. What do we pay him for anyway? Don't we have policy for this sort of thing?"

"Can't reach him, he's on vacation." Byrne stated, reasserting himself. "Hell of a thing to have to handle when he hasn't even officially started. Soon as he gets in next week, he may have to go to an NIH meeting in Washington."

"Oh yeah? What's our chances for getting that program project grant he's working on?"

"Good. We've survived the almost-final cut. But this thing will impact heavily on the grant. We're after a million for each of five years, and the institutional overhead is 43 percent of that. If publicity starts erupting, that could be the end of it."

"Why us?" O'Connell moaned. "Why doesn't this happen to Doctor's Hospital? They're out there in the burbs ripping off our referrals and getting fat skimming the cream. All their patients are Blue Cross-Blue Shield, and we're down to less than half. I don't mind ethical dilemmas, but why do we have to get such a nasty one?"

Perlmutter tried to get back to solutions. "What should we do here, team?"

"Well, it's murder," Byrne said. "Maybe we can wait a few days and take it up with McKennen when he gets here. Can you do anything with Notestein? If he'd just get those parents to sign the op permit, the kid would be off to surgery. Case closed."

"I've got a call from the head of trustees. He wants to know what's going on." Perlmutter picked up the pink message slip his secretary put on his desk. "He says solve this quick because the legal responsibility is on them."

"Yeah, now the hospital trustees start talking about responsibility. Why don't they give us enough operating budget to get the obstetric renovations funded and some paint on the walls, and that Bovie in the OR is shooting sparks again," O'Connell said. "They should be worrying about finding us decent funds for new equipment next year."

"Okay, okay," Perlmutter said, trying to focus. "So maybe we tell Notestein to just get the parents to sign the op permit. And by the way," he added, "which one of you is handling the amniocentesis screwup if we get dragged into it? O'Connell, you call our head lawyer right away. And Byrne, you get McKennen here yesterday. We need all hands on deck for this one."

Alan Lu sat in his corner office in the Terminal Tower, overlooking the northwest sweep of Lake Erie. The phone was perched on his shoulder while he polished his thick glasses. Problematic clients, he thought, shaking his head. He preferred dealing with other attorneys. They spoke the same language, even trusted each other a little. It was the club that he'd earned admittance to and a culture that had replaced the one he lost when his parents sent him to boarding school in the USA. He was talking to Byrne or O'Connell, one of the junior administrators from Cleveland's major medical center, a large account these days. He dealt with both of them and couldn't tell one Irishman from another since they all talked the same.

"Look, I'm telling you," Lu said, "laws are made for making people do what they don't want to do and punishing them when they don't. Not for this sort of situation."

"I *have* looked it up," Lu ansered into the phone. "There is damn little case law, and what there is really isn't on point. In general, hard cases don't make good law."

"Well, I know Perlmutter wants a clear answer on this ..." Lu wished Byrne or O'Connell, whoever, would stop using the word, "Mongol."

"Yes, I am very clear that you pay me to keep your legal matters in order, but this is different ... And we're talking about a baby with Down syndrome, right? How is it different?" Lu shook his head. Did he really have to give lessons in elementary law and basic human sensitivity? He flicked a bit of lint from his silk tie.

"Look. It's not a personnel action, it's not fraud, it's not community activists starting a lawsuit, it's not real estate, it's not about your investments and endowments ..."

"No, I am not being sarcastic." Lu kept his voice even. "I'm just telling you that this is different, and the law does not have a clean answer for you. Be thankful you're not at Women's Hospital and the lab that did the amniocentesis. Somebody's going to have a real mess to clean up there."

"What? No, I wasn't joking. It's a shared venture with Children's lab? Then you'd better tighten your seatbelt on that one."

Lu uncapped his Waterford fountain pen and scribbled on a yellow pad: "Call meeting to organize defense for the lab mistake." He covered the rest of the page with curlicues, spirals, and boxes while the hospital administrator went on and on. In one of the boxes, he wrote, "Forty? Fifty? Bil'ble hrs?"

"The most useful thing I found," Lu said, "was an article in the *Stanford Law Review*. It says, in layman's terms, that adults have the right to request that no heroic care be given at the end of their life. This has different interpretations, because what's heroic in medicine yesterday is routine care today, right? You cannot take the Shulder baby to surgery unless the parents sign an op permit … No, dammit, wait, I'm getting to that. What you can do is ask the judge to make the baby a ward of the court and then request that the judge sign the op permit. The most common precedent for this is the Jehovah's Witnesses babies. When they need a blood transfusion, the courts always grant the docs permission if they make the case that the transfusion is lifesaving. Some of the parents are relieved when the judge takes them off the hook …"

"Then what?" Lu continued. "With Jehovah's Witnesses the parents resume custody after the transfusion. In this case I guess the court could remove custody of the baby from the parents permanently or return him to their care after the surgeries. It gets more complicated for the judge if there are a series of surgeries needed over time … You said the baby won't live unless he gets the operations. And," here Lu referred to some notes on his yellow pad, "there's about a 10 to 40 percent chance of death at one of the what? Four or five major surgeries in the first year of life if you include the heart operations? And another 10 percent chance of serious but not fatal complications on top of that. And what are the odds that the first heart operation will succeed? I told you this case is different. It's a flip of the coin whether the judge will agree with you and grant a court order for surgery, or whether the judge sides with the parents if they don't want the surgeries.

Either way the hospital gets blamed for the amnio mistake and letting an innocent baby die. Wait till the Right to Lifers get a hold of it."

Lu tapped his pen on the pad, leaving a small blotch of ink on the doodles. "The other thing to think about is the politics. An election year is coming up. Our city prosecutor drools for cases like this. Remember Boston, where the prosecutor took young Dr. Edelin to trial for a late abortion? What a circus! So if you can, side with the parents but get them to sign the permit. If you do, all this goes away. No publicity. No legalities. If you force the operations, the hospital will look like the bad guy."

"What do you mean, 'Is that it?' Remember, we don't make the law, we have to work with what we've got. My advice? Don't make waves. Let the doctors handle it. Keep it out of court. Keep it quiet. If you can't, maybe you should call Draper Pryce in New York. They're a PR firm. Someone said they're the best."

"No," Lu said carefully, "I'm not kidding. We lawyers do our best work keeping clients out of the courtroom."

"Of course, I'll come to a conference with the parents. Let the doctors do the talking though."

Lu hung up the phone and clasped his hands behind his head. He worried that more of these cases would be coming his way. He worshipped the law, usually so applicable to the questions that came to him. Contracts mainly. Why couldn't the medical profession be as professional as the legal system and sort out its own problems? If not, then cede the solution to the law altogether. It would be easier, really simple, if the doctors could be left out of it. In China, such problems used to be set before the village elders, and they would decide.

All they had to do was follow the law. Leave it to the lawyers. Case law would have to be written first, of course. Then it was just a ladder of responsibility, with the courts having the final say. What was so difficult?

"No ... no ... no." Like an idiot, Mac just kept saying no into the receiver while some crackly voice seemed to be asking if Mac could hear him. Finally, with one hand cupping the phone, and his other hand jamming the phone against his ear, Mac could just make out the words of someone yelling at him over the afternoon trade winds.

It was an administrator at Children's Hospital in Cleveland. Said he was sorry to interrupt Mac's vacation when he hadn't even started as chairman. Took a whole day to track Mac down. Then he got to the point. Notestein in neonatology had a Down's on his hands with a TE fistula and a bad heart anomaly. The parents were refusing to sign the op permit. Kid's pneumonia was getting worse from the fistula. Already on a ventilator.

Mac's ex-brother-in-law had chartered a forty-footer and a drafted a crew to sail with him down to Antigua for race week. For Mac, just sailing across the Anegada passage was bad enough. He vomited most of the night into a garbage bag, seasick as a Michigan farm boy. After his seasickness finally eased, he started to enjoy the voyage and contemplate his new job. After they made it to Antigua, they celebrated their first day's finish at the patio bar of the Lord Nelson Hotel—they'd come in last, but a respectable last—and that's when Mac heard the bartender calling his name and holding up the phone.

"Are the lawyers in it yet?" Mac asked the Cleveland admin guy on the phone.

"Yup."

"So what's the question?"

"We'd like you to materialize here instantly and solve the whole mess."

Mac liked this administrator already. His kind of guy. "Short of that?" Mac asked.

"Well, just between us, what do you think?"

"How old is the baby now?" Maybe the baby was already beyond saving. Would make the problem moot.

"About four or five days."

"Jesus," Mac said. He didn't think a baby could last that long with an unoperated fistula, but he really didn't know because they'd always operated on them immediately. "Who's the attending?"

"Notestein."

"Well, he's the most senior."

"McKennen? Just between us again, Notestein is a major reason the search committee picked you. Because his division is fucked up, and we wanted someone to clean it up."

Mac didn't have any response for that.

"McKennen? McKennen? You there?"

Mac thought about hanging up the phone and going back to his beer. Island phone connections were notoriously rickety. He could hang out in the bar with the guys. Look at women. Spend a few more nights in the boat's muggy cabin.

"Tell you what," Mac finally said. "I don't know if it will help, but I'll catch the first plane out. May take me a day or two. I don't think I can do or say anything helpful by phone."

"McKennen, you're a champ. If the whole place hasn't gone up in flames by the time you get here, go see Dean Kennelly. He's taking the point on this mess. And look, after this? Keep your little pediatric problems to yourselves."

Mac shelled out his whole share of the boat charter, left his drunken shipmates at the bar, and wondered how he'd get back to Cleveland.

⌒

That same afternoon Sophia sat in her office next to the lab and did nothing. Just sat there till Martin called to take her home. How can you think, make a rational decision, when you're feeling so godawful and depressed? Her lower abdomen still felt pummeled, her head exploding. She tried to remember the hardest problems she'd ever faced. PhD training. Usually she attacked them along similar tangents: Read and understand some of the issues. Experiment. Sleep on it. Read some more. "Live the questions," Martin said, and she'd discuss her problem with professors, other grad students. Then some days she found she'd lived her way into an answer. But this was different. Either/or, live or die. Both choices replete with nightmares. There was so little time.

She needed someone to talk to, someone who'd know what to do. She tried to call McKennen in Boston. They said he'd left for his job in Cleveland. She called the pediatric office. They said McKennen wouldn't start work for a week. Would she like to leave a number?

Frustrated, Sophia held the phone for a minute, then called Amy.

Back in New York, Amy picked up immediately. "How's it going, Soph?"

"Still stinks."

"No resolution?"

"Nope."

"I wish I could tell you what to do, kiddo."

Sophia heard a commotion over the phone. "Bad time?"

"Not really. It's just never a good time with Rocky anymore."

All of Amy's boyfriends were Rocky. Sophia couldn't remember which Rocky this was.

"I'm sorry, Amy."

"I'm sorry, too, kid. Call me anytime."

Sophia thought of calling the vet who put down that dog she'd found, but she knew that was ridiculous.

The phone rang. A woman's voice. Anyone. Sophia craved sympathy.

"Yes. I do have a baby in the nursery at Children's Hospital … Sure, thanks for calling … I'm sorry, I didn't catch your name. Do you work with Martin?"

"A reporter?"

"How does it feel? *Feel?*" The adrenaline shot past the waning effects of Sophia's sedatives. "How in the hell did you get this information?"

Sophia heard the reporter say how her readers could really learn from hearing how a mother of a Down's infant with birth defects felt.

"I'm sure you're right. Would my feelings be on the inside or the outside when your readers wrap dog shit in your newspaper?" Sophia slammed down the phone. She was breathing hard. She looked at the empty vase on the corner of her desk. She shoved it. It fell to the floor. Crashed. Glass all over. She felt a little better. The phone rang yet again.

"*What?*" she yelled.

"Jesus, Soph! It's me. Martin. Sounds like it's past time for me to come and get you. You're officially discharged. I put your bag in the car. Want me to bring a wheelchair?"

Home in Chagrin Falls, Martin and Sophia sat across from each other in their breakfast nook. Though the refrigerator was littered with Scotch-taped photos, their kitchen walls were bare except for the kitchen clock, so large that the second hand was constantly hurrying. Dishes pushed back, the morning newspaper purposely sat on the kitchen counter for dinner scraps. Nuked, week-old spaghetti lay half eaten on their plates. Before they'd left the hospital, Notestein told Martin that he'd arranged a meeting for them the next day with most of the relevant hospital people.

"Let's just sign the damn op permit and get it over with," Martin said. They both had a glass of champagne, one of the bottles that Martin had long before laid in for the homecoming celebration. Sophia fingered her glass, the delicate stem of the flute. The set, a wedding gift from Amy, was missing one glass. Martin had accidentally put it in the dishwasher.

"You're supposed to be the one with the right brain, Martin. Why can't you imagine what the baby's life will be like over the next year? Or over the next ten years?" Neither Notestein nor Fenderson was too clear on long-range outcomes. Down syndrome kids have a spectrum of IQs. But no one really knew what happened to kids with Down's and TE fistulas and half-formed hearts.

"The intern told me," Martin said, "that their attending had never heard of such a case. A series of major operations for sure. Not too much left to imagine."

Sophia played with her knife in the soft butter. Martin watched her. She wished he could help. "Life-threatening operations," she continued. "The heart operations carry a major risk, not only of death but of brain damage."

"More brain damage?" Martin said. "Couldn't he be spared that, at least? I mean with the IQ he's missing already?"

"And Martin, we haven't even begun to discuss what our lives would be like, taking care of a kid like that."

"'Would' or 'will'? That is the question," he muttered, and put his head in his hands. Finally he straightened up and said, "I don't think they're handling this very well."

"What do you mean?"

"Why aren't we getting more help on this?"

"From whom?"

"Well, from some damn experts," Martin said.

"We've talked to the surgeon, the neonatologist, the social worker, the nurse, the senior resident, the odious intern. Isn't that enough? I sure as hell wish McKennen was around."

"Yeah, but we haven't talked to anyone who takes care of kids with Down's or with anybody who has one."

"You're right, Martin, but there's as much difference among parents who have a kid with Down's as there is among the kids with Down's.

"Yeah, maybe."

"And the doctors who care for kids with Down's? Don't you think they'll just say we have to cope?"

"I guess," Martin said, his head down. "But you always seem to know the answer before we even ask for help. Dammit, Sophia, suppose there is no right answer here."

She stared at Martin as if he'd lost his mind. "There's always a right answer. Even if it has only a nanometer edge over the wrong answer. There is. There has to be."

"If it's that small a difference …"

"Don't go there," Sophia said. She picked up the butter and put it in the fridge, wrapped the garbage in the newspaper, then sprayed hot water over congealed spaghetti sauce on the plates.

"Discussion over, I guess," Martin said. "I'll do the dishes. You rest."

"I got them. We'll make a decision tomorrow. Fenderson's deadline. I promise."

For her, cleaning up wasn't a chore. It was automatic, a necessity, like breathing. Martin watched her for a moment, then shrugged, poured himself a bourbon, and headed toward his study. He sat on his leather couch, listening to *Carmina Burana*. *Fortuna imperatrix mundi*, he hummed. He identified with the medieval goliards, those satirical scholar-poets who were barred from the academies and the church, wandering the land. He rattled the ice cubes. "Fortuna, the bitch—how d'you say that in Latin?" Martin rubbed his cast where his arm ached beneath the plaster. He sipped the bourbon, picked up the newspaper, and thought of Sophia. A small column on the front page of the *Plain Dealer* noted that twenty thousand people were dead after a volcano erupted in Colombia. An entire town, *poof!*

The phone rang. Martin swayed over to the stereo and turned it down.

"Who? Shulder? Yup, that's me."

"You're the father of the baby in the NICU, right?" asked Lydia.

"Yeah."

"I'm just calling to see if you need any support from us on that, and to ask a few questions."

A psychologist? "Nice of you to call, but aren't you're working a little late?"

"That's all right, sir, glad to help in any way. This must be tough for you and your wife."

"It is tough, but Sophia's probably the one you should talk to. She's pretty broken up."

"What do the doctors tell you? What do you think you're going to do?"

"Complicated. Needs an operation. Maybe two. But that won't fix everything. So my wife is … my wife and I are still deciding," Martin said, sipping his drink.

"You think you won't sign for the operations because he's …"

"Just because he has Down's syndrome? No, that's not the point."

"You certainly are remarkable to be handling this so well, Mr. Shulder."

"Thanks, thanks a lot. Folks haven't been all that sympathetic. My wife sort of feels that it might put the baby through more pain and stuff if we go ahead with the operations."

"And how do you feel?"

"Me? I dunno. Seems to me if the baby is born, we might as well do everything we can."

"And the risks, the limitations?"

"Mental retardation? Yeah, but maybe they'll have a drug for it someday. Say, why is this of particular interest to you? Doesn't this happen all the time?"

"Well, Mr. Shulder, it isn't often that issues of withdrawal of support come up for us."

"Don't be silly. We're just thinking about whether to go ahead with the operations or not."

"Would you ever consider it, do you think?"

"Nope. I don't think so. All that 'pulling the plug' stuff? Well, maybe yes, maybe no. Depends on what the doctors say."

"But don't the doctors want to do the operations?"

"You're right. They do want to start a series of operations."

"So back to what you're going to do."

"I guess I could go either way," Martin said. "It's really Sophia's, my wife's, decision."

"And if it were your decision alone to make?"

"On my own? I mean it's like nothing in the kid is right—stomach, heart, or head, and for sure not all of it can be fixed. But I guess I'd go along with the doctors. Who wouldn't?"

"Thanks, Mr. Shulder. And call any time if you feel like talking."

"Thank you. Thanks a lot. Let me get your number down—hello? Hello?"

Martin put down the phone, sweating lightly. He held the icy glass of bourbon on his forehead. Damn nice of the hospital to look after parents like that. He put down his drink and rubbed his cast. Have to take care of that arm. Be more careful next time.

17

Day Five

All night, Sophia slept little. Exhausted, she waited for morning light, and as soon as she saw the first signs of blackness turning to gray, she stole out of the bed, showered quickly, and left a short note for Martin, who lay face up, snoring softly, his cast on his chest, his legs spread across the tangled covers as if he'd been dropped unconscious from the ceiling.

The door to the baby's room was open. She went in and adjusted a tuck in the sheet on the crib mattress. She closed the miniblinds against the coming day's morning light. She took a last look at the pristine changing table, the bentwood rocking chair, the murals of elephants dancing along the wainscoting that Martin had finished the day before she went into labor.

She closed the door and left for the hospital.

On her drive into Cleveland, the morning paper was arriving at newsstands, on porches, and on office desks throughout the area.

DA Inquiry on Doctors Pulling the Plug on Babies with Birth Defects

by

Lydia Knowles, Staff Reporter

CLEVELAND, Ohio—Confirmed reports from the intensive care nursery at the Children's Pavilion in Cleveland indicate that doctors may be allowing an infant with birth defects to die without receiving life-saving surgery. When contacted at his office, Philip Lawton, the first-term district attorney for Cuyahoga County, said, "My office will be opening an inquiry, if the facts are as you suggest."

Spokespersons at Children's Hospital were not forthcoming when asked about recent cases. A hospital surgeon, speaking on condition of anonymity, said, "I think we should operate on these infants just like any other babies." Dr. W. McKennen, newly appointed chief of pediatrics at Children's Hospital, was unavailable for comment. Sean O'Connell, in charge of public relations for the hospital, said he was unable to discuss an individual case without parents' permission, nor could he confirm or deny that such a case was currently in their nursery. When asked what the hospital policy was regarding life support of babies with birth defects, he said that the subject was currently under review. He noted the long tradition of excellent care of mothers and infants at the medical center, which spanned four decades.

Some parents' groups and advocates for the handicapped are concerned this problem may be greater than previously thought. Is hospital care in neonatal intensive units being withheld from babies with birth defects?

Sheila Manley, the mother of a six-year-old child who suffered oxygen deprivation at birth, runs the Challenged Children Support Group in Cleveland. "At first," she says, "doctors said my Jill would never walk or talk. We fooled them. Jill can now take some steps with a walker and she likes to be read to. I don't know what my life would be like without her."

William Krug at Harvard University School of Medicine, head of one of the country's leading programs in neonatology says, "Sometimes continued life for a newborn who has an array of life-threatening anomalies at birth may be worse than compassionate care that allows the infant to die without surgery." When asked if he personally ever supervised such a case, Dr. Krug had no comment.

Reggie Arsenault, who was wounded as the captain of an infantry regiment in Vietnam, is currently head of Vets for Handicapped Rights in Washington, DC. When contacted, he said, "I'm glad the medics brought me back when I came in from the field with half my skull blown off. My parents sure as hell wanted everything done for me. I did what my country asked of me. I think if they're letting babies die, maybe the docs should be taken off life support."

Thomas Weller, a pediatrician and former Jesuit priest, the author of a recent well-reviewed book on medical ethics, said in a telephone interview, "I don't think we should ever give up on life. It is sacred. We doctors need to do all we can to preserve it." Dr. Weller then quoted extensively from his book, noting that these kinds of decisions may become more complicated in the future when doctors have yet more powerful technologies to sustain life.

The father of a recently born baby with Down's syndrome now in the intensive care nursery at Children's Hospital denied that euthanasia considerations were delaying life-saving surgery for his son.

Will babies continue to die in the hands of doctors who play God? According to Congressman Itaravich, an inquiry to the Department of Health Education and Welfare indicated that draft regulations regarding right-to-life decisions for newborn babies were under consideration. "If this practice is widespread," he said in a telephone interview, "it's truly abhorrent; hospitals where such things happen should be closed down."

That same day, on the flight back to Cleveland, Mac thought about Billy's birth almost twenty years ago. His wife had been in labor for eighteen hours. He was in the delivery room. During his internship, sleep deprived as usual, he was hardly conscious of what was going on. His wife wasn't too conscious either, after all those miserable hours of labor and some Demerol. Just before the delivery, the obstetrician asked Mac to leave the delivery room.

When the obstetrician came to find him in the waiting room, it was clear that no happy event had occurred.

"I think the baby's a Mongol, Mac. I don't know if we should let your wife see him. Sometimes it's best if they're just institutionalized right away. It's a tragedy, but you're a nice couple, young, healthy. Hell, you could have a dozen kids. I gave your wife a shot, and she'll be sleeping for a few hours. I can give you a number to call, and they'll pick up the baby. They'll take care of him, and you won't have to worry."

Wham. That was the sixties, antediluvian times. The amazing thing is that the news didn't really change much for Mac. He was already wadded in cotton wool—overwhelmed by work, by the prospect of having a baby, of being a father with his youth unspent, before even feeling like an adult. So he just plodded on, dealing with the immediate.

Though that first morning, Mac had rebelled. He'd decided they should keep the kid. His wife never knew there was an option not to. He tried to protect her from the truth, the prognosis. Mac told her about the exceptions. The kids with IQs in the nineties, wonderful kids, great personalities, always hope, just hang on. He worried more about cheering up his wife than the consequences of caring for a kid with Down's. After all, the baby's care would be her responsibility.

Christ, it was awful. Here Mac was a trained, at least partially trained, expert in birth defects and child development, completely at sea, unconscious. He went to work, his escape hatch. He tried not to think about it. But he'd learned one thing since. Those who need the most help, like him and his ex-wife, often don't ask for it. Or rather they ask for it in indirect ways. Ten days after Billy's birth, Mac came home from the hospital and found his son lying on the floor, crying. His wife was in a chair, not reading, not smoking, not doing anything. She stared dully at Mac and said, "He won't eat. He hates me. I've created a monster."

Mac did the usual inept things he imagined fathers did. He picked up the baby, made up a bottle, and with difficulty got it into him, then sat with the kid limp in his lap and tried to talk with his wife. He didn't understand her then, and she wouldn't talk to him much. He totally missed her diagnosis. How did he not see how depressed she was? "I appreciate your trying to help, but there's nothing you can do" was the most he could get out of her. In the next weeks, she let herself go. Drank too much. Didn't get dressed or leave the house all day. She took care of the baby all right, at least the externals. She changed him, bathed him, fed him. The baby grew. But they were both apathetic, and nothing changed for months. Sure, he should have looked for help, but in those days there wasn't much around. It was either a psychiatrist or nothing. Seeing a psychiatrist stigmatized you, and it was expensive. His wife wouldn't go anyway. Slowly things improved a bit, and his wife went back to school part time. They got out to socialize with the other residents. Mac thought things were going to be okay.

When his son was eight months, by now smiling and reaching, trying to roll over, he came home from the hospital and found his wife's things had vanished along with her. She left a note. The baby was with the neighbors. She'd been having an affair with a graduate student and they were going to California. She would contact Mac. She was sorry, so sorry about the baby.

Today, things were beginning to be different for both the child and the parents. So many things were standard now in big cities: support groups, social service, counseling, new antidepressants, in-home programs, special infant development programs, coordinated medical care for Down syndrome. In other parts of the country, of course, kids with Down's were still being warehoused in institutions. Mac and his wife weren't stupid back then, just ignorant of how much support was needed to contend with the issues, and too proud, tired, ashamed, or embarrassed to ask for the little help that was available. What benighted times. If Mac hadn't known, being in pediatrics, then who could have known? How they made themselves suffer.

But somehow over the next months, Mac fell in love with Billy. Mac adored his son's complacency, his serious calm, even though his developmental landmarks kept slipping further and further behind. Maybe Billy's calm came because he was insulated from all those additional neurons that were sparked among the kids who bounced around the sandbox in the park, using toys, interacting with others. Finally Billy learned to hold a marble between his thumb and forefinger, but nothing smaller. Even now Billy needed triple-sized buttons on his shirts.

The pure stream of lovability in his son diverged when he was about two and a half years old. He became stubborn, and frequently more than a rivulet of savagery appeared. Maybe it was his partial realization that he was different from other children, maybe he recognized his mother's betrayal. Mac couldn't handle it. Home day-care workers were calling him out of rounds. They quit every other week. Mac caved and put Billy in a residential facility. Mac, a pediatrician.

In the past five years, things turned around some, and Mac felt more like a father than a visitor in his son's life, but still, the way he and his wife had dealt with Billy was Mac's dark and dirty little secret.

⁓

Through the plastic top of the incubator, with her forearms pushed through the portholes, Sophia looked down at her own hands. One hand stroked her baby's head, careful of the scalp vein IV. Her other hand lay open beside the baby, motionless, like a foreign object. He was connected to a mélange of electronic monitors, of different brand names and vintage. His chest was moving rapidly. There were no doctors around, and the nurses, signing out at the end of their shift, left her alone. With the day nurses coming on duty, Sophia thought, it felt like the changing of the guard at a military cemetery; their charges were respected, but not in much need of immediate care. One of the monitors indicated her baby was receiving twice as much oxygen to breathe as normal babies, twice as much oxygen as Sophia was breathing.

How easy it would be to pull the monitors, the oxygen, the IV, the endotracheal tube, unplug the incubator, wrap the baby in a blanket, and just hold him. The way it would have been back in the days when Sophia was born. Her baby was not the way he should be, and goddamn it, neither was she. "We're both messed up, little guy," she whispered to him. She felt a small regular thumping when she placed her fingers on his chest. The baby startled, then fell back into his drugged sleep. Sophia tensed. Had little guy sensed something? What his mother had just contemplated? But she wouldn't do it. Disconnect her little guy? It would be the mirror image of the surgeons cutting her baby open again and again. There was no logic to how she felt.

At noontime Martin met Sophia in the hospital cafeteria. They pushed an uneaten sandwich back and forth until time for their meeting.

Sophia hated the conference space next to the NICU. Too many people there for the business about to be transacted, and too many people glad to stay away. Stuffy and overcrowded, it smelled of stale food. Someone had taken the trouble to wipe down the table and straighten up the usual mess before they arrived. The blackboard was newly erased, and the light boxes on the wall empty of x-rays.

Attendees dragged into the conference room as if they were going to an execution. Sophia sat in a straight chair next to Martin. Her stitches still ached. Dressed in a gray sweater and dark slacks, she was the center of attention.

Notestein made the introductions. Sophia knew Alicia, the primary nurse for Baby Shulder. Then there were the social worker; the nursing supervisor of the NICU; Kurz the senior resident assigned to the NICU; and Sean O'Connell, a hospital administrator. The hospital lawyer had a Chinese name. He wore an intelligent expression behind thick glasses; for a second Sophia thought he looked like a grown-up version of her baby. She wished the unhelpful Lennie could have come. Dr. Kracton, the pediatrician, was not present, nor was Fenderson. That morning, Sophia had asked if a specialist in Down's syndrome were available, but they couldn't turn one up on such short notice.

She watched the second hand on the institutional wall clock jump forward in sudden leaps, five seconds at a time.

One arm across his lap and a hand covering his mouth, Notestein reminded Sophia of a twisted pretzel. Not the compassionate, omnipotent healer she needed.

"We want you to know that we are all concerned with the care of the baby and want the best for your family."

He looked over his glasses at the group, then continued as if leading a seminar. "Let me just review the issues we need to talk over today. The stat chromosome report came back and confirmed what we already strongly suspected, that your baby has Down syndrome, or trisomy 21, whichever term you prefer."

Sophia thought about which she would prefer. She licked her lips. Her mouth was dry.

"About 4 percent of infants with this condition have a blocked gastrointestinal tract, and your baby meets this description. There is an abnormal connection from the baby's stomach to the bronchial tubes, which is allowing gastric acid to get into the lungs. We strongly suspect that the baby has a complex congenital heart defect that is severe but probably amenable to heart surgery at some point. But if we don't hurry up and fix the gastrointestinal problem, the baby will succumb due to pneumonitis."

Notestein looked at O'Connell, as if for some token of praise.

Sophia wanted to leave the room. The discussion was pointless. Again, she remembered the burn patient. Could it be, she'd wondered at the time, that two people could have opposite views and both be right? With Martin last night, she'd felt so sure of herself. Opposing views, both right, cannot coexist with logistic outcomes—null or one, life or death. When she spoke, telling the group that she and Martin feared that putting the baby through the surgeries was the greater of two evils, Notestein nodded.

"It's not uncommon to go through a period of anger, depression, and rejection when you first hear news of this sort. Some of us sensed some degree of ambivalence in your feelings about the operation."

"Of course, we're ambivalent," Martin broke in. "How could anyone not be? We've been in an emotional storm about this." Martin paused and took a deep breath. "But you're wrong if you think that because we're disturbed about it, we're pawns of our emotions and we can't make up our minds. Of course if the baby dies, we will wonder if we did the right thing for the rest of our lives. But if the baby lives, we may feel the same way."

Martin reached for Sophia's hands to quiet them. He'd surprised her, pleased her, even though he lacked her ability to imagine how life with a sickly infant would be. Martin would try to help, but she knew it would really be her baby to live with. And whether the baby lived or died, she would have to live with the decision.

Notestein ran his hands through his few remaining tufts of hair and fixed his eyes on the administrator looking for his input, but O'Connell wasn't biting.

"Listen to me," Sophia said. "Twenty to forty percent of Down's babies with these anomalies die in their first couple of years regardless of what's done."

Notestein looked up quickly. "Who told you that?"

"It's in most of the texts," she said, not looking at Alicia.

"We don't like to cast numbers like that in stone," Notestein said. "There are amazing medical advances all the time."

"Helpful things, like curing cancer in rats," Martin muttered.

After a pause, the social worker leaned forward eagerly and said, "Sophia, we've talked together a lot in the past few days. You talked on the phone today with my counterpart from the clinic who works with these children. You know how happy they can be."

Apparently, the social worker had been briefed. Sophia remembered their discussions: embarrassing monologues by a young woman with too much jewelry and affectation and too little information. Even now the scent of her perfume mixed with the nervous sweat in the room.

"If they're so happy, why do you routinely carry out abortions in the first part of pregnancy when the amniocentesis shows Down's?" Sophia asked.

There was another pause. Sophia and Martin had agreed beforehand that they should try to avoid confrontation. To buy just a little more time.

"Sophia, Martin." Notestein was consoling. "You know we don't understand what happened with the amniocentesis. That's a problem they're dealing with at Women's Hospital."

Again, Sophia saw Notestein glance at the administrator for support.

"Lots of parents have felt exactly like you at a time like this," Notestein continued. "Yet they learned to love their infants with trisomy 21. There are worse things. Why not put off long-term decisions?"

"I thought there was no time," Martin said. "I thought you said the surgery permit had to be signed even before today."

"Well, that would give you more time to get used to the idea. I think we'd better get the first operation done and then think things through some more in the next few weeks."

Martin raised his eyebrows and took a deep breath. "Doctor," Martin said, "you are not hearing us. We agreed to meet with you to discuss all the options for our baby, but it sounds like you just want to get us to sign for surgery so your problem goes away."

Sophia gave his hand a squeeze.

"Now, Martin," said Dr. Notestein, "I'm not sure it's your decision to make alone. Who speaks for the baby?"

Sophia looked at the doctor in amazement. She was the *mother*, for God's sake. What did he think they were doing here?

"Doctor," Martin said, his hand on Sophia's knee, spoke for her. "If it's not our decision to make, why have people been asking us all week why we won't let the baby have the operation? And if it's not our decision to make, why don't you sign your own damn surgery consent?"

O'Connell stirred in his seat and cleared his throat. Nobody else spoke. O'Connell sat up straight in his chair. "Mr. Shulder, I'm afraid we may have to do something like that if you don't reconsider."

"What do you mean?" Sophia asked. She had the feeling that a crowd of people was observing her through a one-way window.

"It's arguable that it could be illegal for you not to consent to the operation."

"I don't understand," Martin said in a low voice. "What kind of gobbledygook is that?"

The lawyer looked at Martin and Sophia through his heavy glasses. "Reagan is about to sign some kind of executive order about it, making it clearly against the law for anyone, parents or doctors, to refuse a life-saving operation for a seriously defective child."

"Then why have us sign a piece of paper 'permitting' something if there is no choice?" Sophia asked. "We know you don't do surgery on infants with some defects like anencephaly or even trisomy 13. We know this."

"It's our baby." Martin appealed to Notestein, the only person he thought might have the power to help. "It's our decision. You said so yesterday. Tell this guy."

"I'm sorry, Martin," Dr. Notestein responded. "I'm not in the habit of letting my patients die."

"And I'm not yet in the habit of having my baby tortured," Sophia snapped.

Notestein winced.

"The baby is brain damaged," Sophia continued. "His heart is no good. He'll need at least several heart and stomach operations, and his chances still won't be great. We have talked about this; God knows we have thought about it. Five or six months ago you would have recommended abortion without a second thought. That's if your damn amniocentesis was accurate. And none of us would be sitting here now."

Around the table the hospital staff froze in some kind of diorama.

"Don't string it out. Stop torturing us and the baby." Sophia sunk back, emptied out.

Martin was breathing hard. He grasped the edge of the table. "Who's being helped here?" he said softly. "Our baby was brought here because this is the best place for a sick baby, come what may." He turned toward Sophia. "We just need more time."

Sophia was crying now, quietly.

"We're out of time. Just sign the permit, Sophia, and things will be better," said Dr. Notestein.

"But why?" Sophia stopped herself from crying. "For

whom is that best?" She paused for a moment, then looked directly at Notestein. What would you do if the baby were yours?"

Notestein was caught off guard. "That's not the point, Sophia," he said.

That was exactly the point, Sophia thought.

"We are not free agents," Notestein said. "There are laws. We must respect a human life."

"You mean," Martin said, "we're constrained by laws to do what may be wrong? Everybody's about patients' rights to die peacefully and stuff like that. You don't keep everybody alive, no matter what. What if we brought our lawyers in here like you?"

"Well, I think that's it for today," Notestein huffed.

"Martin, Sophia, we've talked this over as much as we can," said O'Connell. "We expect to file for a court order later this afternoon so we can proceed with the operation." The administrators and staff scraped back their chairs. Sophia and Martin walked out of the conference room in a daze.

Alicia followed and tapped Sophia's sleeve. "Do you want to see him?"

"Yes," Sophia said, then turned around. "Just a minute." She walked back into the conference room and heard the tail end of a sentence: "… the parents not handling it very well …" She confronted the ring of faces, stared at them for a beat.

"This is my baby, *my* baby, that you're talking about." Sophia turned and slammed the door of the conference room.

There was silence as people looked everywhere except at each other. Finally the lawyer said, "I'll file with the judge today. Tell your boss"—he nodded to O'Connell—"prepare for the worst."

Mac arrived at Cleveland Hopkins airport in the early afternoon with a backpack that smelled of damp and dirty shorts and T-shirts. He took a cab straight to the medical center, but the taxi was stopped by a police barricade a block away because of a demonstration. He made his way on foot, megaphones blaring, "Hey, hey, ho, ho, baby killers got to go! Life is right, right for life!" Mac waded into the crowd and headed for the main entrance. Someone shoved a sign into his hands, a cartoon baby and the caption, *My Heart Beats, Don't Kill Me.*

A policeman saw the poster in his hand and shoved Mac away at the door. Mac started to explain, but the officer and pointed to the line that held back the protesters. Others in white coats, scrubs, or suits entered the complex unimpeded. No choice. Mac walked back into the noisy group, where he received smiles and pats on the back. Some applauded his attempt to storm the bastille. Mac handed the poster to a girl who looked like she was skipping seventh grade. He circled the building, entered the emergency entrance, and found his way to Kennelly's outer office.

"Mac," the dean said, coming out of his office, his arm outstretched for a handshake just as he'd done on Mac's recruitment visits. "So glad you're here." He nodded towards his office and led Mac inside. "You know Notestein, of course."

Mac had been chosen by the search committee for the chairmanship and Notestein hadn't. Notestein didn't like Mac, and Mac didn't like him.

They sat in a triangle around a glass coffee table to discuss the problematic baby. The dean took a big breath and opened with, "The chief of staff asked me to handle this. I'll tell you why, Mac. You've heard about the case we want your help on. There's more. The mother is Sophia Shulder."

Jesus H. Christ! Both Notestein and the dean observed Mac's reaction like he was a lab rat.

"You knew Sophia Shulder," Kennelly said, "back in Boston, and for that reason, at least partly, we think you can help."

"Mac, I need to know how well you know Mrs. Shulder."

Composing himself, Mac said, "Well enough." Not well enough even to know Sophia was pregnant. "I knew her in Boston for a couple of years before she moved here. Our labs were on the same floor. Our paths only crossed in occasional interdisciplinary seminars. I mentored her a bit on the academic labyrinth. Reviewed her recent grant application for her."

Kennelly raised his eyebrows at Mac's last comment. Something in Mac's response was bothering the dean. He shook his head. Notestein looked out the window.

"Well, that will help," Kennelly commented. "Perhaps you mentored her well. Stanton over in biochemistry told me she got a fundable score on her NIH grant. Not bad for an assistant professor. But here's the thing …" The dean got up and motioned to Notestein. "Could you step out for just a moment?"

Notestein, not pleased with any part of this, got up and left.

"The thing is, Mac, as dean I have to wade in murky waters sometimes. You saw the morning paper?"

"Not yet. Why?"

"The Shulder case is on page one."

"Shit. So that's what's going on outside! I thought it was about the abortion clinic."

"You named it. Same crowd, much bigger today," Kennelly

said. "I know our priority is the baby and the family, but there are a lot of dimensions to the Shulder case that I have to deal with besides the bad publicity. A few examples: we have the best cardiac surgeon in the United States. I brought him here from Stanford last year at great expense. Now he's intimating that he might take a higher paying job in Texas, where such sensitivities don't seem to exist. Our Cuyahoga county prosecutor has subpoenaed the hospital records for the baby. Also we have the mess with the amnio. And here. Take a look at this." He handed Mac a page printed like some poster from a prison wall.

NOTICE

DEPARTMENT OF HEALTH AND HUMAN SERVICES
Office for Civil Rights

DISCRIMINATORY FAILURE TO FEED AND CARE FOR HANDICAPPED INFANTS IN THIS FACILITY IS PROHIBITED BY FEDERAL LAW. SECTION 504 OF THE REHABILITATION ACT OF 1973 STATES THAT

"NO OTHERWISE QUALIFIED HANDICAPPED INDIVIDUAL SHALL, SOLELY BY REASON OF HANDICAP, BE EXCLUDED FROM PARTICIPATION IN, BE DENIED THE BENEFITS OF, OR BE SUBJECTED TO DISCRIMINATION UNDER ANY PROGRAM OR ACTIVITY RECEIVING FEDERAL FINANCIAL ASSISTANCE."

Any person having knowledge that a handicapped infant is being discriminatorily denied food or customary medical care should immediately contact:

Handicapped Infant Hotline
U.S. Department of Health and Human Services
Washington, D.C. 20201
Phone 800-368-1019 (Available 24 hours a day) - TTY Capability

In Washington, D.C. call 863-0100

OR

Your State Child Protective Agency

Federal Law prohibits retaliation or intimidation against any person who provides information about possible violations of the Rehabilitation Act of 1973.

Identity of callers will be held confidential.

Failure to feed and care for infants may also violate the criminal and civil laws of your state.

Kennelly continued, "Our people in Washington tell us that in a few weeks, they think this will have to be posted all over the children's hospital, especially in the NICU. If care is withheld from any kid for most any reason, the feds will investigate and even pull federal funding from the medical center.

Mac held the poster between his thumb and forefinger and handed it back to the dean. "So Washington wants to decide the most difficult medical cases imaginable. Like using a sledge hammer to build watches."

"You got it, Mac. Bad as it is, it may get worse. So maybe you can understand why I have to ask. We don't need any surprises. Is, or was, there anything more to your relationship with Mrs. Shulder?"

Oof. Mac never saw that coming. The dean was serious. Mac clenched his fists. This was way over the line, but after a moment he figured that the dean wasn't judging him. He needed to find out, doing his job. This information would matter. Possibly Mac's help could screw things up even more. He tried not to look shifty. "Admired her from a distance. That's absolutely all."

"And she has, or had, no feelings for you?"

"Not that I'm aware of." Mac held his gaze.

Relieved, the dean shook Mac's hand. "Well, good. Sorry I had to ask." He got up, opened the door, and waved Notestein back in. "Okay, Notestein, your turn. Fill us in on the baby."

Notestein sat back on the couch, feigning a relaxation that Mac could tell he didn't feel. "Her baby had a normal amnio, but was born with Down's syndrome that took her pediatrician a couple of days to diagnose."

So that was the "amnio" mess the dean had referred to. This was worse than the worst Mac already knew about.

Notestein continued as if he were uninvolved, offering the full account of the baby's condition.

"Who's been talking to the parents?" the dean wanted to know.

Notestein ticked off nearly ten names on his fingers.

Kennelly asked the obvious. "What about you, Dr. Notest-ein?"

Well," Notestein grimaced. "With so many involved, I thought I'd keep myself in the background. Parents are obviously worried sick at the prospects of multiple surgeries both for the TE fistula and for the heart."

"Can't say I blame them," Kennelly said. "But here's the thing. 'The cardiac guy' as you call him already is bringing in about 10 percent of the hospital's revenue this year. We're building him a whole new operating wing and a cardiac ICU for his postops. Apropos of nothing, he also happens to be a born-again Christian."

"The one-year survival rate for that heart anomaly is still about 70 percent at best," Mac said.

"Shit," Kennelly said.

Kennelly stood up and walked around his desk, sat down, and ran his hand through his thinning hair. "I sincerely want all this to go away," he said, "without any further damage to the Shulders or the reputation of our hospital and medical school. Mac, I want you to talk with the Shulders."

Sure, and fix the rest of the world too. At least Mac could try to help Sophia, poor woman. He wondered what the Stanford surgeon's starting salary was. He wished his were a significant fraction of whatever it was. But pediatricians sometime in the past must have taken a vow of poverty as indicated by their average national salary. Mac resisted the urge to salute the dean, and said all he could say: "Okay."

Steve was tired—tired of the nursery and tired of his internship as he tried to organize the data on each of his nine patients in the NICU. He transcribed the lab reports. He also needed information from the nurses' notes and the x-ray reports. All these pieces of information were scattered in different logbooks, on clipboards, at the bedside, or in the chart at the nurses' station. Frequently he had to call one of the labs, and wait on hold until someone looked up the latest urine culture. He could not keep the reams of data clear in his mind. The blood counts blurred into the electrolytes and blood gases. The numbers became meaningless. Afternoon teaching rounds were an hour-and-a-half ordeal, and Notestein was running late. This wasn't education, it was some form of torture.

"Ready, Stevo? Let's round."

Dr. Kurz gathered his minions—two medical students and two interns. Dr. Notestein strolled into the nursery, his puce clipboard and long white coat marking his status. None of them had seen the morning newspaper.

Steve disliked them both. Kurz because he insisted that his interns and students present their patients in a formal, ritualized manner. Kurz thought that if you just followed his outline and supplied the data, you wouldn't miss a thing. Everyone knew Kurz hoped to be the chief resident next year, and he usually kowtowed to the attendings. Notestein was just the opposite; he usually wanted the big picture but was capricious. It was hard to predict when he might peer over his steel-rimmed glasses, his lips pursed, with a look that implied you were an idiot.

"Steve, we'll start with your intermediate kids," Kurz ordered.

Steve could feel the students and the other intern relax. They were off the hook for the time being.

Steve read from his notes. "Baby Jimenez is a twenty-four-day-old full-term infant that is weaning off tincture of opium for opiate withdrawal." He went on and on with all he knew, finally finishing up with, "Mom has abandoned. Kid is going into foster care when he graduates."

"Steve, Stevie, Stefan. From the top again, this time by systems, if you please." Kurz checked to see whether Notestein approved.

"You know what," Notestein said. He looked exhausted for some reason. "I think that for these not-so-sick kids, a thumbnail is sufficient. Let's move on."

Steve felt confused. Pleasing the attending and shortcutting rounds were good, but not at the price of pissing off the senior resident. He avoided Kurz's eyes as the group trooped to the next infant.

They were almost an hour into rounds when they stood next to the Shulder baby's incubator.

"Let's see," said Steve's fellow intern, as if all of them were not intimately aware of the baby's problems. She ran through them fully, then smiled at Dr. Kurz, who failed to hide a self-satisfied smirk.

"That was a good one, Kurz," Dr. Notestein said. The two med students with them looked puzzled. "We'd thought the cardiac problem was the usual one with Down's causing too much blood flow to the lungs. But our Dr. Kurz here, without the help of the cardiologists, realized the problem wasn't too much blood flow to the lungs but too little blood flow to the body because in fact the baby has a hypoplastic left ventricle. Kurz can take you through it after rounds."

Steve envied Dr. Kurz, who was damn smart but never let you forget it.

The intern rattled on. Steve's feet hurt. When she finally paused, Notestein scratched something on his clipboard.

"Do you think this kid is encephalopathic?"

"Excuse me?"

"Encephalopathic. Depressed. Zonked," Kurz said.

"Oh, right." Steve's fellow intern fixed her glasses on her nose and brushed some hair from her face. Then in medicalese, she laid out the ways the baby was sicker than squat.

With that, Notestein was ready to move on. "Next case," he said.

"Sir?" Steve asked. He felt as if something had pinched him. "I'm wondering where we are with this kid?" Steve instantly kicked himself for not keeping his mouth shut. It wasn't his case.

"Steverino, we just discussed it!" Kurz walked to the next infant's incubator.

"I mean the bigger picture. I know surgery is all ready to operate if the parents sign the consents. But what's happening?"

"Now that's a good question, Steve." Notestein raised his hand to stop Kurz who was heading the group toward the next incubator. "There was a thing about these sorts of cases in the paper this morning. We had a high-level meeting with the parents earlier today, but they're stalling, possibly motivated by our obstetric colleague over at Women's Hospital. We're going to court to get an injunction, a court order compelling the surgery as soon as our lawyer can find a judge. Not much to do until then. Probably too late anyhow."

Just wait? With the child dying? If they were going to let the child die anyway, why not pull the plug now? The team moved to the next baby, Notestein looking at the clock on the wall.

It didn't make any sense to Steve. "Sir? I'm on tonight. Do we have a 'Do Not Resuscitate' order on the baby?"

"No, we don't," Notestein said, tersely. "Now enough about this case. We're waiting for the injunction. We'll let the media chatter about it. Let's move on. These people have to go home."

Steve listened distantly as his fellow intern went through the drill for the next infant. What if the Shulder baby coded tonight while the attending was at home asleep? What should he do? A full-scale resuscitation? Would they tap a pneumothorax? Replace the endotracheal tube? What about cardiac compressions and meds?

"Pardon me, sir." Steve knew he was annoying the hell not only out of the senior resident but also the attending this time. "But I have just one more question on the Shulder baby."

The whole group turned and stared at Steve. He too felt he was beginning to whine. But there was something important here that was not being addressed. Why was he the only one who thought so?

"Maybe it isn't right after all to get an injunction, especially with the baby as sick as he is now."

"Stevenooski! What is it with you and this case?" Kurz was seriously pissed. "This may be that rare happy time when you should be glad you're only an intern. You are just one of the line workers in this great healing factory. There are the medical issues, then there are the legal issues. Two separate things. That's why they pay our attending the big bucks. Now, we're stealing time from the rest of the kids. Let's go. I'm on call tonight too. So be sure and wake me if you want to talk about this yet again."

Dr. Notestein winced at the "big bucks" comment and waved for them to hurry it along. The group moved to the next baby.

Fuck them. Steve still felt mortified about talking trash in front of the mother. He owed her. He needed some support from his peers. Didn't these people study religion or philosophy in college? Didn't they have any questions? Steve thought about the senior's last comment. Wasn't that the defense at the Nuremberg trials? They were just doing what they were told by their superiors?

Steve couldn't help himself. "Just one more thing," he said very rapidly. "Shouldn't we get the mother some sort of help?"

"Help? Jesus," Kurz said, looking at his watch. "She's talked to Notestein, the social worker, the surgeon. She's tying up a whole bunch of resources in this hospital. Help? I'd like to drop kick her into Lake Erie. And I'm beginning to feel the same about you. Your job?" Kurz said, waving his hand to include all the babies in the NICU. "Your job is simple. Just keep them alive till the end of your shift. Now *c'mon!*"

The students grinned like apes, seeing that Steve was the one drawing Kurz's ire instead of any of them.

Steve rolled his eyes at the nurse, who had remained silent beside the incubator. "Don't look at me," she whispered. "It's the first day I've had the baby. Alicia knows him, and she's on tonight."

With the help of his new secretary, eager Emily, Mac reached Sophia, who agreed to meet. She was still in the NICU, could be in Mac's new office in half an hour. His stuff from Boston had arrived, and the boxes were stacked perilously high against one wall. He had a nice view of the park in front of the art museum, but the spacious office had little in the way of furnishings. His predecessor had died six months earlier from pancreatic cancer. No golden years for him. All Mac had inherited was a great leather chair and a mahogany desk. Emily had to bring in a folding chair for Sophia. Mac asked to meet Sophia alone, without Martin, and she'd offered no objections.

Emily not only showed in Sophia promptly at 4:00 p.m. but also dragged in a cart with some tea in paper cups and some pastries. Sophia sat down and got right to it. "Mac, I'm glad you took the job, and I'm glad you called. But I assume they want you to get me to sign the surgical permits."

"Hi yourself, Sophia. I know you've been hit by tragedy, but being able to fix it is way more than I'm capable of. I'm so, so sorry. Now have some tea."

"I was hoping for more than tea."

"Maybe a *petit four*?" That got Mac a slight smile. "Okay," he said. "Let's talk about real stuff. First the amnio mistake. I've been on the phone since I arrived today talking to everyone I could think of. Somehow your tube of amniotic fluid was mixed up with another woman's. The whole slew of them are now doing everything in their not-inconsiderable power to find out how it happened and how to make sure it never happens again. You should know that the other woman chose to continue her pregnancy and was ecstatic that the reported lab results were wrong. I promise to keep you in the loop."

Mac rolled his chair around so the desk was no longer between them. "Let's talk about your baby. Does he have a name yet?"

Sophia looked down at her cup of coffee, not drinking. "Not yet. Jewish boys are named on the eighth day, but not if they're sick."

"I guess I knew that."

"Mac, I don't know what to do."

"I've assumed that Martin is pretty much wanting to do whatever you decide?"

"Yes."

"What I know of you, Sophia, is that you've always been a pretty decisive person."

"Right. But for me, it's if, if, if. If the baby just had Down's. Well, okay then, we could deal with it. If the baby just had the hypoplastic heart, and not Down's, I could decide whether the risks of surgery would be worth the pain and suffering for the baby. If I'd known I was carrying a baby with Down's, I would have had an abortion, no question. What terrifies me is that if I make a decision I'll make it about me, not the baby."

Mac took a chance, took her hand. She didn't pull away. "That's all very clearly thought out. Believe me, I understand why it's so hard."

Sophia sniffled.

He sat there and held her hand. One of the hardest things for doctors to do sometimes was just to keep their mouths shut.

"And I know what you're going to say now," she said.

"I don't know what I'm going to say, so I'm interested to find out."

"The baby is going to die without surgery."

"Right," Mac said. "And the baby may die with any one of the surgeries in the offing."

"So I'm stuck. I don't want the baby to suffer with a series of surgeries that may not be successful."

"That may be where you're a little off track," Mac said. "With the drugs we have on offer, we can nearly eliminate pain and suffering." He never completely believed that himself, but it was one of the things doctors reflexively said. "I think," Mac added, "that there may be one thing that's not yet on the table. How will you feel if the baby dies, and you haven't yet made a decision that you can live with?"

"You're telling me, Mac, that not making a decision is a way of making a decision. Don't you think I know that? That if the baby dies, it will be on me. For life." She pulled away.

"Maybe," he said, "we ought to stop talking about decisions, and start thinking about choices. It's a given that there is no choice here that we could call a good one."

"The least bad choice?"

"I hate to say so, but right."

"At night," Sophia said, "I see a child growing up like Rosemary's baby, furious at her mother, and the mother running this way and that, scared for her child but also furious with her child for ruining her life."

Mac winced at the allusion. That movie gave neonatologists, in particular, nightmares. "But that's my point. You're predicting a whole lifetime for two lives," he said. "You can't know for sure. One thing we're better at is predicting over the short term. We know it would help your baby's lungs if we close the fistula and help the baby's circulation by increasing the blood flow to the body. Neither will cure the anomaly. But what if we could see whether the heart and gut surgeons could work together and do both with one operation? If so, we can see how your baby does and take time to decide on what's next. How does that sound?"

"Show me," Sophia said. "It actually sounds like something Martin suggested."

Mac sketched a simple cartoon. He had no idea if the surgeons would agree.

"Okay," said Sophia, with a great sigh. "Let's do that. And, Mac, right away. I can ask for a 'Do Not Resuscitate' order, right?"

"Sure," Mac said. "Your prerogative. I don't think any lawyer or administrator would get in the way of that one,"

"Okay, then I want a DNR on the baby, before and after the operation. Starting now. Is that unreasonable? Scratch that question. That's what I want."

"Will Martin go along with all this?"

"He'll be vastly relieved."

"Okay," Mac said. "We'll see how flexible the surgeons will be."

After Sophia left, Mac made all the calls. The two surgeons agreed, each unhappily. Sophia would sign the permit first thing in the morning, and Sophia's baby would be operated on tomorrow afternoon. Mac called Notestein. Sophia wanted a DNR starting immediately. Notestein wasn't cordial but said he'd get right on it. Next Mac called Sophia and then the dean. They both asked the same question. "Can we trust the surgeons to do both operations?"

Mac responded, "I think so. The cardiac surgeon is going first."

"Excellent," the dean said. "He thinks he can walk on water."

Mac left for his new apartment hoping all would settle down tomorrow, and that his second day wouldn't be as hard as his first.

18

Day Six

At night the pace in the nursery slowed, and some nurses preferred it to the daytime job. Black night at the windows, beeping monitors, gawky green and red plastic ventilators hissing life-breath into babies in plexiglass incubators. The nurses in blue scrub suits, bowed over their charges like votaries at the altar, night and day, seven days a week, year in and year out. A continuum of care for the ill that stretched back millennia.

At 2:00 a.m., Steve sat near the chart rack, completing his notes. He stretched and yawned after finishing the one for the Shulder baby, his last for the night. He had been glib and cavalier with Dieter. Thoughtless. Acted like an adolescent, not a professional, not a doctor. Which wasn't hard because he didn't feel like one. He'd asked Kurz whether he should apologize to the mother, but Kurz had said, "What's the point? I mean, what you said was right, it was just the way you said it."

But Steve brooded over it. The episode with the mother had thrown a switch. The doctors were wrong. The mother was right. What business did they have operating on this baby? Thirty years ago there would have been no thought of doing extensive heart or gut surgery on a newborn, any newborn. This year a tidal wave had wiped out ten thousand people in Bangladesh. Busting your ass to save one Down's syndrome kid wasn't even a faint consideration in most countries.

He finished his note with,

"Plan: per Dr. Notestein."

No new orders since yesterday and now Alicia told Steve that Notestein had left early. Steve wondered, Do we intubate the baby if he arrests? Do we run meds? Do we wake Notestein up and haul his ass in here if the kid codes?

The delivery room called for a pediatrician to attend a routine caesarian section. Steve walked over the bridge to the obstetric floor in Women's Hospital. He scrubbed and gowned, then checked the overhead warmer and the resuscitation equipment. The anesthesiologist showed him the OB record. All perfectly routine. The obstetric team were at the point of clearing the bladder off the uterus, and the chief OB resident looked over at Steve. He nodded. Ready.

With a rapid incision, the OB resident incised the uterus, reached in, and pulled out the pink baby. They clamped and cut the umbilical cord and handed off the baby to Steve. The baby was full term and good sized. Steve placed the baby on the resuscitation table and suctioned clear amniotic fluid from the baby's nose and mouth. He listened to the chest, but the baby wasn't breathing and the heart rate was falling. Steve picked up the bag and mask, turned on the flow of oxygen, and gave the baby a few puffs from the bag. Almost instantly, the baby took a few big breaths then wailed lustily and waved his hands in the air. The OB nurse dried the vigorous baby and held him at his mother's side while the obstetricians sewed up the op site. Steve smiled at the mother's expression of relief and joy as she turned her head and saw her pink son.

At that moment Steve's pager went off with an emergency call to the NICU. He tore out of the operating room and galloped across the bridge. Panting, he pulled off his mask and gown. The head nurse pointed to the Shulder baby.

At the Shulder baby's incubator, Alicia pointed to the cardiac monitor. Heart rate had slowed. Skin was blue. Steve put his hands through the portholes of the incubator and did a rapid reexamination. With his stethoscope, he strained to hear the baby's faint lung sounds. He couldn't hear the ductus murmur anymore. Neurologically, the baby remained out of it.

Alicia disconnected the ventilator and started to ventilate the baby with the anesthesia bag. Finished with his exam, Steve said to her, "Better up it to 100 percent oxygen. We've got to call Kurz. Let's get some blood gases and start some epinephrine. Let's extubate and ventilate with a mask."

Steve took over the bag and mask ventilation while Alicia went for the emergency cart with the medications. Some of the nurses were leaving for their break. Alicia was taking her sweet time with the emergency cart. The baby was going to die anyway. But he might linger on for days, even a week. It was insufferable. It was wrong.

Alicia was sweating. They were just keeping the Shulder baby alive so the lawyers and administrators could continue to dither. It was cruel. Something in the conference with the parents had changed Alice. She was ashamed of her hospital colleagues, the way they ganged up on the parents. The baby was too far gone now. If they were really going to do something for him, it should have happened days ago. She took the sterile drape off the top of the emergency cart and wheeled it over to where Steve was hand bagging the baby. The cardiac monitor showed the heart rate was down to eighty-five beats per minute.

"Jesus, Steve. Your bagging isn't helping," Alicia said.

"I know," said Steve. He gave the bag and mask to Alicia.

The mean blood pressure dropped to eighteen. "Do we have a DNR on this kid?" Alicia asked.

"Not a time for kidding," Steve said. He pulled out the endotracheal tube and tossed it on the emergency cart. Alicia continued the ventilation with a bag and mask while Steve slowly injected the epinephrine in the umbilical vein catheter. "Damn," he said. "I can't find a flush on the tray."

He bent to open the meds drawer on the resuscitation cart, pulled out a vial of saline. As he was about to flush the IV line, something made him pause. He looked at the vial. The label was orange, not pink. KCl, not NaCl. Potassium chloride, not sodium chloride. What the hell? He was so tired. What difference would it make? Steve pushed the contents of the syringe into the IV line.

In less than a minute, Alicia looked up at the cardiac monitor. "What's that, Steve?"

Steve raised his head and saw the classic sine wave of potassium toxicity. I dunno," Steve said. "Where the hell is Kurz?"

The bizarre tracing on the monitor slowed until the monitor showed a straight line. The alarm started to chime loudly, impossible to ignore. Alicia hit the intercom button that set off the cardiac arrest alert for the nursery.

Dr. Kurz came around the corner on a run.

Kurz listened to the lungs while Alicia continued ventilating the baby.

"Poor breath sounds on both sides. Noisy. Can't be sure whether I hear the heart or not."

Kurz suctioned, and some blips appeared on the cardiac monitor.

"Fuck, Steve. Look at the endotracheal tube. There's a solid plug of goo in there. Good you pulled it. Get me a laryngoscope and three-point-five tube so we can reintubate. One mL of 1:10,000 epi, then about twelve mL of bicarb."

Alicia walked into the treatment room and waited until she heard the resident start to swear. She picked up a laryngoscope and loosened its light bulb, then hurried back.

"Damn, this baby is still hard to bag," Kurz said. "What took you so long?"

He opened the laryngoscope blade in preparation for placing a tube into the infant's trachea. The light at the end of the blade failed to go on.

"Laryngoscope doesn't work. Get another."

Alicia walked back to the treatment room with the laryngoscope, tightened the bulb, and after a minute, returned to the Shulder baby. Steve was at the senior resident's side, handing him meds while the charge nurse gave cardiac compressions. Kurz had a new endotracheal tube in his hand.

"Why not just stop?" Alicia said. "We're still not seeing much activity on the cardiac monitor. It's been about fifteen minutes since we started the code. Maybe we don't really want to get this one back anyway." She held onto the laryngoscope despite Kurz's outstretched hand.

Everyone paused. The charge nurse said, "Let's quit."

Steve said, "Agreed."

Kurz looked at the ceiling. "Okay, but I'm not the one telling the attending that we called off a code without a couple more rounds of meds."

Steve said, "It's okay. Let's clean things up, and I'll make the calls."

"Thank God," said Alicia.

Kurz looked at his pager. "Stat emergency room call," he said, and galloped out of the NICU.

19

Day Seven

The phone rang at 4:00 a.m. Sophia awoke from a half sleep. She pushed on the alarm clock, but the ringing didn't stop. In an instant, she was fully awake.

"Mr. or Mrs. Shulder?

"Yes."

"This is Dr. Calvert, Steve, Steve Calvert, at the NICU at Children's. I'm afraid your baby has taken a turn for the worse, much worse."

"Is he alive?"

Sophia listened to the faint buzz on the phone.

"Ah, well, actually, no. He had an arrest about forty minutes ago, and we couldn't get him back."

"Why, why did he ... arrest? What caused it?"

What do you mean, why? Steve thought. Everything caused it. How the hell do you think we can keep a baby like this alive with no surgery, his lungs filling up with gastric acid and his heart failing? Nobody did anything to help the baby—that's what caused it.

"Aspiration, sepsis, closing ductus," Steve said. "They aren't, we aren't, entirely sure."

"Do you want us to come in now?"

"Well, sure, if you want. But there isn't anything that you actually need to do at this point. There are some papers to sign, and you may want to talk with the attending in the morning."

"What happens to the baby now?"

"We'll take him downstairs to a holding area."

"The morgue?"

"Yes."

"Don't."

"Don't?"

"Not yet. I'm coming in. Now. I want to see him. Not in the morgue."

Sophia pulled some sweat clothes out of a drawer.

"Is that it?" Martin asked, sitting up.

"That's it. He's died. I'm going in."

"It wasn't supposed to be this way."

"I know. I know."

"C'mere, Sophia. Hold me a minute."

Sophia put her arms around her husband. She felt dead and impatient. She needed to get to the hospital. She wanted to hold her son.

"I'll drive you."

Sophia could see that Martin's heart wasn't in it. And as usual when she was hurt, she wanted to be alone.

"I'll be fine. I just want to see him for a while. That's what I have to do now."

"You okay? You sure?"

"I'm sure." Sophia said it in a way that Martin would know she meant it. "But I would not say I'm okay."

The twenty-mile trip was fast, free of traffic. She drove automatically. Whatever feelings emerged she pushed back, racing on through empty streets. She parked in the hospital parking lot and stepped over puddles from the night's rain. A cloudy dawn was just breaking. She walked through the empty hospital corridors to the NICU. She wondered how much of herself had died with the baby.

The night nurses were organizing their flow sheets for change of shift, but Alicia came over and gave Sophia a silent hug. She sat Sophia in a rocking chair behind a screen. The baby was bathed, the IVs, monitors, and catheters had all been removed. Gently, Alicia placed Sophia's baby in her arms. Swaddled in a white terrycloth blanket, only his face, with his eyes closed, was visible. To Sophia, he seemed serene despite his mottled pallor. Someone had combed his thin hair down over his forehead. With his round, swollen face, he looked like a baby Napoleon, king of the world. Alicia put the baby's identifying wristband and his pink "I'm a Women's Hospital Baby" stocking hat on a side table beside Sophia, then left them alone.

Alicia told Sophia that she was working odd shifts and would be back in the NICU later in the day if Sophia needed her, but now she had to sign over her patients.

There were no doctors around, and nobody paid much attention to Sophia. She looked down at her baby and rocked in the chair. Her feelings could no longer be tamped down, whited out. They escaped like wraiths, each bearing a hurtful weapon to hurl at her. She prayed that the suffering, her baby's, hers, meant something. Was for some purpose. She could think of none. She prayed for her baby to be in some happy place, a heaven, then hated herself for her hypocrisy. For a moment, she felt that maybe she could have been a good enough mother, then knew that she had failed her child—her only important test. Trying not to cry, she bit her lip so hard that it bled. She welcomed the pain. She endured the next minute and then the next. With the lifeless bundle on her lap, she stroked his hair, his cheek with her index finger. "I'm so sorry," she murmured, "I'm so sorry." On the other side of the screen, the activities of the NICU continued, the stereo tuned to an early morning AM music station. Dimly she heard the words, over and over. *Hey Jude, don't make it bad …*

Later Sophia tried to sleep a for a few hours in a butterfly chair in her office. In the morning, she walked back to the NICU. She met with Dr. Notestein for five minutes to sign the autopsy permit, brushing off his attempts at earnest warmth. The hospital wanted it, and Sophia was beyond fighting. Martin was too angry to come back to the hospital this last time. The permit required only one parent's signature.

Standing at the scrub sink with nowhere to go in the NICU, she felt like one of the monitors with the sensitivity knob turned to max. The inputs overwhelmed her: the sights, sounds, and smells—betadine, plastic, and freshly sterilized laundry. Bright fluorescent tubes, brighter pools of light on the younger infants with jaundice. Phones rang incessantly, and the unit secretary paged nurses over an intercom.

Her baby's incubator looked the same but already held a preemie two hours old, breathing with the assistance of a ventilator. Sophia reached into the laundry supply shelf and put on a yellow gown. Though she had no baby to touch, she automatically scrubbed her hands in the sink and walked slowly into the nursery. The head nurse was about to call out to stop her when Alicia motioned that it was okay. Sophia paused and looked at each infant in its incubator, those dying and those recovering, the big ones with asphyxia and the tiny or medium-sized preemies. Some of the nurses sympathized with her, others averted their eyes. The doctors were busy, two or three in a group at the workstation. A few students watched Sophia.

At the side of Baby Eugene's incubator, she stopped. Iris sat in a rocking chair, her right hand through the incubator porthole, stroking Eugene's leg with her finger. She was the only other mother in the nursery at that moment. Iris had seen Sophia during the past week and thought she recognized her as the scientist who had shown her class around the lab in the medical center last spring. Cautiously Iris smiled at Sophia when their eyes met

Iris had wondered what all the commotion was about with the Shulder baby. Everyone seemed so tense whenever they were around the baby or the parents, but they never seemed to do very much like they did for the other real sick ones, putting tubes in and out, taking x-rays and stuff. This morning Iris saw that the Shulder baby wasn't there. Iris had been in and out of the nursery enough times to know that that meant one of two things. Either the baby had been moved out of intensive care to the intermediate care unit across the hall, or it had died.

Iris had been in the nursery twice when a baby died, and once when another baby "tried to die." That was what they said about Baby Eugene when he bled in his head. Usually you could tell it was bad because an alarm would go off on the baby's monitor, then the nurse would call over another nurse and yell for the doctors. They'd quickly get all this equipment around and work real hard. Then sometimes the baby would come back. You knew it hadn't when they put up a white screen around the incubator so the other parents couldn't see.

With Sophia staring at her like that, Iris realized what must have happened. It made her nervous.

"How's your baby doing?" Sophia asked quietly.

"Oh, he's coming along okay," Iris said. "Your baby didn't make it, I guess."

"No … no, he didn't." Sophia faltered. "He died last night. I wasn't here."

"Baby Eugene almost died in the middle of the night about a month ago. I had to come racing down here."

Across the nursery, Eli Kurz grabbed Alicia. "What in the fuck is going on? What is she doing here? She want to do in another one?"

"Eli, just shut the hell up," Alicia said. She headed toward Sophia and touched her on the arm. "How you doing?"

Sophia tried to smile. "One hell of a night." Alicia stayed at her side.

Iris wondered why Sophia wasn't crying if her baby had just died. She thought about that for a minute.

"You want to touch Baby Eugene?" Iris asked.

"May I?" She looked at Iris, and at Alicia too, for reassurance. They both nodded.

Sophia reached in and stroked Eugene's leg like Iris was doing. Sophia was tentative, hesitant.

"That's okay. He won't break. He likes it," Iris said.

Some of the nursery personnel had stopped what they were doing to stare at Sophia and Alicia, standing with Iris beside Eugene's incubator. The women, unaware that they were the focus of attention, watched Baby Eugene yawn and stretch contentedly.

"He's so little," Sophia said with awe.

"I know what you mean. His size sure does take getting used to," Iris said. "What happened to your baby?"

Alicia didn't move.

222

"He had defects we thought were too bad for him to get operated on. So he died. It was awful," Sophia said.

"Whatcha mean 'defects'?" Iris asked, interested.

"It's kind of complicated." Sophia looked to Alicia for help.

"He couldn't swallow food, and his heart was not formed correctly. He had a chromosome problem," Alicia explained.

Sophia said to Iris, "Would you mind if I sat down?"

"Oh sure, I don't mind." Iris didn't. Sophia looked kind of beat up, but nice.

"The doctors say they're going to operate on baby Eugene's head in a week, but they don't say it's up to me," Iris said.

Alicia pulled another rocking chair over for Sophia. The Gilded One, as some of the nurses called the bejeweled social worker of the NICU, was waving urgently at Alicia from the doorway.

"Just because you didn't allow no operation, your baby died?" Iris asked.

Looking squarely at Iris, Sophia saw only mild interest. No hostility.

Alicia strode to the door, blocking the agitated social worker, who was prepared to storm the nursery and exorcise Sophia's feelings.

"We, my husband and I, we thought he had so many problems and would need so many operations and then would never develop normally anyway. He would never have normal intelligence. He had Down's syndrome. We thought it was just better to let him go, not to put him through all that," Sophia said.

Iris thought some more. Where she lived, people often

died for a lot less. Sophia was pretty, and Iris wished she were as pretty as that.

"You have any other kids?" Iris asked.

"No," said Sophia. "I've spent most of my time in school."

Iris grinned. "That's what my teachers and folks said I should been doin'."

"Did you want to get pregnant?" Sophia asked.

"Sort of," Iris said. "Eugene's father thought all the birth control got in the way. I thought, well, if it happens, it happens. And I kinda like babies. Better'n school anyway. But I didn't expect all the problems like Baby Eugene's got."

"Yeah," said Sophia. "Nothing's supposed to go wrong, is it?"

They looked at each other like veterans, aware of the knowledge they shared that most women didn't have. Or need.

"Isn't that like, illegal, not to let your baby get operated on?" Iris asked.

"Well, yes," Sophia answered. "It kind of is, but it's not exactly clear, at least to me. We just talked, argued about that with some of the doctors, but our baby died."

Sophia put her hands over her eyes and lowered her head. She wasn't crying. But she felt awful again, as if hungover when she already had the flu. She looked up when she felt a gentle tap on her arm. Iris was stroking her the way she did Baby Eugene. Sophia left her arm within Iris's reach, then covered her face with her other hand and abruptly started to sob. Suddenly there was quiet in the nursery, the only sounds coming from Sophia, the bleeps of the heart rate monitors, and the pop radio station.

⌒

The next day after rounds, Steve was leaving the hospital when he saw Alicia waiting by the lobby information desk.

"I thought you were off earlier."

"I was," said Alicia, "but I wanted to be with you."

Arm in arm, they walked down the block for scrambled eggs at a diner on Euclid Avenue before going back to sleep at Steve's apartment.

Later in the morning, they were still exhausted. Only half awake, with the autumn sun pouring through the window on their naked skin, Alicia muttered, "I really didn't hop on that arrest."

"Look, Alicia, you did the right thing. No one in the unit really wanted that baby to go to surgery, not after days of jaundice and hypotension."

They dozed off again, each wondering how they would feel when they looked back on what they had done.

Alicia woke up about noon. Steve stirred as she disentangled her limbs from his. "A slow code is what they call it," Alicia said.

"Doesn't matter what they call it. It's killing a baby. That's what we did." Steve put his face in his hands.

"I know. I know," Alicia said. "The baby wasn't suffering ... he was zonked. He didn't move for the last three days, even when we stuck him for blood tests."

"I felt if we were going to let him die, we should just let him do it," Steve said in a monotone. He avoided her eyes.

"We are all going to die, Steve."

"Yeah, but not in a few days, on a ventilator, with pneumonia and sepsis and God knows how many more venipunctures."

"Dammit, Steve, we gave him morphine. Did we want him dead to end our own pain?"

Steve looked at Alicia for a beat, then ran to the bath-room, slamming the door. Alicia heard him vomiting. She got up and collected their dirty scrubs from the floor. A used vial of potassium chloride fell out of Steve's pants and rolled on the floor. She picked it up and put it in her pocket. She knew the cardiac signs of potassium poisoning as well as any intern.

PART III

Between the conception
And the creation
Between the emotion
And the response
Falls the Shadow
—T. S. Eliot

2 0

Name Day

There were just a few people in the chapel; no family members had flown to Cleveland for the ceremony. Sophia's mother was down with the flu, her brothers preoccupied. "Maybe you just weren't meant to have children," Gertrude had hypothesized over the phone. Her mother was talking about herself. Martin's parents called regularly. Sophia sensed they thought it was for the best that the baby died, that Sophia and Martin should get pregnant again as soon as possible. Like replacing the dead family dog with a goldfish.

Byria Marchand from the lab, dressed in slinky black, was in the chapel with her latest boyfriend. Lennie Stackpole's office had called in condolences. Alicia from the nursery sat in the back row, ill at ease. Funny, Sophia thought, Alicia seemed so confident when she was immersed in the high-tech hardware of the NICU. Baby Eugene's mother, Iris, was there, surprisingly, accompanied by an older woman. Probably the baby's grandmother. Over her shoulder, Sophia was pleased to see her boss, the chairman of the biochemistry department, with his plump wife, the woman who had thrown her baby shower, a veiled black pillbox hat perched on her head.

Sophia cringed when she saw Dr. Kurz, one of the pediatric residents, in the row behind them. There were a couple of other people she didn't recognize, among them a nervous young woman with a notebook in her lap. Mac slipped in late. He smiled at Sophia and gave her a small wave. Sophia faced frontward and tried to compose herself.

Martin sat beside Sophia, wearing his one suit, a relic from a previous decade, a faded blue plaid. He held her limp hand. Before them was the small white coffin, closed and topped with a simple arrangement of fall flowers—gold and crimson, yellow and white. The ceremony had been set up on a day's notice.

As the canned organ music stopped, the fresh-faced minister, new to the Unitarian church in their small town, approached the podium. He was garbed in a black robe, as though this were his college graduation.

"Dear friends of Sophia and Martin." The microphone squealed, and he jumped back. Turning red, he tapped the microphone. "Testing, testing." He started a second time. "Dearly beloved, we are here to mark the passing of the baby of Sophia and Martin."

He stopped, flushed again. Holding his hand over the microphone, he leaned toward Sophia and Martin and whispered, "What was the baby's name?"

"We hadn't really decided yet," Sophia whispered back, thinking maybe Isaac after her father. She had not wanted to give the baby a name before she was sure that he would live.

"Martian, it's Martian," Sophia heard her husband say too loudly. There was a little stir among the people behind them. Sophia tensed. Martin was drunk. For God's sake, it was eleven o'clock in the morning. She had missed the cues.

"He means Martin," Sophia said quickly. Now she wouldn't

ever know the name of her dead son. Why hadn't they decided? It was her fault, of course. She'd been overwhelmed, unable to decide a single thing. Two days ago Martin had found her sitting in her car in the driveway, motor running, unsure if she needed to stop for gas on the way to the hospital—an immense, paralyzing decision.

Nervous titters reached them from the rear. When things went bad, they only got worse. Her husband was not the empathetic soul she thought she'd married. That she hoped for and needed. But she reached for his other hand anyway and held it tight. A spring inside her slowly unwound. She had a sudden vision of the Princess Turandot, and a gurgle arose deep inside her, coming out of nowhere and filling her. Her father, her baby. Maybe she should just do in Martin too. Off with the head of everyone who couldn't meet her expectations, everyone she was supposed to love.

The minister was looking less distracted, as if he were onto something. Like Sophia felt in the lab, when order suddenly appeared in the chaos of a data printout.

"This baby," the minister intoned, "came into the world for only a short while. Before we started this ceremony, Sophia asked me why the baby should have lived so short a time and suffered during almost all of it. I don't know, Sophia. Many individuals wiser than myself have addressed the questions of suffering, of tragedy, of the bad things that happen undeservedly."

Sophia pondered. Maybe it wasn't so undeserved. Her baby had suffered for *her* sins. She was the one who'd forgotten the birth control pills. She had worked in the lab around God knows what kind of chemicals during her first trimester. She'd had all those doubts, harbored the unthinkable thought that she did not want this baby, any baby.

"We often tend to blame ourselves," the minister was saying. Sophia lifted her head. Someone came in late, stirring the row behind them. A hand on her shoulder—Amy had made it from New York. A warm feeling washed over Sophia.

"That usually leads us nowhere," the minister continued. "We must accept whatever responsibility we hold, but that doesn't give us enough understanding to help us get on with our lives. For that, some of us need faith. It helps us believe that there is meaning to these awful events. That somehow, for instance, this baby's brief life is part of some grand purpose that we cannot know." He paused, looking at Sophia and Martin.

"Sometimes we simply try to balance the sad, dreadful happenings, the suffering, against the good that we know and appreciate in the world. Generosity, beauty, love."

The minister closed his eyes for a moment before facing Sophia and Martin again.

"I don't know either of you, and I don't want to take liberties. But if I had to guess, I think your baby was a messenger. He has died. We cannot foresee the long-range effects of his having lived, on us, the living. If I have any consolation to offer, I think it is that you are on the right track, seeking the meaning of your son's existence. And I think, I believe, that someday you find what that meaning is."

His words touched Sophia. He was trying. The minister stepped forward, holding his hands out to the Shulders and indicating a moment of silence. A tinny requiem emanated from the small speakers at the back of the church, but it helped, Sophia thought. It helped a little.

As the minister dropped his hands and turned away, Martin leaned toward Sophia and whispered, "B for content, C

232

minus for style." His face was almost blank, his "I'm fine" expression glued on. She tapped him gently on the knee, three small strikes. She knew she would end their marriage, probably sooner rather than later.

21

The Buck Stops

Opportunity always knocks at the worst times. Mac had just returned from the funeral for Sophia's baby. Though it was a crisp fall day in Cleveland, he felt sweaty and unchairman-like, still unpacking boxes in his new office and sorting books onto oak-paneled shelves.

"Sir? Can I have a minute?"

A young doctor in slept-in scrubs stood in Mac's doorway. His hair was greasy and flyaway, and his bearing, his face, was the personification of anxiety. He looked like he was about fifteen years old. Mac had talked to most of the nearly thirty pediatric interns and residents during his visits, but despite their group photo on his desk, he didn't yet know all of them.

"Sure, what's up, son?" Mac waved him toward the captain's chair, a going-away present from his colleagues in Boston.

"I'm Steve Calvert. One of the interns."

Mac reached out and shook his hand. "What rotation are you on now?" His scrubs told Mac it had to be either the PICU or the NICU.

"The nursery."

The intern looked around, taking in the picture window and its panorama of downtown Cleveland, the new wood bookcases, the large desk with its stacks of paper, and Mac, settling into his leather chair. It was good to have a break from the unpacking, and Mac wasn't contemplating any big problems ahead.

In his large horn-rimmed glasses, the intern looked more like a scholar than a doer, the kind of intern who preferred the library to the messiness of clinical medicine, with its daily routine of time-dependent and not-always-thorough diagnosis and treatment.

"I've been meaning to get together with you folks again in the next day or so," Mac said, enjoying the leathery depths of his new chair. "Glad you dropped in."

The intern hesitated, and Mac guessed he was having second thoughts. God forbid his first intern contact was a psychiatric case. With the stressfulness of internship, such things were not unheard of.

Steve Calvert took a deep breath. "I may have killed a kid."

"Excuse me?"

Mac assumed he meant that one of his patients died a tough death. He heard they had a DOA the night before in the emergency room.

"Feel like talking about it?" Mac asked. It was obvious. He was here, wasn't he? With some more prompting and a few false starts, the intern told his story. It was the Shulder baby of course. When things are bad, things just get worse. Steve told Mac how the baby had coded, that he might have flushed a line with potassium instead of NaCl.

Steve shed some tears, but after blurting out the story, he looked a bit better.

Mac, on the other hand, felt worse, no longer savoring the respite from unpacking. Good God, Sophia's kid! He felt growing anger.

"Steve, this is tough."

He sat there nodding, a grateful expression on his young, young face.

"Can you tell me how it happened?" Mac expected Steve would say he'd just been tired and hadn't double-checked the vial.

"I thought," Steve said, "they were wrong to keep the kid going. He was yellow, had pneumonia, was on a vent. The parents still hadn't signed an op permit. He was infected. And … I don't know. I just couldn't stand it anymore."

Whoa. No accident, even if it was colored by the feeling that another's suffering was simply unbearable.

"Did you talk with the senior resident or the attending about it?" And just to make sure, Mac asked, "There wasn't a DNR on the baby?"

"No, no. I don't have much rapport with either of them. No DNR." He looked down.

"Did you talk with anyone about it?"

"No."

Steve looked a little squirrelly when he said that, but Mac chose to believe him. That made his job a little easier. He wouldn't have to mop up with a number of others. So Mac had to face this singular problem alone. What was the right thing to do here? For Steve, the department, the parents, the hospital, the medical school, colleagues, pediatrics, himself … the list went on. Where was the guru on the mountaintop when Mac needed him?

Mac was curious, though; What did Steve expect him to do?

"So why have you come to talk with me about it?" Not a kind question, but important under the circumstances.

"I feel terrible. I made a mistake, but actually I'm not even sure about that. I thought someone had to know."

"I understand," Mac said, and he did, having felt like Steve at times in the past. Many doctors have. Older ones. Ones who don't talk about it. So Steve doubted that he'd made a mistake? Sophia felt that whatever she'd done was a mistake. At least Sophia now knew that she'd finally made a choice, late in the game though it was.

Steve had not done anything like this in the past. His internship was overwhelming; he was lonely and vastly exhausted, on call every third night for the four months since his internship began. He had come from one of the big schools in upstate New York where the med students don't get a lot of hands-on experience with patients. The oldest son of parents who ran a hardware store in Omaha, he had made a big dent in their savings to attend medical school.

"So, Steve. What do you expect is going to happen now?"

"I don't know, Dr. McKennen. I may lose my job." Was that what Steve was hoping for? Mac sat back, now uncomfortable in his highbacked leather chair. "Steve, here's what I want you to do. Go home. Get some rest. This evening write up everything that happened just before and during the Shulder baby's code. And what your thinking was. Then I want to see you here tomorrow morning at 8:00 a.m."

He left, head down. That would give him something useful to do. Mac needed some time to think about this.

The next morning Eli Kurz huffed into Mac's office after morning sign-out rounds. Kurz was acting chief resident while the official chief was on vacation. Mac had met Kurz along with the rest of the resident staff. Smart, but not high on empathy, he was all about systems and charting and blood chemistries. Mac heard he was a good doc, but treated his little patients like poorly oiled machines.

Kurz announced that Steve Calvert had left a message asking for sick-call coverage. Not just a day, but at least a week. He'd left town overnight, claiming a family emergency in New York, but Steve's folks lived in Nebraska. No details. No lead time.

Had Mac approved this emergency leave? Fortunately, Mac could tell Kurz he hadn't, thereby preserving the possibility of staying on the right foot with one of his senior residents, who he would depend on in the coming months.

Steve, Kurz said, was a hyperanxious intern, not great with the technical stuff, and tiresome, always asking, "How come?" instead of just doing his job. Made the simple difficult. Kurz thanked Mac, as if he had done something.

"Tell me about the death of the Shulder baby," Mac asked.

"Happened fast. Looked like a blocked endotracheal tube. The team was good. They had him extubated and were bagging and running meds. When I got there, the baby was asystolic. Didn't have much reserve. We did the usual resuscitation but, frankly, didn't drag it out very long. Didn't start cardiac compressions." Kurz gave Mac an apprehensive look.

"Not a problem," Mac said. "It probably turned out okay in the end."

"Were they really planning to do a repair on both the heart and the TE fistula at the same time. Never heard of that before."

"Me neither. Maybe just a rumor. Thanks for coming in, Dr. Kurz. Sorry to hear an intern decamped."

Mac heard that Kurz was the one who'd made the correct

diagnoses on the Shulder baby, even before the cardiologists. Maybe a potential academic. Mac didn't know whether he liked him much, but he'd keep an eye on him. "Just one last thing, Kurz," he said. "By any chance was there a DNR on the Shulder baby."

Kurz looked at his new boss as if he were bereft of his senses. "No, Dr. McKennen," he said as if talking to a child. "No DNR."

2 2

Bermuda

A week after the funeral, Sophia and Martin arrived at the airport in Bermuda. The top of their rented Austin Mini was pulled open to the sun as Martin drove to their pink hotel opposite Hamilton's small harbor. Balmy warmth caressed Sophia's face and arms. Martin's parents had paid for the trip. "Good to get away," they'd insisted. Sophia wasn't so sure. Work was her anesthetic. But on the plane from Cleveland, she'd suddenly felt her stomach relax and untwist, an unexpected respite. It left her almost breathless and hating herself.

The tropical panorama was working its magic on them even before they turned into the gravel drive of Somerset Resort. Martin slowed to take in the view. Palm trees lined the drive, and white-roofed cottages hid beneath medleys of exuberant red and yellow blooms. Beyond lawns stretched a white beach lining a translucent lagoon, the water a definition of aquamarine. The sea breeze was laden with the scent of flowers in perfectly manicured beds. Like a recalcitrant child, though, Sophia resisted the loveliness, so overpowering at that moment that it seemed oppressive.

"Martin, why did the baby die?"

He looked across at her uncertainly. "I dunno," he answered. "Maybe it was the infection, his heart, all that gunk in his lungs. That's what the doctors were saying."

"No." Sophia pursued it. "I mean, I feel like I've had the experience but missed the meaning."

"Meaning as in the eternal scheme of things? I don't think there was any. I wish there were. If that amnio for the chromosomes had been right, you would have had an easy abortion in the first trimester, and that would have fixed it. I still don't see why you wouldn't let me talk to a lawyer. We could have sued their asses off."

Fixed it? An *easy* abortion? Martin was continually pissing Sophia off these days. His deep voice grated. Even his intelligent comments seemed ridiculous.

Unlike the arrogant administrators of Children's Hospital, the ones at Women's Hospital had practically groveled before Sophia and Martin. Days after the baby died, the hospital people finally laid the blame for the mistaken amnio on a lab technician who'd mislabeled the test tubes. In return for a lawsuit waiver from the Shulders, they promised that corrections would be made so no mistakes of that kind could happen again. And Women's Hospital would make a bequest of $500,000 for pediatric research at Children's Hospital, a grant memorializing "Baby Doe," so named to maintain confidentiality for the parents.

Martin turned into the driveway between a row of huge royal palms and soon reached their pastel-painted cottage. Sun bounced off its stucco walls. Martin removed their small bags from the Mini, and Sophia stooped down to pick up a GI Joe doll, forgotten by a previous occupant. She cradled it in her arms.

"Don't," said Martin.

"No, I'm okay," Sophia said. "I'm just testing my maternal instincts to see if there's anything left. I'm not really sure about babies. Not before, not now." She looked at Martin and saw his concern, his desire to help. And his waning patience.

They unpacked in their room under a slow-moving ceiling fan. Suddenly Sophia stopped and sat on the bed, fingering the yellow chenille bedspread. A precise throwback to her childhood.

"Martin, what do you think happened to that reporter? She acted like there was more going on than people were saying. That's probably how reporters always feel. Conspiracy paranoia. Maybe that's why they're reporters. I kind of feel that way too. Like I still can't see everything that happened."

"Honey," Martin said, rummaging in the tiny freezer for some ice cubes. "There wasn't anything else. It was just a dumb mistake."

Sophia considered. The events surrounding the birth of their child might be construed in many ways, but in her mind, a dumb mistake couldn't come close to covering it.

"Sophia, c'mon, this is supposed to be a 'Let's put the bad stuff behind us' vacation. Let's have a drink and hit the beach."

Sophia urged him to go without her. After he headed into the glaring sunshine, she ran the hot water in the over-sized tub, poured in the contents of a miniscule plastic bottle emblazoned with a Somerset Resort logo. She soaked for a while in the bubble-filled tub. Then she wrapped herself in the plush hotel bathrobe, and lay on the chenille bedspread. Sophia couldn't halt the scenarios crowding her head. They would not have cherished the baby. He could have lived with foster parents. He could have been happy. The anomalies might have been fixed. The images dissolved, the child passed out of childhood, grew up, yet remained a child. Sometimes a gross caricature of a child.

After her father died, their dog, Boots, spent her nights in the basement near the warm furnace. Gertrude insisted. Boots hated it, but Gertrude insisted, and it was Sophia's job to put Boots in the basement for the night. Sopha would open the cellar door and call, and Boots would appear from the living room or kitchen, whining anxiously. Every night the same routine. Sophia would show her a biscuit and toss it down the cellar stairs. Boots would gallop down after the biscuit, only to hear the door close behind her. After gobbling the biscuit, Boots whimpered at the door. That stupid dog never learned. Sophia loved Boots anyway, never questioned her right to live. And when she could, Sophia would smuggle Boots up to her room for the night.

She reasoned, there are people all over the world who care only about the stuff of survival—food, sex, a roof over their heads. Not about intellect, reasoning, literature, art, discovery, or making fine distinctions. Places where the presence of a child or an adult with Down's wouldn't cause a ripple on the societal pond. She pulled up the bedspread to insulate herself from the draft of the fan, and figured that her baby would probably have died in infancy no matter what.

With a start, Sophia awoke. Each time she awoke, it was as if the baby had died again, at that very moment. The same loop would start replaying its grim questions once more. My baby died. Did I love him? Did I not love him?

Martin had left a note on the bureau while she was sleeping. He'd changed his mind. He was going to rent a motor scooter, not go to the beach. His arm in a cast, that was such a better idea.

Sophia left her bikini in a drawer and put on her old one-piece bathing suit; it hid her sagging belly and incipient stretch marks better. Wrapped in the robe, she walked out to the pool, where a few adults lay prone in the afternoon sun. She pushed an orange air mattress into the water, clambered onto it face down, and delicately pushed away from the pool's edge. The water was pleasant, nearly body temperature. She dangled her arms, inching herself forward. Was she losing her mind? If she wanted to die, she could do it with sleeping pills. A coma, then sleep. Like the baby. According to Freud, the love of a mother for her firstborn son was as pure a love as existed in the world.

Sophia rolled carefully onto her back and into the water, enveloped in warmth. Like the womb. The water lapped the sides of the pool, the breeze flapped the fronds of the palm trees. What would Sophia be doing now if Martin's salary and hers didn't add up to more than $40,000 per year? What would she be doing if the therapy of a jaunt to Bermuda was not an option? If she and two children, no husband, barely survived in a cramped third-floor apartment in inner-city Cleveland? Would the drudgery blunt her middle-class sensitivities? When one problem is resolved, why does life simply become more difficult? Does the "problem" define us, give us purpose? If only she could fix her psyche. Become normal.

Stupid to have left her sunglasses and paperback in the room. *The Great Gatsby* was Martin's recommendation. Sometimes he felt like Gatsby, he said, on a great quest. Sophia was sincerely hoping that Gatsby would get his due punishment by the end of the book. Shaking her head, she tried to fling out her thoughts along with the drops of chlorinated water in her hair. She had trusted intelligence. She had believed in the indivisibility of the intelligent and the good. Now she grieved for her infant son. For being right, and for being wrong. For failing.

23

Night Call

It was 3:00 a.m., and Sophia couldn't sleep. Until this moment she'd believed she was coping. After their week in Bermuda, she worked fifteen-hour days in the lab. She remembered her father's favorite advice when her report card carried a less than an excellent grade, "Work hard at whatever you do, because there will be no action, no thought, no knowledge, no wisdom in the world of the dead."

And the work was going well. But this afternoon, when the nurse who had cared for her baby called, Sophia realized that she had been numb for weeks. At Alicia's insistence, she finally agreed to think about getting help. Maybe. But from where? Martin, for all his touchy-feely poetic friends, didn't believe in therapy, thought one could do it oneself. Sophia had not asked how that was working for him. McKennen had come to the funeral. That was nice, but she didn't get a chance to say more than thanks. Mac had called her at the lab while she'd been in Bermuda, and Byria had written down a message and phone number. "Call anytime," it said on the pink slip of paper Sophia shoved into the recesses of her purse. So she did.

As she sat in the dim, chilly living room, phone in hand, she heard. "Who? Say again? Sophia? Give me a minute. I was sound asleep." She waited for Mac to wake up. She wondered vaguely whether he had a wife or a girlfriend.

"Sophia. I'm so glad you called."

That was unusual. Most human beings would not be happy to be awakened in the middle of the night.

"What can I do for you?" he asked, his voice sleepy but sympathetic.

"I have some questions about my baby and don't know who else to call." There was a pause on the line. "Look," Sophia said, "I'm sorry I called you at this hour. This obviously can wait. Maybe I can stop by your office, or we could get some coffee in the cafeteria some morning, and I could ask you my questions."

"Actually, Sophia, I'm awake now. Nothing else scheduled. Shoot. What's on your mind?"

Sophia felt a tear escape. Another, and then they flowed. "I don't really know why I called." She could feel him register her sobs.

"I think I understand. Why not just take some time and tell me how you've been feeling?"

Sophia didn't know why she'd called. Martin, sound asleep upstairs, would have been appalled. This "feeling" business was what art, literature, and music were for. A clunky phrase of Freud's, one of Martin's favorites, crossed her mind: "Art manifests ego mastery." Martin would be proud of her for remembering it.

"Sophia?"

"I'm here."

"Maybe if we start at the beginning. How'd you feel about the pregnancy?"

"Ambivalent, I guess, would cover it."

"Of course," McKennen's husky voice reassured her. "You had a great career in front of you, and the career didn't want a competitor showing up."

He got it in an instant.

"How did Martin feel about your being pregnant?" he asked.

In fact, it wasn't any of his business, but somehow in the dark living room in the middle of the night, Mac didn't seem to be prying.

"He could be sweet. We tried to be a team. Sometimes he drives me nuts." At a recent seminar on neuroscience, she'd heard that positive affective emotions were triggered by neurotransmitters from the neocortex draining into the deeper limbic system in the brain.

"Well, sure. You're married. Comes with the territory. But you two decided to have a baby together despite the ambivalence."

Sophia heard Mac sigh. She felt her tension give way. The phone was quiet, but Sophia sensed no urgency on Mac's part to end the call.

"I killed the baby, you know," Sophia said. The sentence popped out of her almost like a hiccup. Her body stiffened again, expecting a burst of outrage from Mac.

"No, Sophia. You did not." His voice was calm.

"But I never signed the op permits. Martin would have. I didn't let him. That's why the baby died."

"That's not why the baby died, Sophia. And you agreed to sign the op permit for the combined operation we talked about."

"Yeah, but it was too late."

"Look, Sophia. We were dealing with a rare combination

of serious anomalies, piled on to the diagnosis of Down's syndrome. Not operating may well have been the best for your baby, or not. Maybe your baby died not from the fistula or from the heart problem but from the combination. We just don't know."

Sophia knew she hadn't murdered her baby, but she sure as hell was responsible for his death. Even if it would have happened during surgery or somewhere in the first years of his life. It was clear enough. Why was Mac being obtuse?

They were quiet for a moment, and then he responded to her unspoken comment. "All parents blame themselves when an infant dies. They always find some way to think they somehow caused it."

Platitudes. This wasn't the Mac she thought she knew in Boston. Suddenly she was sorry she had called him hours past midnight. But she still wanted Mac to see her point.

"They wanted to operate multiple times, first to correct the TE fistula and then to correct the heart malformation. And more operations would have been necessary for both the heart and the esophagus."

Unruffled, he replied, "And you didn't want them to do that." Was he being sarcastic?

"Yes … no." Sophia shook her head in frustration. "Of course I wanted my baby fixed. But they couldn't do that."

"So?"

"I was so angry."

Mac was silent.

"I was furious."

Somehow this was still insufficient to draw a reply from Mac.

"They were pushing me. Forcing me."

"Forcing you to do what?"

"THEY WERE FORCING ME TO HURT MY BABY! Sophia screamed the words. She looked around in the dark, not seeing, eyes wide, breathing hard, then collapsed back into the white chair, exhausted and soaked in sweat. Almost like she felt after delivering the baby.

Another minute passed before Mac said, "So you were in an impossible situation. You didn't really know what to do."

Sophia sniffled and nodded as though he could see her, though on second thought she was glad he couldn't.

"In some ways, the way you wrestled with the problems," he paused, "that seems to me like a heroic response, Sophia."

She shook her head. For a moment she'd believed that Mac understood. But no. He didn't understand that it was easier not to allow the surgery. Easier for Sophia. Not to have the baby with all of his problems. She didn't tell him. "You don't understand."

"Help me here, Sophia." Mac's voice bordered on plaintive, as though he were the one who needed help.

Sophia closed her eyes, seeing images of being with her baby. How happy she was after the birth, for being ready, for the brilliance of the baby's warmth and light on their first day together. Then how it all darkened, as if she'd forgotten the lesson her father had instilled in her: One can survive only by being smart enough to discern the consequences of your actions. She had forgotten. But who can be that smart?

Sophia was uncertain how much time had passed when she heard Mac's voice, gentle again.

"What would have happened if you'd signed the permits?"

"The baby would have lived," Sophia said instantly.

"Maybe. And maybe only with an inordinate amount of suffering, for both you and the baby."

"I don't know what I want. What's best. I don't know why I called you."

"Absolution?"

"No, dammit! Just acceptance." Sophia felt she had to get off the phone, urgently. "Thanks, Mac. Thanks for listening. Maybe coffee some morning." And she hung up without waiting for his response, more alone than ever in her life. Mac hadn't really offered much in the way of help. He was holding back. Finally, she dozed off, still in her chair. As the milky light of morning came through the curtains, she awoke with a hot face and a sense of embarrassment. She shook it off, went upstairs to have a shower, then left for work before Martin was awake.

24

Christmastime

Driving their new white BMW along Carnegie into Hough, Sophia felt like a sitting target. The car, another dead-baby gift from Martin's parents, stood out even more than she did on these slippery streets, populated almost exclusively by black people. She wished she still had her old Karmann Ghia.

Iris was the only mother in the NICU Sophia had really talked with. At Alicia's urging, Sophia and Iris exchanged phone numbers the day Sophia's baby died. Baby Eugene "graduated" from the hospital nursery in late November, a couple of months after Sophia's baby died. Now he was nearly four months old, and when Sophia made another one of her ill-judged calls, near midnight, Iris, who said she was up with her baby anyhow, seemed glad enough to hear from her.

"Of course I remember," Iris finally said. "How you doing?"

After a bit of surprisingly candid talk, Iris said, "It is tough. Having a baby. And not having a baby. You want to stop by sometime and see how big Baby Eugene's got?"

A week later, Sophia took a left onto 238th Street, sparsely lined by leafless trees and one-family homes with run-down porches. Old snow lay piled along the street where the plows hadn't bothered to complete their job. A bunch of kids, bundled into colorful jackets, stopped their hockey game and eyed the BMW as Sophia cruised down McKinley Street, looking for numbers on the front doors. Cars were parked with their front wheels on the sidewalk, and Sophia followed local custom. Nerves jangling, she slid out of the car and banged her elbow on the horn with a brief blast of mechanized noise. Shit, she thought, they'll think I want a military escort into the house. As she reached the porch, Iris opened the front door. "Well look who's here, no kidding. I wasn't sure you'd make it."

Iris looked at Sophia, friendly but appraising. Sophia was dressed for the lab, the bare basics for days when no meetings were scheduled: turtleneck sweater and wool slacks under a standard black London Fog raincoat. No makeup, no jewelry except for her wedding band. No diamond; it tore her rubber gloves used during experiments.

"I know, Iris," Sophia said, with no formalities. "I'm White, you're Black. You live here. I live out in the burbs. You're young, I'm ancient, we're nervous. Now, where's that kid of yours?"

Iris was disarmed.

"Well, come on in. The little monster is making happy after his nap."

Sophia entered an unlit hall with a small living room off to the left. Iris took her coat. The living room contained a well-worn upholstered sofa, paired with a matching overstuffed chair, both adorned with hand-crocheted doilies. Baby Eugene, all seven pounds of him, was lying flat on a white sheet on the middle of the floor. With some effort, he raised his head to gaze at Sophia. Then he started to cry. Close behind Sophia, Iris swept the baby up into her arms, carefully supporting his large head. She sat down in a rocker next to the fireplace and soothed him.

"Don't worry, Sophia. The only white faces he's seen are the doctors and nurses who stick him with needles. He's a little gun-shy." Turning her face into his, she crooned something in motherspeak. Baby Eugene smiled, gurgled, and drooled. Parallel currents of envy, guilt, and relief jolted Sophia.

"Have a seat." Iris looked back at Sophia. "My mom's making up some lunch for us. Be ready soon. What's been happening?"

"Not much. Work," Sophia said. "I went on vacation for a week with my husband." She paused. "To Bermuda."

Iris was dressed for company: tight white jeans, a gold sweater, gold earrings. Sophia thought she looked older, more mature, more in control than when she had seen her months ago in the nursery.

They considered each other for a silent moment.

"Bermuda, where's that?" said Iris.

"About six hours on a plane from here, out in the Atlantic off North Carolina. It's beautiful."

Iris changed the subject. "Well, I'm kinda bored being here all the time looking after Eugene. Eugene's not the new thing on the block anymore. Not many of my friends still come by. They're interested in bigger boys than Eugene." She slowed down. "So how you doing?"

"Mmm," Sophia said, "hard question. How about I hold Baby Eugene for a little?"

"Good deal, girl. He's all yours. I'll go help Ma."

Iris gave Sophia a clean diaper to cover her shoulder and deposited Baby Eugene in her arms. He nestled his head against her breast, pawed at her contentedly while Sophia looked around. A large photograph of John F. Kennedy hung on the wall behind the couch. A portrait of Martin Luther King Jr., enveloped in heavenly clouds, was over the fireplace—or rather a well-wrought *trompe l'oeil* of a fireplace painted on the front wall. A small black-and-white TV occupied the corner, its sound turned off. A cigarette-scarred coffee table and some standing lamps with dubious wiring completed the decor. Iris appeared in the doorway and caught Sophia pretending that she hadn't been carrying out a survey.

"I know, it isn't much, but it's ours. C'mon back and meet Ma. She's been cooking for hours. You better be hungry."

Sophia stood up with Baby Eugene. Iris held out her hands.

"No, I'm all right." Sophia said. "Let me keep him for a minute."

The kitchen, at the back of the house, was steamy and well lit. Iris' mother was stout and barely five feet tall. Sophia couldn't even guess how old she was, though she remembered her from the funeral.

"Mom, this is Sophia, from the hospital."

"Poor baby. I'm so sorry about your loss. C'mon here and give me a hug."

Mattie engulfed Baby Eugene and Sophia as though she were Sophia's grandmother.

"Now you sit yourself down at the table here and eat."

Iris and Sophia followed directions.

"Gimme Baby Eugene now, Sophia. Iris, get some bowls down and set the table. Go on, girl, now pitch in." She shook her head. "This daughter of mine always been a way-having child."

Mattie slung Eugene on her hip and turned back to stir,

while Iris saluted her behind her back. Sophia opened her purse and laid a small gift-wrapped package on the table.

"Well, what do we have here?" Iris said.

"I wanted you to have a baby gift, so I brought you something totally useless. Consider it an early Christmas present for Baby Eugene."

"Great. I love presents," Iris said as she ripped off the silver wrapping. Inside the May Company gift box was a crystal angel, wings and all. Iris took it out and held it up against the kitchen light hanging low over the table.

"Looky here, Eugene, an angel. Another one just like you, baby. Sophia's brought him to look after you. That's real nice, Sophia, you shouldn't have done it."

Mattie put Eugene down in the car seat that engulfed him.

"Why, it's so nice. Thoughtful too," Mattie said. "It's a gorgeous thing. Our first Christmas decoration. We're always way behind. Now sit down and eat."

Iris leaned over to give Sophia a half hug. Sophia was pleased. She could box the presents from her baby shower and bring them to Iris. The clothes would still fit Baby Eugene.

Sophia and Iris gossiped about the NICU staff. Mattie monitored Sophia's intake of the steaming beef stew and hot biscuits.

"Mostly they just seemed like people doing their job," Iris was saying. "Told me what was going on. Asked if I had questions. You were the one they were always picking on."

Sophia finished her stew and before she could refuse, Mattie refilled her bowl. "Our babies were different" was all she could think of saying.

"Not so much. When Eugene had that bleed in his head, it was bad. Sometimes I wonder whether maybe we shouldn't have kept him on the ventilator when it happened. It's still bad. He has seizures and had to go back twice for surgery. The shunt in his brain keeps getting blocked."

Iris wasn't eighteen yet. They'd never talked about how Sophia felt about the operations. Sophia said, "You mean we both had decisions."

"Sort of," Iris said. "For you it was a decision you had to make. For me, it was a decision they made for me, and I let them."

Mattie stood at the stove, her back toward them, but Sophia saw her stiffen.

"I wish that were true," Sophia said. "But I didn't have the guts to decide, and my baby died. The way I … I was a coward."

It was quiet in the kitchen. Mattie rinsed some dishes.

"You kidding?" Iris threw her soup spoon on the table. "I wouldn'a known what to do either, if they had given me a choice."

After setting three stemmed glasses and a bottle of plum wine on the table, Mattie pulled up a chair. "We love the baby we got," she said. "We'll be fine."

25

Brouhaha

In the early winter cold Mac sat in his office chair in his lined raincoat, windows open because of the paint smell. He'd just got off the phone complaining to Ellen Larkin in Boston about the mess that had greeted him in Cleveland. Whether it was the parents' or the hospital's right to deny life-saving surgery for a newborn. Imagine what would have happened if they knew that the case involved more than a touch of euthanasia on top of a botched amniocentesis. Mac hadn't told anyone, even Ellen Larkin, what Steve, his errant intern, had told him in the sanctity of his new office. After a day or two with no word from Steve, it had become clear that Steve was not just absent, he was well and truly gone. After the Shulder baby died, Sophia and Martin took off for some vacation retreat. After all that, Mac just kept his mouth shut. Maybe it was cowardly. He was afraid—for himself, his new job, and the reputation of his department and the medical center. And he also thought it would be wrong to blame an intern or Notestein or the Shulders, who'd already contended with their amnio mistake and buried their firstborn.

Ellen told Mac that his replacement at Harvard, one Dr.

Krug, when interviewed on TV about euthanasia, had talked about how some newborns with birth defects would be better off not being kept alive. His Germanic name did not help validate his point of view. He was getting shelled in the media. The reporter at the *Plain Dealer* had uncovered new "Baby Doe" cases, as they came to be known, all over the country. President Reagan saw the Krug interview and was outraged. He ordered Health, Education, and Welfare to do something. Across the country, right-to-lifers were revitalized. More picketers in front of the hospital accused them of playing God and bumping off babies who had nothing more than a hangnail. Never mind that Nancy Reagan had just toured the intensive care nursery in Orange County and asked the neonatology team why they were keeping all those tiny babies alive. "Isn't it very expensive?" she asked, and, "Wouldn't we be better off not letting them suffer?"

Meanwhile, Mac no longer felt like a department chair. Instead he'd become a full-time committee member, 7:00 a.m. to 6:00 p.m. and sometimes nights too. He never knew that God made so many committees. More than all the grains of sand on all the beaches of the world. Committees of medical staff, department chairs, the dean and a flock of associate deans, medical ethics people, hospital and malpractice lawyers, every kind of administrator including some he'd never known existed (risk management types), med school alumni, even the board of trustees. The clergy showed up in force. The Children's Hospital, the medical school, and the university all had task forces for this and task forces for that. Consulting ethicists were called in; they charged a bundle and justified it by talking in tongues. Big words like *justice*, *equity*, *beneficence*, and *maleficence* were paddled about. The Futilitarians seemed to have the upper hand much of the time. The Academy of

Pediatrics set up their own committees and concluded that medical professionals were being victimized. Now it was Us vs. Them—Them being the media, the government, Health and Human Services, President Reagan. Anyone who dared stick their noses into "our" business. The whole mess was selling lots of papers. Though that Lydia lady at the *Plain Dealer* made quite a name for herself, at least the med center had managed to keep the Shulder family out of the spotlight. And thank God, it didn't come out that Mac had a son with Down syndrome.

Mac began attending in the nursery, Dr. Notestein's sensitivities be damned. Before Notestein failed to head off the Shulder debacle, he'd screwed up another case in the nursery, a preemie born at the edge of viability. A cute tyke—Eugene Malone. Major brain bleed, and they never even talked to the mom about DNRs. The kid was almost off the ventilator when Mac took over as attending. The mom was just a teenager, but Mac had to hand it to her; she was in the nursery every day for months until they sent her home with her baby. If Sophia and Martin had had a baby like Eugene, they would have reacted differently. The odds were worse for Baby Eugene, but the outcome was less certain too. Mac had heard that Martin blew this way and that about the surgeries, like a toy boat in a bathtub. As for Sophia, she'd run up against a problem with no good solution, and her gears jammed. All that fine-tuning of her intellect was of no use.

Would Sophia's feelings have changed over time if her baby had lived? Perhaps. Could she have been helped by a skilled professional? Definitely. Would Martin have gone along with saving the baby? For sure. Was it possible that Sophia delayed the decision for all the wrong reasons, and some of the right ones? Absolutely. Did her baby die because of the choices she made? In part. But in the end, it was Steve, not Sophia, who killed her baby. And in her bizarre middle-of-the-night phone call, Mac didn't have the guts to tell her the truth.

As the meetings dragged on, Mac tried to hide behind his new pipe and look sage, mostly doing his best to keep his mouth shut, thinking about how he was going to spend an anonymous, unrestricted gift to the department, the result of a settlement that had been worked out with Sophia and Martin to forestall a lawsuit over the amnio foul-up.

Mac already knew that he was attracted to Sophia, now in part for what they'd both lived through. And it was clear that sooner or later he'd have to come clean with her. Unlike Mac, Sophia was fully conscious of the maelstrom she'd experienced. After his son was born, Mac had just plowed ahead. There was only one choice: to keep Billy at home as opposed to putting him in an institution. Two decades later, while Sophia's case was being discussed, analyzed, and used to develop codes of ethics, rules, and bylaws, he kept his head down. Now things were going to be different. Difficult medical cases were going to be handled according to regulations promulgated by Reagan and his ilk. More process, channels, committees, lawyers. There would be preordained outcomes resulting from an amorphous and fickle chemistry of committees, catalyzed by the loudest minority, and agreed to by a sullen majority. "The bland leading the bland," someone observed. What really irritated Mac was that committees always assumed that the best solution would appear as long as the right processes were followed. His knowledge of medicine and his experiences with Billy and with Sophia were of no help whatsoever in formulating generalizations. His ethics would remain situational.

At the end of his whining phone call to Ellen Larkin, she'd said unsympathetically, "Welcome to the world, Mac. You took the job, and that's what you're there for."

Finally, Mac wrote a letter. He hoped that HHS would reverse its decision to launch regulations instituting investigating teams, Doc Squads, that would visit any nursery where a whistleblower believed that insufficient life support was being provided to a newborn with major birth defects.

The Honorable Margaret Heckler
Secretary, Health and Human Services
Washington DC, 20013

Dear Ms. Heckler,

I firmly believe that the proposed amendment in the Federal Register is antithetical to good ethics, good medicine, and wise legislation. That is to say, hotlines for hospital personnel to report "bad" medical behaviors to government administrators and Baby Doe investigations resulting from this form of legislation will not be helpful.

Life and death decisions regarding seriously malformed or otherwise severely impaired infants should best be left to health professionals, families, and other qualified, concerned advisors who are on the scene. While there ultimately may be some abuse as in any practice that deals with desperately ill patients, old or young, legislation is a blunt instrument intruding into the very sensitive areas of medicine and medical ethics.

A better approach would be to ensure optimal interactions between skilled caregivers and fully informed family members by supporting increased postgraduate education in this area. I urge you to study these issues further before endorsing or proposing new regulations.

Sincerely,

William McKennen, MD
Max and Esther Weizmann Professor of Pediatrics
Chairman, Pediatric Department, Case Western Medical School

2 6

War of the Roses

In early February, Martin walked into their empty house in Chagrin Falls and tossed his coat, damp from the light snow, over the top of the closet door. When he'd come home from school as a kid, there was always action—dogs, cats, and gregarious parents. The quiet of his own house was disturbing. He and Sophia had more or less ignored the holidays this year. She wasn't up to visiting her family in Boston, and his family was snowed in on Mackinac Island.

Sophia worked at the lab, often and late, catching up on the time she'd missed. She said that work was an acceptable way to deal with her grief.

What's an acceptable way for me to handle my grief? Martin wondered. Shit, it had happened. The unpredictable. Could've happened to anyone. Not such a big deal. On the other hand, they could have operated, and the kid would've gotten better or not, could have died later. If he had lived, he would have been almost five months old by now. At that age, lots of kids would squeal with delight when Daddy showed up after work. Martin remembered the way his father came swinging through the door. Nathan would pick him up and ask what great things Martin had done that day. Martin learned fast that his dad wasn't interested in anything about him that was not great. If someone had bullied him, if his bike had been stolen, Nathan didn't want to hear about it. But Martin knew his dad was a genuinely nice guy; he could actually relate to his son wanting to act in plays and read rather than playing football and making money. It was okay to dramatize other people's angst. It was not okay to talk about one's own.

Martin stood up, looked out toward the forest shrouded in mist behind their house. How would it have been if he were the one with Down's syndrome? If he were a mongoloid walking into the room, Sophia would look up at him, barely hiding her disgust and sadness when she saw who it was, then return to her crossword puzzle. Not so different from the way it was now.

Martin poured himself some bourbon and took it into the living room where Sophia had folded the glittery wrapping paper from their few holiday presents and placed the papers on the coffee table. Martin mused about being a "househusband," a phrase he'd seen for the first time in the *New Yorker* a week ago. Take care of the kid and the laundry. Write a little.

When Sophia opened the door about ten that night, Martin looked up from the couch. "Heard you drive up. Had supper? There's a fresh pastrami and rye in the fridge with your name on it."

After dropping her coat, she washed up. Someone had put out clean towels in the bathroom. In the kitchen, the breakfast dishes were washed and put away. She took the sandwich and a beer out of the fridge and collapsed with Martin on the couch in the living room. "Wiped," she said. "Thanks so much. Just what I needed. What are you watching?"

"An old movie about a couple of sweethearts, George and Martha, remember? *Who's Afraid of Virginia Woolf?*"

"All I remember is Burton and Elizabeth Taylor being so awful to each other."

Both were too tired to get up and go to bed. Martin flipped channels and stopped when a woman on the screen dropped the garage door smashing her husband's sports car.

"Now why would she do that?" Martin asked.

Sophia yawned and raised her head. "Easy enough to understand. Probably because he dumped turpentine on her prize roses?"

Martin flipped channels. "Glad we're not like that."

"We will be," Sophia said, "if you don't lighten up with the bourbon."

"We will be if you don't get home before ten o'clock most nights. I'm going to sue your lab for alienation of affections."

"Not the fault of the lab, Martin. Sue me."

"All right, how much you got?"

"Basically half the mortgage on the house."

"Me too," said Martin.

"I'm exhausted." Sophia made an attempt to get up. "Aren't we too tired to be having this discussion?"

Martin pulled her back on the couch. "Maybe it's the best time. We're too tired to throw anything at each other. Even insults."

"That's why the kitchen's so neat. You rat. This is a set-up."

"Nice try."

"C'mon, Martin. If this is the end, no poesy?"

"Why should a foolish marriage vow
Which long ago was made,
Oblige us to each other now ...
We loved, and we loved, as long as we could ..."

It was as if Martin had prepared the poem as well as the sandwich that night. Later they remembered that neither of them had slept so well in almost a year.

27

Baby Eugene

The most recent improvement in Mattie's neighborhood was a McDonald's, which had gone up five years ago. "Over a million sold," bragged the updated sign over the yellow arch. Iris was Mattie's first and only child, fathered by a guy named Rawlings who was a part-time security guard at the Coca-Cola plant. The only present he ever gave Mattie was gonococcal pelvic inflammatory disease.

"Irisssss," Mattie hissed. "Where you going looking like that, girl?"

Iris was thinking herself fine in a gold-sequined top, navel peeking out, and a short black skirt that was shiny and seriously tight. Three-inch hoop earrings that hurt after a couple of hours and black leather boots that did the same completed her outfit. Mattie also thought her daughter looked fine but knew that a bit of maternal disapproval would confirm Iris's feeling that she was sufficiently out there.

Iris switchwalked across the kitchen to give her mother the full effect.

"Goin' out, Mama. Calvin's asked me to dinner at the club tonight. And I am ready!"

"It's not enough I raised you? Now I got to take care of Eugene too?"

"C'mon, Mama, you know Thursday nights are *Wheel of Fortune* reruns. Eugene won't be any trouble. He's been sleeping well. Catching up on his weight. I've fed and changed him. Give him his theophylline and a bottle, and you're done. C'mon, Ma, do it, do it, do it. Me, you, and Eugene will go on a picnic up at the park this weekend and I'll do the food."

Mattie smiled and turned away. It had long been clear to both of them that Mattie could never refuse her daughter. And Mattie had seen some changes come over Iris in the past few months. Caring for Eugene, finishing high school, choosing better friends. Sopha had even helped Iris find a part time job helping out in a lab at the medical school.

Iris didn't wait for an answer; a short honk from Calvin's low-riding Chevy with the twin antennas on the back fenders and she was out the door. Calvin was new. Mattie liked him. He knew his cars, had a steady job, and as far as Mattie could see, he thought almost as much of Iris as Mattie did. Mattie poured herself half a tumbler of peach brandy and headed for the TV. She was tired after an hour's extra work in the neighborhood community center for old folks.

"Eugene, Eugene, Eugene, you sassy little brat. You're so good for your momma. C'mere and give your grandma some love."

Eugene was already almost seven months old. The intracranial hemorrhage had slowly resolved, leaving a large cyst that was putting pressure on his brain. The increased pressure was making Eugene sleepy, and sometimes he vomited for no apparent reason. Iris didn't notice anything wrong, but Mattie was worried. The last resident to see Eugene at the hospital pediatric clinic was also concerned. She'd written out a referral to the neurology clinic, but the earliest appointment was in late June.

Later, after the eleven o'clock news, Mattie gave Baby Eugene another bottle. He'd taken a couple of ounces of formula, not a lot, but at least he didn't spit it up on her pale pink lingerie. Mattie got up from her easy chair and carried Eugene on her bosom as though he were a brooch, then got ready for bed.

Mattie was feeling the lonelies lately, what with Iris taking up with Calvin, and the disappearance of Sam, a neighborhood tomcat that usually hung out at Mattie's.

"Baby Eugene, you're sleeping with your grandma tonight." She hunkered down in her soft bed, on her back, with Eugene at her side, his head in the crook of her arm. Under the synergistic effects of exhaustion and brandy, Mattie was out in minutes. Eugene's nose and mouth were buried in her breast, slung sideways over his face.

By 2:00 a.m., the street noise from Carnegie Street had diminished somewhat. Baby Eugene's airway was partially obstructed, and carbon dioxide was building up in his blood stream. The oxygen level in his blood dropped precipitously. Baby Eugene slipped into an irreversible coma and stopped breathing.

Turning into McKinley Street, Sophia saw the rotating lights of an ambulance and police car casting red and yellow streaks across the porches of the houses. Iris had called, and Sophia, waking slowly, thought at first it was another NICU nightmare. Iris, crying and barely coherent, said that Baby Eugene had died suddenly at home.

Iris and Mattie stood on the porch of their house. Iris

was sobbing. Her mother, standing with a wool overcoat over her nightgown, looked dazed. Eugene's small body in a white baby blanket was strapped to an adult stretcher inside the ambulance. A pair of patrolmen walked out of the house.

"Christ, John. She mashed him. He weighs next to nothing, and she's got to be over two hundred fifty pounds."

"I dunno, he's not bruised or anything. No blood on the sheets, maybe it's crib death or something. It's not like it's child abuse. Weird-looking baby anyway. Maybe there was something wrong with it. I don't think we need to call the detectives tonight. I don't want to wait around for them to show up."

A growing group of neighbors drifted toward the scene. The neighbors hadn't heard any scuffle or gunshots, but the bright lights of the law indicated clearly that something untoward had happened. Sophia ran up the steps.

"God, Sophia, after all he's been through. He just died sleeping with Ma. Goddammit!" Iris's mascara was running down her face. Sophia hugged her and Mattie.

"Hey, look, folks," one of the policemen broke in, "we're going to close up here. The body of the baby goes to the morgue, and some detectives will be out in the morning to ask you some questions." He turned to the group in front of the house. "Now all you folks get off the street. The show's over."

He turned back to Mattie. "We're real sorry about your loss, ma'am." Then he walked stiffly to the patrol car, backed off the sidewalk, and drove down the street. The siren growled as they blew through the traffic light at the corner. A few minutes later, the ambulance carrying Eugene left more quietly.

The last of the concerned neighbors offered their consolation and drifted back to their own houses, relieved that the angel of death had stopped elsewhere. Sophia, Mattie, and

Iris sat themselves around the kitchen table, Sophia and Mattie grasping mugs of lukewarm tea. Iris moaned.

In a way, Sophia envied Iris. Eugene had responded the way he was meant to. Baby Eugene ate, he slept, he smiled, he cried, and he gurgled. That was how he expressed his appreciation, his life. Then he died. Long after all the IVs, monitors, ventilators, and strangers caring for him, he'd been home, and loved, for months and months.

"God, Mama, I should have never gone out. I shouldn't have left him."

"I dunno, baby." Mattie said. "It's like he just gave up. For the life of me, I don't know why he chose now, after fighting so hard to get out of the hospital. God, what he went through."

28

Dinner

Adam Stanton, the chair of biochemistry and Sophia's boss, received the Lasker Award, America's equivalent of the Nobel Prize. A posh affair at the University Club downtown celebrated the occasion; one waiter for every two people at the long dining table resplendent with a regal array of crystal wine glasses, sterling silver cutlery and serving pieces, and silver-rimmed plates.

Happily, Sophia and Mac were seated next to each other. Though they'd chatted a number of times in the halls of the medical center, Mac hadn't really talked with her since her nighttime phone call almost a year ago. He was spending way too little time in his lab because of all the meetings the Shulders and their nameless baby had engendered. Sophia and Martin had separated without much acrimony. Mac imagined that they had retreated from each other in the belief that shared pain was magnified pain. It had happened to his own marriage after Billy was born.

Sophia struck up a conversation. "Mac, I never thanked you enough for your kindness after my baby …"

There was a slight hush in the dinner table conversation.

Sophia was known in the university medical environment—not only as a rising star in the biochemistry department but also because of the furor over her baby. As more Baby Doe cases appeared in the news, Sophia had become both a heroine and a pariah.

Mac flushed. "I'm sorry I didn't do more," he murmured. When the lawyers heard that Mac attended the funeral, they sent around a memo directing hospital staff to not talk with the Shulders "until some resolution could be put in place."

Trying to maintain Sophia's attention, he added, "Of course, I'm still involved in some of the aftershocks. Notestein retired soon after that. How did he do?"

"Believe it or not, I don't especially remember his performance in the whole drama. He kept a low profile. He just wanted the operations done."

That was Notestein, all right. Basically, he had survived at the med school by being a nice guy. Somebody once said that "vagueness and procrastination are a comfort for nice guys," and that fit Notestein to a T. Mac had more than urged him to retire.

"So, Mac, have there been any big changes since the birth of my baby?"

Sophia read the papers, watched the news on TV. She'd heard about the difficulties raised around the country when babies with similar problems were born. Mac was aware that some of their dinner companions were listening to their conversation. Nonetheless, whatever the social context, he knew Sophia truly wanted an answer. That's when Stanton, just a few seats down, knocked over his wine glass. Some of the dinner guests rose to protect themselves from the red wine rapidly advancing down the damask tablecloth like a smear on a thin-layer chromatograph.

In the midst of the uproar, Mac seized his moment. "My son has Down's, Sophia. He's in his twenties now and has been living in a protected home environment near me the past year. Doing fairly well. He has chronic leukemia too, but under control."

He didn't know what he expected. Sophia dropped her head and stared at her hands folded in her lap.

"I couldn't," she said, almost inaudibly.

"I know, Sophia. In many ways, I couldn't either."

Sophia rose and stood behind Mac for a moment. Then she hugged him, her face against his, and whispered, "I'm so sorry." She headed for the restroom.

Mac wanted to talk with Sophia some more, though in her absence he had more wine and was at no loss for words with the pharmacology professor on his left. She became animated after Mac's exchange with Sophia. She leaned in and asked him what he thought about the sanctity of life. She seemed like a nice enough woman, but with Mac's cover-up with Sophia, his guilt about Billy, too much wine, and the whole goddamn mess, something in him broke.

"Sanctity of life? Yes, I have thought some about sanctity of life. I've seen plenty of newborns die. Also, kids in car accidents. Anencephalics. Leukemics. Hemophiliacs. SIDS. Kids who were victims of abuse."

Mac paused, sipping even more wine to fortify his argument. "I'm told this is all part of God's plan and we just have to take that on faith. Right?"

She was nodding, if not in agreement, then in anticipation of what he was about to say next.

So was Mac. "To tell the truth, the amount of pain and raw suffering I've seen little children endure creates a significant torque on my faith. I believe in a higher power, but sometimes I think there's some cosmic need for human sacrifice."

She was frowning now, but there was no stopping Mac.

Sanctity of life—something about the phrase still irritated him. Mac leaned toward her, brandishing his butter knife. "That's why people like you," he continued, having no idea to whom he was directing his tirade, "make up rules about sanctity of life. Because you want protection. In those corners of the world where rulers don't care and there's no rule of law, in small, insignificant countries where there are wars—what happens? You've got cultures of casual killing. So I guess that 'sanctity of life' business protects people like you from people like me."

She recoiled and turned for safety to her dining partner on her left. Mac knew he'd been grotesque. Of course, life was sacred, but only for ourselves and our own, and even then, only until it wasn't.

His alcohol-fueled thinking was, to put it euphemistically, alinear, but he felt good.

After dessert, and a cup of strong coffee while he listened to congratulatory speeches for Stanton, Mac bumped into Sophia at the coatroom. On impulse, he asked if she'd like to have a drink or some coffee before leaving. She hesitated, a puzzled look in her eyes, but agreed. They found some comfortable seats in the club's anteroom in front of a huge, unlit fireplace. Sophia asked more about Mac's son, whether he had ever faced decisions like hers. In his day, he told her, the default option was warehousing such kids. But at birth, his son had had none of the additional problems like Sophia's baby.

Sophia and Mac were quiet for a minute until Mac could no longer ignore the elephant in the room. He looked at the damn beast squarely and followed his intuition. For too long, Sophia had been convinced that by delaying surgery, she alone had killed her son. That was Mac's fault. He blurted out, "No, Sophia, no. It wasn't you. Your baby died when an intern put an overdose of potassium chloride in the IV line. I'm sorry."

She lurched out of her chair as though Mac had struck her. With her cup in hand, she stood over him. He thought she was going to throw her coffee on him. He put his hand on her arm, but she backed away. "Goddamn you, Mac. Why didn't anyone tell me?"

It was the obvious question, and Mac had no good answer. After she paced in front of the fireplace for long, silent minutes, she sat back down and grilled him. How did he know? Why did the intern do it? What about the DNR? Did anyone try to stop the intern? What would have happened if the intern hadn't done it? Why wasn't *that* in the newspapers? What happened to the intern? And, repeatedly, the hardest question of all: Why hadn't anyone, why hadn't Mac, told her?

He did his best to explain. There had been the press and the government all closing in. And the lawyers. The intern's disappearance. Steve's act might have been wrong, but not necessarily causative. Then there was the damage the news would have caused to the hospital. Mac was overwhelmed with all the ad hoc committees and the demands of his new position. He'd considered calling her and Martin after the funeral but rationalized that any more information would only bring them more pain.

Mac's tonic water was long since gone, and Sophia had barely touched her coffee, but eventually her ire ran down; she seemed less angry. Possibly even relieved. Some of the responsibility for the baby's death lifted from her. But their parting that night was not amicable.

29

Losses and Wins

When they figured out who screwed up the amnio, it wasn't the mistake that doomed Dieter: it was his lying about it. Mac taught medical students that they would make mistakes no matter how hard they tried not to. A mark of a talented physician was not only minimizing mistakes, but handling the consequences. Dieter, therefore, would not have made a good physician. It might have been malicious of Mac, but he made sure Dieter never went to medical school. Steve, too, was a casualty. He never resurfaced, and Mac had to say that he was relieved. He'd decided that the slow code for a dying infant with multiple anomalies did not have to see the glare of publicity. But then there was the potassium chloride that turned a slow code into actionable behavior. Mac had been untruthful with himself.

Mac's initial enthusiasm for his job dissipated in nonstop committee meetings like air leaking slowly from a tire. He knew he wouldn't last, and he started looking ahead for work in outpatient medicine for kids with chronic problems. Few administrative responsibilities. No life-or-death decisions.

Was there anyone who profited from that debacle, Mac

wondered. Kurz, the senior resident and a smart guy, got his coveted chief residency in pediatrics, probably by not rocking the boat. Just do what you have to do to keep the babies alive. The reporter from the *Plain Dealer* followed the Baby Doe story along until interest died out, but afterward gained small fame as an authority on all matters medical. Martin Shulder couldn't really be called a casualty. He and Sophia would have divorced eventually anyway, and the death of their baby seemed to give Martin the impetus to leave academia, live off his father's generosity, and publish a novel that gave him no little credibility on the creative writing workshop circuit. Maybe there was one other who benefited as well: Sophia's baby. He died, thanks to Steve, a day, maybe a week sooner than he would have if things had gone on as they were. But with the possible success of the initial innovative surgery, Sophia and her baby might even now be on the slippery slope of more and more surgeries. And perhaps that would have created an insufferable life for her and her baby. Or perhaps the baby would have survived the operations, led a fulfilled life, and Sophia could have found fulfillment in motherhood. Maybe another guy to love. Maybe someone like Mac. When that thought occurred to him, he didn't think it through. He just picked up the phone, what the hell, and called Sophia in her lab.

30

Cleveland, August 1986
Sailing

It had been a year since the Stanton dinner. Mac's attempts to apologize to Sophia had thawed her just a bit. Over coffee together in the med center's cafeteria, Mac learned that Sophia had sailed with her family when she was growing up. He happened to have access to a great sailboat. It belonged to a stockbroker whose son had arrived in the ER last Fourth of July when Mac was covering for one of the residents' volleyball tournaments. The stockbroker carried his kid in with blood dripping down both his legs. Some wild teenagers had thrown firecrackers out of their car window, and they exploded at the boy's feet, shooting gravel, shrapnel-like, into both his legs. Mac cleaned up that mess, and the grateful stockbroker took him sailing on a number of weekends—with an invitation to use his wooden keelboat, a beautiful twenty-five-foot sloop without an engine, whenever Mac had the time.

A pleasant summer weekend was forecast, a propitious moment for Mac to ask Sophia to join Billy and him for a sail. Once on board, Sophia seemed kind of nervous. Maybe because she hadn't sailed since she was young. Or because of her uneasiness being with Billy for the first time. But as they coasted along at a gentle four knots, eating tuna fish sandwiches and kibitzing with Billy, Mac saw Sophia slowly relax, and he was able to coax her into taking the helm.

By the time they turned back toward the marina, a strong breeze was coming up. The sky darkened. Not a bad squall for Lake Erie, but since the damn lake is so shallow, it can kick up a hell of a chop in no time, especially when the wind has a long fetch toward Cleveland from the northeast.

They operated near their limit as the boat, under reefed main and small jib, surfed downwind toward the entrance to the harbor. Now and again they hit the back of a wave, and warm gray-green water washed into the cockpit, soaking all three. Sophia had an apprehensive frown on her forehead but gripped the tiller with determination. With one last shove from a breaking wave, they rounded the breakwall, the knot-meter pegged at six. Soaring into the now-quiet water toward their slip, the mainsail chattered when Sophia slackened the mainsheet. Mac clambered up to the mast to drop the mainsail. He yelled to Billy to throw off the jib sheet, so they'd slow down while Sophia glided them in alongside the dock.

A bewildered expression was on Billy's face as he jerked at the jib sheet. "Can't!" Billy shouted back at Mac. The jib sheet was jammed on the winch. The boat was heading straight for the pier, fast, with no room for turning around.

Imagining the coming collision, tourists on the pier stared at them wide-eyed. With a dock line in one hand and the main halyard in the other, Mac felt like a moron for being up on the foredeck.

Holding the tiller between her knees, Sophia looped a

spare rope around the jib sheet. "Now help me, Billy. Pull hard on this." She put the rope in his hand and Billy pulled with all he was worth, taking the tension off the stuck jib sheet and allowing Sophia to yank it off the winch.

The untethered jib relieved the driving pressure on the boat. Mac let the main halyard go. The mainsail came down with a rush. Sophia pushed over the tiller. The boat swung into the wind and shuddered to a dead stop alongside the pier.

The tourists, who moments before were expecting a maritime disaster, cheered and clapped. One of them caught the line to tie up the boat.

Mac let out a whoop. His crew wore big grins. Sophia hugged Billy, "You did great!"

Holding Sophia, Billy yelled, "Cheated death, Dad. Cheated death!"

Ezekiel 37:14

I will put My Spirit within you and you will come to life ... Then you will know that I, the Lord, have spoken and done it.

Historical Chronology—Baby Doe

April 9, 1982. Baby Doe is born in a community hospital in Bloomington, Indiana. The infant has Down syndrome and tracheoesophageal fistula with esophageal stenosis and was born with perinatal asphyxia. Parents choose not to approve transfer of the baby to a tertiary hospital for life-saving surgery after consulting with a family friend, an obstetrician. Nurses object to lack of treatment. Hospital officials turn to Monroe County superior judge for opinion. The judge rules that, given differing medical opinions, the parents' wishes should be respected. In light of objections to his decision, the judge asks the county child protection committee to review his decision. They uphold the judge's opinion. County prosecutors seeking a court order to perform surgery are denied. The Indiana Supreme Court refuses to hear the case. On April 15, 1982, while the Monroe County prosecutors were en route to Washington, DC, to appeal to the US Supreme Court, Baby Doe dies.

April 30, 1982. Memo from President Reagan to Richard Schweiker, secretary of the Department of Health and Human Services (DHHS), requesting enforcement of federal laws designed to prohibit discrimination in the care of handicapped infants.

May 18, 1982. DHHS memo from Betty Lou Dotson, director of the DHHS Office of Civil Rights, to health care providers who receive federal funds. It notes that Section 504 of the Rehabilitation Act of 1973 prevents discrimination against the handicapped, including withholding of nutritional substances or medical treatment from infants, solely because they are handicapped.

March 7, 1983. DHHS Interim Final Rule (Baby Doe I). Notice that must be posted conspicuously in delivery, maternity, nursery, pediatric, and intensive care units throughout the nation, stating that discriminatory failure to feed and care for handicapped infants is prohibited by federal law. The notice encourages whistleblowers to call a DHHS hotline with anonymity guaranteed. Under the aegis of DHHS, Baby Doe squads will do on-site investigations of hotline reports. Over four hundred investigations were carried out with more or less rigor over the lifetime of the Baby Doe Rules.

March 21, 1983. Presidential Commission Report, Deciding to Forego [sic] Life-Sustaining Treatment, is made public (despite the administration's opposition to publication).

April, 18, 1983. Baby Doe I Rule is declared invalid by Judge Gerhard Gesell of District Court for the District of Columbia. Elucidation of his decision: DHHS lacked a rational or factual basis for its rule and had not allowed for public comment before implementing it. More specifically, he termed the rule "arbitrary and capricious, and virtually without meaning be-yond its intrinsic *in terrorem* effect."

July, 1983. Revised Baby Doe Rule (II) is published and pub-lic feedback invited. It is nearly identical to Baby Doe I.

October 15, 1983. Baby Jane Doe is born in Port Jeffer-son, New York, with myelomeningocoel, microcephaly, and hydrocephalus. Parents do not authorize surgery. US Court of Appeals, Second Circuit, ruled that Section 504 of the Re-habilitation Act did not apply to decisions for treatment of seriously ill newborn infants.

February 13, 1984. Final DHHS Baby Doe Rule. Encour-ages establishment of hospital ethics committees and urges those concerned about the care of newborns to contact these committees and state child protection agencies.

1984. Child Abuse Prevention and Treatment Act signed into law by President Reagan. Amendments include three condi-tions wherein therapy can be withheld legitimately: when the patient is irreversibly comatose; when treatment is virtually futile for prevention of death and is thereby inhumane; and when further therapy would prolong the act of dying. If these conditions are not met and therapy is withheld, child abuse or neglect may be present. Enforcement of these transgres-sions is a state, not federal, responsibility.

April 15, 1985. Federal Register. DHHS, Office of Human Development Services. 45 CFR Part 1340. Child Abuse and Neglect Prevention and Treatment Program: Final Rule. Mod-el Guidelines for Health Care Providers to Establish Infant

Care Review Committees. The rule threatens to cut off federal grants to states unless states establish programs and/or procedures to respond to reports of medical negligence, including reports of medically indicated treatment being withheld from disabled infants with life-threatening conditions.

June 9, 1986. US Supreme Court rules that Section 504 of the Rehabilitation Act does not allow the federal government to intervene in medical decisions made by hospitals, parents, or physicians regarding the care of handicapped newborn infants.

2011. The review by Michael White is the best short summary of the thicket of conflicting regulations and recommendations regarding life-and-death decisions in the NICU that exist to this day.

Sources

Adzick, N. S., E. A. Thom, C. Y. Spong. "A Randomized Trial of Prenatal Versus Postnatal Repair of Myelomeningocele." *New England Journal of Medicine* (2011): 993-1004 doi:10.1056 / NEJM oa1014379.

Annas, G. "The Baby Doe Regulations: Governmental Intervention in Neonatal Rescue Medicine." *Public Health and the Law* 74 (1984): 618–620.

Anonymous. Burn Case. Sophia's memory of the burn patient relates to a true story that was featured on *20/20* on ABC on April 22, 1999. The former patient has worked as a lawyer in Corpus Christi, where he's represented clients who have been severely injured. He is blind, and believes in the right of severely injured patients to refuse life-saving therapy.

Aviv, R. "The Death Treatment." *New Yorker* (June 22, 2015).

Ballard, D. W., Y. Li, J. Evans, R. A. Ballard, and P. A. Ubel. "Fear of Litigation May Increase Resuscitation of Infants Born Near the Limits of Viability." *Journal of Pediatrics* 140 (2002): 713–718.

Beck, Martha. *Expecting Adam: A True Story of Birth, Rebirth, and Everyday Magic*. New York: Times Books, 1999.

Berube, Michael. *Life as We Know It: A Father, a Family, an Exceptional Child*. New York: Pantheon, 1996.

Caplan, Arthur L., Blank, Robert, Merrick, Janna: *Compelled Compassion: Government Intervention in the Treatment of Critically Ill Newborns (Contemporary Issues in Biomedicine, Ethics, and Society)*. New York: Springer, 1992.

Carr, Janet. *Down's Syndrome: Children Growing Up*. Cambridge, UK: Cambridge University Press, 1995.

Clowes, B. "Shouldn't Abortion Be Allowed for Serious or Fatal Birth Defects?" *Human Life International* (blog). May 22, 2017. https://www.hli.org/resources/abortion-serious-fatal-birth-defects/.

Dillard, Annie. *For the Time Being*. New York: Vintage Books, 1999.

Dick L. Willems, *A.A. Eduard Verhagen, and Eric van Wijlick*. "Infants' Best Interests in End-of-life Care for Newborns." *Pediatrics* 134 (2014).

Dorris, Michael. *The Broken Cord*. New York: HarperCollins, 1990.

Edwards, Kim. *The Memory Keeper's Daughter*. New York: Viking Penguin, 2005.

Fruitman, D. S. "Hypoplastic Left Heart Syndrome: Prognosis and Management Options." *Paediatric Child Health* 5, no. 4 (May-June 2000): 219–225. doi:10.1093/pch/5.4.219.

Gawande, Atul. "Annals of Medicine: Whose Body Is It Anyway?" *New Yorker* (October 4, 1999).

Guillemin, Jeanne H., and Lynda L. Holmstrom. *Mixed Blessings: Intensive Care for Newborns*. New York: Oxford University Press, 1986.

Gustaitis, R., and E. W. D. Young. *A Time to Be Born, A Time to Die*. Reading, MA: Addison Wesley, 1986.

Hattori, M., Fujiyama A., Taylor TD., Watanabe H., Yada T., et al."The DNA Sequence of Chromosome 21." Nature 405 (2000): 311–319.

Hentoff, Nat. "The Awful Privacy of Baby Doe." *Atlantic Monthly*, January 1985.

Johnson, Harriet McBryde. *Too Late to Die Young*. New York: Picador, 2006.

Katz, Jay. *The Silent World of Doctor and Patient*. Baltimore: Johns Hopkins University Press, 2000.

Kay, Rosemary. *Saul*. New York: St. Martin's Press, 2000.

Kuebelbeck, Amy. *Waiting with Gabriel: A Story of Cherishing a Baby's Brief Life*. Chicago: Loyola Press, 2003.

Lantos, John. *The Lazarus Case: Life and Death Issues in Neonatal Intensive Care*. Baltimore: Johns Hopkins Press, 2001.

Luce, John, and Ann Alpers. "Legal Aspects of Withholding and Withdrawing Life Support from Critically Ill Patients in the United States and Providing Palliative Care to Them." *American Journal of Respiratory and Critical Care Medicine* 162 (2000): 2029–2032.

Lyon, Jeff. *Playing God in the Nursery*. New York: WW Norton, 1985.

McHaffie, Hazel E., I. A. Laing, M. Parker, and J. McMillan. "Deciding for Imperiled Newborns: Medical Authority or Parental Autonomy?" *Neonatal Intensive Care* 15, no. 1 (2002): 33–38.

Miller, William Ian. *The Mystery of Courage*. Cambridge: Harvard University Press, 2000.

Mitford, Jessica. *The American Way of Birth*. New York: Dutton/Penguin Books, 1992.

Moreno, Jonathan. "Ethical and Legal Issues in the Care of

the Impaired Newborn." *Clinics in Perinatology* 14 (1987): 345–390.

Murray, T. H. *The Worth of a Child*. Berkeley: University of California Press, 1996.

Oe, Kenzaburo. *A Personal Matter*. New York: Grove Press, 1988.

Paone, Donald V. *To Be or Not to Be: Reflections on Modern Bioethical Choices*. New York: Blue Skies Press, 1999.

Pernick, Martin S. *The Black Stork: Eugenics and the Death of "Defective" Babies in American Medicine and Motion Pictures since 1915*. New York: Oxford University Press, 1996.

Pinkerton, J. V., J. J. Finnerty, P. A. Lombardo, M. V. Rorty, H. Chapple, and R. J. Boyle. "Parental Rights at the Birth of a Near-Viable Infant: Conflicting Perspectives." *American Journal of Obstetrics and Gynecology* 177 (1997): 283–290.

Pless, J. E. "The Story of Baby Doe." *New England Journal of Medicine*. 309 (1983): 664.

Rhoden, Y. K., and J. D. Arras. "Withholding Treatment from Baby Doe: From Discrimination to Child Abuse." *Milbank Quarterly* 63, no. 1 (1985): 1-34. https://www.milbank.org/wp-content/uploads/mq/volume-63/issue-01/63-1-Witholding-Treatment-from-Baby-Doe.pdf.

Sheiner, Marcy. *Perfectly Normal: A Mother's Memoir*. Lincoln, NE: iUniverse, 2002.

Shelp, Earl E. *Born to Die: Deciding the Fate of Critically Ill Newborns*. New York: The Free Press, 1986.

Singer, Peter. *Rethinking Life & Death: The Collapse of Our Traditional Ethics*. New York: St. Martin's Press, 1996.

Stinson, R., and P. Stinson. *The Long Dying of Baby Andrew*. Boston: Little Brown, 1979.

Van King, prod. *Dangerous Medicine*. Episode 147. Aired November 28, 2000, on Arts and Entertainment Network.

Verhagen, E., and J. Sauer. "The Groningen Protocol—Euthanasia in Severely Ill Newborns." *New England Journal of Medicine* 352 (2005): 959–962.

Wall, S. N., and J. C. Partridge. "Death in the Intensive Care Nursery: Physician Practice of Withdrawing and Withholding Life Support." *Pediatrics* 99 (1997): 64–70.

Weir, Robert. *Selective Nontreatment of Handicapped Newborns.* New York: Oxford University Press, 1984.

Werth, Barry. *Damages: One Family's Legal Struggles in the World of Medicine.* New York: Simon & Schuster, 1998.

White, Michael. "The End of the Beginning." *Ochsner Journal* 11 (2011): 309–316.

Zhang, S. "The Last Children of Down Syndrome." *The Atlantic,* December 2020. https://www.theatlantic.com/magazine/archive2020/12/the-last-children-of-down-syndrome/616928/

Acknowledgments

To all of you, thanks for your support, expertise, and help...

Mary Ellen Avery, Stephen Taeusch, William C. Taeusch, Randy Revell, Enid Pritikin, Judy Revell, Phil Holcomb, Andy Schell, Pam Satran, Ginny Horton, Cameron Tuttle, Joel Gardner, David Betz, Carol Edgarian, Tom Jenks, Deborah Thorp, Paul Sniderman, John Murray, Jessica Vandeveer, Michael Epstein, Colin Partridge, Susan Sniderman, Alma Martinez, Roberta Ballard, Margot Clements, Barry Smith, Carol Clements, Kate Gunn, Peter Singer, Judy Fletcher, Lewis Buzbee, Squaw Valley Community of Writers, Ann Packer, Nicholas Nelson, Sean Reynolds, Sandra Scofield, Joy Johannessen, John Paris, Chris Adrian, John DiBene, Elena Fuentes-Afflick, Phyllis Koppleman, Jay Koppleman, Barbara Gingold, Kirsten Barrere, Ellie Hajdu, Graham Schofield, John Robert Marlow, Alan Greenberg, Feigie Bailey, Leslie Wilkof, Deborah Nulman, Ilana Blumberg, Daniel Weizmann, Rama Weizmann, Zehariah P.B. Zivotofsky, and Ethel Zivotofsky.

hwtaeusch@gmail.com Newnovelstory.com

Made in the USA
Middletown, DE
07 April 2024

52722555R00182